lock the door shut the wind

turn off the light ar

BLUSHES IN THE DARK

HJ FURL

Copyright © 2022 by HJ Furl

All rights reserved. No part of this publication may be reproduced or transmitted, in any form or by any means, without permission of the publishers or author. Excepting brief quotes used in reviews.

Any reference to real names and places are purely fictional and are constructs of the author. Any offence the references produce is unintentional and in no way reflects the reality of any locations or people involved.

CONTENTS

Blood Beasts	05
Captivity	14
Deceit	20
Jess	60
Knight	87
Mae	119
Pig Beach	141
Primordia	146
Red Sparkle	204
The Arrival	215
them	231
Two Girls	253
Belle	278
Occasionally	295

Blood Beasts

I HAVE TAKEN TO EATING ON THE PATIO since Farr returned to Dubai. I think of him often as I sip my glass of ice-cold Sancerre leaning back on the lounger for all the world to see. We had a massive row about the buddleia before Farr flew out of my life. I wanted the bush cut down to give our moss-ridden lawn some much-needed sunlight to help the grass grow back. He insisted that we keep the butterfly bush to save the insects. In the end we compromised, we always compromise, and cut the thing level with the wall. I look across the garden at the clusters of Peacocks, Red Admirals, Painted Ladies, Cabbage Whites, gathered on the purple blooms, smiling to myself, I miss you Farr, for all your faults and forceful ways. I wish you were here now forcing yourself on me, kissing me, loving me in our garden of romance, as the sun goes down. Come back soon, honey. I get scared living here on my own.

Lately, I've been joining Farr on protests. By that I mean real protests, not marching round the square chanting and waving banners. Disruptive protests. Squatting on the motorway, holding up traffic. Climbing on the roof of trains. Banging gongs and dustbin lids as hard as we can to make our voices heard in Parliament, broadcasting our opinion with high decibel loud speakers.

Farr's right, he's always right about these things: if we don't act soon to reverse climate change the world's wildlife will disappear. Sure, a few species will adapt, Farr tells me. The question is: how will they adapt? Is the virus a freak occurrence? Or is it the result of humanity tearing down the rain forests, melting the ice caps, exposing us all to new adapting species that threaten our existence?

I finish off my wine and survey our walled garden. The grass is parched and dying. The moss has turned brown. Already, there are leaves drying, curling, falling, to the ground. I feel tired.

The evening draws on. Some swifts fly in and out of our eaves. I take my glass, stand, and walk towards the kitchen door. Some dead leaves rustle underneath our hydrangea, beside the garden wall.

Strange, there's no breeze tonight, not even a zephyr. Can't be an animal. Must be a bird, I decide, a baby bird, pitiful thing, with a broken wing. Maybe I can catch it, take it to the RSPCA.

I open the kitchen door, pop the wine glass on the window ledge, pad across the lawn to take a look. Get down on my hands and knees. The rustling stops. My garden's still, silent. I could hear a pin drop.

Why do I feel so surprised? Probably just my imagination playing tricks on me. I have quite an imagination, in bed. Ask Farr, he'll tell you. I think I'll take a shower, go to bed, read my book, get some sleep, dream of Farr…

There it is again: that rustling noise.

I want to, need to go indoors. I stand and brush the dry soil off my knees. There's something sticky on my calf, warm, stickily familiar. When I was a little girl, I stole two punnets of berries from some boys blackberrying on the mudhills. They started throwing stones at me. One struck me on the back of the head. My hair, face, and eyes were drenched with blood. Blood ran down my back, under my striped tee-shirt, my shorts, into my knickers, down the backs of my thighs, calves. My plimsolls filled with blood. They took me home to Mummy, my tee-shirt wrapped around my head. I had to have stitches, plastic skin, I feel the skin on the back of my head at night, bald, and bare. I need to go indoors. There's something sticky on my thigh, warm, stickily familiar. I scrape it off with the blade of my hand, hold it in the fading light. I sniff, smell it, a feral animal. I resist the urge to taste it…

God, if only Farr were here, this is blood.

I inadvertently smear my face with blood, a frightened little girl once more. My stomach heaves my pizza supper onto the lawn. I get down on my knees and heave-some-more, heave until I'm hollow inside, reach and tear a leaf off the nearest bush, wipe the braque off my face, the thick congealing curd off my leg. I run inside to shower.

Lock the door! Shut the window! Turn off the light! And go to bed!

There it is again: that rustling in my head. Blushes in the dark. My darkest dreams come true. Blood Beasts on my pillow! Slime across my sheet!

My nightmare ends at three-twenty-six in the morning. I wake up in a cold sweat, switch on the bedside lamp, touch my pillow, and stroke the crumpled sheet with my naked leg, wishing Farr were here to curl up with. Pushing back the duvet with both feet, I find normality: no blood, slime, or smells, just clean. I get out of bed and draw the curtains. There's a half-light here, the first signs of dawn. My body feels hot and clammy. I badly need a shower. I think of Farr in Dubai, four hours ahead of me, travelling to work, in fifty degrees, shorts, short-sleeved shirt, his hairy arms and legs, driving me wild, driving me. My phone lies on the bedside table, ready.

I hope he's free.

'Hello, Farr?'

He's free.

My spirits soar, my heart races, 'Darling, it's me, Helen.'

'Hello me,' he drawls, 'What gets you up so early this morning?'

'I was missing you, baby. I had a terrible nightmare, about blood, and slime.'

He mocks me, he makes me feel stupid.

'Slime? Come again?'

Stupid! Stupid! Stupid!

'Don't mock me, Farr. I dreamed I found a pool of slime under the hydrangea. There was blood. I dreamed it made me sick. Dreamed I sicked up on the lawn. It was horrible, horrible!'

'Hey, calm down, Helen. It was probably something you ate. What did you eat?'

Go on admit it.

'Pizza, I...'

'You ate pizza before going to bed?'

I stretch my arms and yawn, 'Yuh.'

'Cheese?'

'Yuh.'

I feel him smile, sorry for me, missing me. I feel childish, I wish I hadn't mentioned the dream.

I distinctly remember the bloody putrid mess in the flower border, sicking up all over the lawn.

'I know, baby,' I love to call him baby, 'know what you're saying. Don't eat pizza before I go to bed at night. Silly me, naughty me, tell me off, give me a good spanking when you get home. When do you get home?'

'Next month,' he promises faithfully, 'I'm flying home at the end of next month, Helen.'

'I can't wait that long! Can't wait till next month!'

'I have an important meeting in ten minutes on biodegradables.'

I can't believe my ears. Talk about changing the subject, 'You have a what?

'You heard.'

I perk up, think of my protest in Parliament Square, 'Biodegradables? That sounds interesting.'

'It is. Honey, is there anything else we need to talk about? Anything that can't wait?'

He's like this with me, Farr. Hot and cold. One minute he's all loving, manly, sexy for me. The next, it's as if he doesn't know me. Still, I can't complain, I don't need to work. He keeps me in clover. I think of the pool of blood, smearing my face and thighs, running inside to shower.

'Nothing that can't wait.'

'Speak to you tonight then.'

I shiver, feel as if something dark and wet just walked across my grave. I speak, my throat's dry.

'Yes, tonight.'

He cuts my call.

I pad downstairs to the kitchen, boil the kettle, make myself a mint tea, rhubarb jam on toast, go back to bed, and read myself a bedtime story about a lion, a witch, and a wardrobe imagining there is a lamppost in my mind, a lamp in my mind, in my mind, my mind, drifts, off, to, sleep.

I wake up with a start.

Silence.

I can't hear any birds. There's daylight in my eyes, dawn. My body feels sticky, sweaty, dirty. I need a shower. Blood-smell creeps thru my window, tang. I can't hear any birds. Sick smell. For crying out loud! I live behind a wall. Blood smell. Birds live, in the trees, behind my wall. I can't hear any birds. The smell pervades my nose. I run to the shower, can't wash of the smell. I wrap a towel around my breasts, my waist, my wet hair, I pad downstairs to the kitchen. The door is open. I locked the door last night. The door is open. Heart, pumping blood, blood-smell in my nose, a metallic smell, a sick smell, I step outside into the garden, I walk to the hydrangea.

The grass is clean! My lawn is clean!

I get down on my hands and knees.

Heart pumping hard, blood-smell in my nose, a sick, acrid, smell, I look under my hydrangea.

The soil is clean! Thank God! The soil is clean!

The wriggling starts.

There's something sticky on my thigh, warm, bloody familiar. I can't scrape it off. I sniff, smell it, a feral animal, resist the urge to taste it. I sit cross-legged on the lawn and pull off the towel.

I feel the wriggling stop. Stuck to my thigh is a black sheath full of blood. The wriggling starts.

The sheath crawls up my thigh, blood beast on my thigh, slime on my.

The dizziness passes, the moment rewinds, context lost. Where am I? Who am I? The tide of memory ebbs…and resumes:

There's something sticky on my thigh: warm, bloody, familiar. I can't scrape it off. I sniff, smell it, a feral animal, resist the urge to taste it. I sit cross-legged on the lawn and pull off the towel, I am naked, I feel the wriggling stop. Stuck to my thigh is a black sheath of blood. The wriggling starts. The sheath crawls up my thigh, blood beast on my thigh, slime on my.

*****

Ecocide! Flaming red letters on a deep-green banner. A slogan on the tee shirt of a rogue priest, glued to the steel of a power plant. The dying grass presses its cold, sharp tendrils into my naked skin: stabs of reproach, of retaliation; under my wavering gaze the roses, buddleia and wisteria grey out, my mind assaulted by alternate realities: sterility, a wasteland of dunes, dusty and brown; this is the endgame, the death of nature, the empty victory of myopic masculine technology.

A rustling footfall somewhere near: something scars the pristine sand with chitinous claws. Huge and hard, the scorpion-shadow looms before me: intimidating, radiating menace. On my back now, my bare flesh glistening, breathing fast, my thighs spread of their own volition. My knees rising, separating in sacrifice, my self-sacrifice, my atonement for what we've done. Forgive me, Mother Earth, for I have sinned…

'You did this,' Farr says, swaying towards my traitorous, willing body. His sting arches, long and smooth, traversing the space between my knees, blindly swaying above my patient thighs, the drop of poison at his tip glistening, distending, growing, 'Your selfish greed which raped the planet!'

I thrust up to meet my nemesis, shameless to the last, panting in anticipation; the pleasure, the pain, the ecstasy…

Absolve me! Punish me! Expiate my guilt!

And reality shifts.

*****

The dark, pulsating, corrugated slime-tube lies quiescent on my thigh amidst the sunburned lawn and drooping floral beds. Its slit-end stares me down, drips haemorrhagic mucus. Slowly quests, sampling my sweat and emanations, seeks its destination, prepares to slither forth…

I strike it off with the back of my hand, turn onto my front. On all fours I'm heaving dry-retching, dirty, naked in the roses. I sit in the shower, cradled in a corner with the spray drizzling down, the healing, cleansing rain.

'Clean for Farr, Helen,' he says, 'be clean for me – you're nature's bounty; everything I do, I do it for you. You are my rose, my English rose; open your blossoms, my special darling, open yourself to me.'

I am transported into his arms, the bed soft beneath me, his muscular body arching above: feverish, rhythmic, powerful, dynamic, relentlessly pounding.

In wanton excitement I see myself through his eyes: curvy, warm, juicy, a throbbing caterpillar in the iron grasp of his limbs, his pincers. The ovipositor, fleshy, hot and mindlessly thrusting, has reached its destination, its home. It spews forth its glutinous load, inserts secretions deep into my willing cavity, my waiting nest.

Sensation fades as I shudder through the gasping crescendo; arousal recedes; a not-unpleasant paralysis seeps into my muscles, my eyelids flutter to a close... and relax...

The seeds spew forth a swarm of nematodes, larvae burrowing and foraging within me. His parting whispered words:

'You'll feel no pain as they, like moles, devour your flesh; their sanitation-hormones grant you unrelenting joy. In this last sacrifice, Helen, you set the world to right.'

I want to scream: 'I did not choose this hell-fag of yours! I am not a grubbing caterpillar but a gorgeous bright fritillary; my destiny – mine! mine! – is unlatched freedom: to leave the earth and soar away and fly!

I lie here mute and feel the rancid churning in my womb.

The words no longer come.

And I no longer care.

Captivity

HER CELL IS DARK, DINGY AND DAMP. There is no door or window, only a grille in the ceiling, where rusty water drips through. In one corner of her cell sits a pail, her toilet bucket. At the centre of the room lies a soaking wet, unkempt bed with a striped-grey duvet, a scattering of pillows, and, bolted to the bare concrete floor, a varnished wooden chair. She squats on her chair in her soiled white button-down dress and cuddles herself to sleep as best she can. On the floor, between her dirty bare feet, her cream bucket bag lies unopened, waiting for her to open it.

She closes her eyes and relives the moment of her abduction. When she left the wine bar alone, merry, not drunk, to catch the late-night train home. Took her shortcut down the dark alleyway in Spitalfields. Such murderous territory. He took her from behind, placed a wad over her nose and mouth, and suffocated her. Her last memory of normality was the tiny pinprick in her neck, slumping to her knees, her green eyes rolling up, revealing her petrified whites, then darkness.

Since waking in her brick-walled box, she has lost all sense of time, of reason. She blinks her bleary, sore eyes open, pushes her grubby hand through her greasy ginger hair and cries.

'Why am I here? What do you want of me?'

She stares up at the grille in the ceiling. The constantly dripping water stains her cheeks blood red. She stands up, feeling the cold from the wet floor beneath her feet, tiptoes to the nearest wall, and runs the flats of her hands over the rough brick wall. Two paces later, she reaches a corner, turns left, four paces: another corner. Accidentally, she kicks over her toilet. Its putrid, foetid contents slop over her feet.

'Let me out of here!' she screams, 'I want to go home!'

She turns left, walking four paces to her third corner. Then she turns left. After four more paces, she reaches the last corner. Two paces along, she turns and tiptoes back to her chair. She stares at her thick coarse rope dangling tantalisingly out of reach from the grille in the ceiling. The rope he lowered her into this hellhole with.

The chair, she stands upon her chair like an acrobat, reaching for her rope. Her rope is pulled upwards and disappears through the grille. She climbs down off her chair, the water drip-drip-dripping into her hair, rusting it ferric red, and cries with frustration. On the floor between her feet lies her bucket bag: unopened, waiting for her to open it.

'Let me out!' she wails miserably, 'Let me out, will you?'

She stares up as her thick coarse rope reappears dangling tantalisingly out of reach from the shadowy hole. Where there is no night. Where there are no stars. Only his dark. Her rusted rain.

He lowered her body, her slumped meat, dead-weight into this hellhole.

Her chair, she stands upon her chair, reaching for her rope like a kitten stretching for her soft pink cotton playball. His kitten. He jerks her rope upwards making her leap and jump and paw and scratch thin air and blurt and cry and plead and beg. Jerks away her rope to freedom. She falls, toppling off of her slippery chair. He jerks her rope up out of the grille, his blank, black face leering at her. Her thick coarse rope disappears through the grille.

Despondently, she climbs down from her chair, the water drip-drip-dripping into her dyed hair, and cries in frustration. On her floor between her feet lies her cream bag, unopened, waiting for her to open. She starts to hallucinate.

Seeing her captor as her lover, she whimpers for him, 'Are we there yet, love?'

'Be there in the morning. Think it's sleepy time, don't you?' his voice is such a loving hush.

She yawns and stretches her twizzle arms, 'Mm! Night, night. Love you.'

'Love you too, baby, with all my heart. Night, night.'

Invisible fingers proudly stroke his kitten's rusty hair. Missing lips kiss his kitten goodnight.

'Why don't you open the bag?'

She sucks her thumb, all child-like, 'What is in the bag, please?'

'Why don't you open it and find out for yourself?' his voice booms.

'Please, may I open the bag?'

'Why, course you can, baby.'

Big emphasis on her nickname bay-bee.

'Now, open the bag.'

'What's in the bag?'

'A surprise! Like surprises, don't you?'

She smiles, speaks all childish, 'Mm! I like surprises, candy and chocolate and dolls and...'

'Do you like butterflies, girl?'

She stares up at his face in the shadow, always in the shadow.

'Oh, yes! Red Admirals! Peacocks! Cabbage Whites!'

'The bag is full of butterflies, insects, all-sorts of lovely creepy-crawlies for you to play with.'

'Would you like to come out to play now?'

'Oh, yes please! Please, say yes!'

He says yes, sighs, and stares down at his captive larvae, his pupating chrysalis, her imago, 'Baby?'

'Mm?'

'Open the bag.'

She opens the bag to discover the bugs have hatched out in its warm silk lining, bred, swollen in size to thumbnail, and multiplied. They swarm all over her. Disgusted, she pushes them away tipping out the contents of her bag: tweezers, comb, lipstick, mirror, tampons, purse, hair brush, tissues. Littering the dirty floor under her chair, scattering the foul-vermin insects everywhere.

She stands up, stamping her feet, tries to shake them off. But the super-resilient, shock-resistant strain survives, crawling up her bandy-thin legs, underneath her dress, in search of her warmest breeding places. Desperately, she slaps, hits, squashes and pinches them flat in a vain bid to kill the devils. She freezes stiff as several bugs crawl inside her soft black cotton panties and nestle in her bald crotch. Still more bugs scamper over her stomach, scouring her deep navel, burrowing inside her under-wired, lacy black bra, nibbling at the soft undersides of her breasts, her erect nipples. They swarm over her, scratching her neck, eyes, ears, nose, throat. Infesting her hair follicles. Penetrating her roots.

Bristling with bugs, she staggers, sways and falls onto the sodden bed, her weak arms held aloft in the shape of the cross. Collapsing in their seething, blood red-treacle mess. Itching her knee, Complaining, as bugs stream up her legs. Shrieking like a baby. Shrill whelps of alarm emanate from her. She is no longer his kitten. She is his distressed sheep. Bleating for his unforthcoming assistance.

She emits a blood-curdling scream, rubbing fat bugs out of her eyes, glancing over her shoulder at the thousands of bugs streaming down the mildewed walls. OMG! Her legs go pole-straight, arms hang limply at her sides. Her eyes bulge. Her lank hair is riddled with bugs. Her jaw flaps open, showing off her pearly, white teeth. A fat bug rests awhile on her petrified upper lip, then disappears down her gaping throat. She screams and screams, hysterically brushing the greedy insects off her torso, scratching her bug-infected body for dear life.

Hordes more bugs scurry up her calves, her thighs, like bestial newlyweds, overwhelming the wretched woman. Every bite makes her itch, whine, and scratch. The bugs feast upon her body, infesting her gullet, swimming in the mucous lining in her lungs. Occupying her every crevice, orifice, and hole. Time is running out for her. She lies sprawled on the bed, moaning like mad, half-dead. The host is half-dead. Not her ghastly bugs. They are alive and thriving inside her.

The entomologist is concerned insects will be forced to find new habitats as humans destroy the environment. He is delighted to find that bugs can live in us. His project is almost complete.

White gabbles, insanely: 'Mind the bugs don't bite, Joanna! Please, mind the bugs don't bite!'

The bugs eat her inside out.

Her captivity ends abruptly.

He plans his next experiment.

Joanna. Joanna. She must be a Joanna, not an Anna, Polly Anna, or Joanne. Now where shall I find her? In the slums? Leaving the office? Boarding a late-night train. Missing her taxicab home? Oh, and she must be wearing a white dress - a virginal, pure, Cabbage White, dress.

Deceit

MARTIN HADN'T DRIVEN HIS 4X4 SINCE THE ACCIDENT. The bedroom was stifling hot. Sian had set the heating too high. He was claustrophobic. He needed fresh air. He slid open the glass partition, stepped out onto the veranda, and chilled as an invigorating blast of frigid air whipped his chest. Martin sneezed, smelling the fug of her stale scent.

Slick watched him from across the road in her copper chrome Fiesta. Their eyes met. She turned cooked-lobster pink, swung her cramped stiff-hurt legs out of the car, and hurried off towards the communal recreation facility and sports hall. He wondered if she'd ever leave him alone.

Sian was lying on her side, fast asleep, shattered. Martin closed the smeared partition between them carefully so as not to wake her, crossing the bare pine floor, sealing his auburn woman in her crystal cube - and went to the toilet. The bathroom was a shrine to his masculinity. It had a black slate floor, marbled walls, a white porcelain toilet, bidet, deep-curved bath, a wash basin.

Martin locked the door, enacting his intimate ritual of body cleansing. First, he sat on his throne, and peed. Then, painstakingly, he set about removing every trace of Sian from his body: her putrid cheesy sediment, her slick body fluids, her acrid body odours. Once he'd smooth-shaved, showered, sanitized himself, and rinsed his hairy hands, he wandered through their lounge to the kitchen to cook himself some brunch.

The lounge was littered with a contemporary sideboard, a vast media unit and coffee table. He had bought a royal blue sofa for Sian to luxuriate on, a criss-crossed, coarse sisal rug for her tantric yoga moves. The kitchen had a dual-purpose fridge, an overhead storage unit full of her seeds, pasta, his nuts, a trendy cooking hob, and a small breakfast bar with three poseur stools, still wrapped in polythene.

Starving, Martin raided the fridge, shredded some plastic ham, beat three big eggs, and rustled up a ham omelette with grilled turkey rashers. Next, he cremated three thick slices of granary, plastering them with low fat spread under thick-cut marmalade, and downed two black coffees. He threw all his dirties in the sink for Sian to deal with later, before hurrying to the spare room.

His new smart casual outfit was laid out neatly for him on the bed. His woman had clearly gone to a lot of trouble to choose him suitable spring clothing: a pair of lovat moleskin jeans, a sea blue, soft cotton chambray shirt, navy-blue waxed jacket, tanned leather brogues. He felt remorseful.

These clothes must've cost Sian a fortune.

He snipped off all the price tags then cautiously opened the mauve envelope lying on the bed. The gilt embossed card read:

Thanks for last night's sex, Darling. Fondest Love, Sian xx

Martin returned to the bedroom, lump-in-throat, his beautiful Celtic princess lain out on the bed, ready for his silent kiss. One of her beige-tanned knees was protruding awkwardly at a right-angle from under the ruched candyfloss duvet emphasising her sexual exhaustion. Her lover admired her maternal breasts heaving, gently, with the rhythm of her breathing, resting snugly in their quilted nest of furled down. Her nipples still erect, strawberry red, from having sex. He was struck dumb by her native Welsh beauty. Could almost hear the crash of the waves. Taste the smack of salt on her lips. Feel the sand on her skin. From when she first made love to him, clinching him, clamping him inside her, loving, stark naked on Morfa Dyffryn beach.

*****

Martin stood without using his arms, stripped off his olive t-shirt and shorts, and tested the sand with his toes. The heat was bearable. He flexed his biceps for Sian, stretched out on the beach mat, taking in the vista before him. The sky was clear, azurite blue, the sand tinged with ochre, liberally strewn with bladderwrack, flotsam, jetsam, amber froth, and plastic, along the tideline.

The glass-clear water, slapping the shore in teasing ripples, herald of the rare, becalmed sea, looked deceptively inviting. Not to Sian though. Impish, elfish, Sian dressed only in a soft turquoise cheesecloth dress, her arms, and legs bare, tanning under the searing sweltering summer sun.

Amaze me, Sian. You really do! Tell me girl, what's going on it that strange mind of yours?

Martin cast his gingerbread brown eyes over the deserted beach. He and Sian had chosen well, nestling out of the cutting wind.

'My Welsh Mistral!' Sian proudly called it.

Nestling where the sandy dunes, stiff with marram grass, met the exposed foreshore. Nestling.

'Our little love-nest, Martin!' she laughed nervously, blushing.

He turned to face her. He couldn't quite make her out. Her undying love for him. Despite his sinful tasks. The trust she placed in him. On many occasions. Her lonesome nights. When he played away. His endless overnight stays: ask-no-questions: discreet inns, guest houses, luxury hotels.

~ 22 ~

All expenses paid. Ask-no-questions. He watched as she drew the hem of her crimped dress high to the small of her slender back pressing it to her front, lowering her head, showing him herself, revealing the fullness of her pale, bare rump, ever the Celtic maiden.

'Look, see, I'm not wearing any knickers!'

Martin blew out his cheeks, 'Sian! Don't do this to me. Please, don't do this to me! You'll give me a bloody heart attack.'

Sian lay flat on her back on the mat, 'Well, darlin?'

He struggled for breath: her knowing allure, her wanton temptation, his guilt at all the women.

'Coming in for a dip, Sian?'

She lifted the hem of her dress, 'You know I don't like it when the water's cold. You know I like to stay warm. You know I want a little baby, darlin. Don't you think it's time we tried?'

Martin ran to the sea, ran away from her: the guilt she racked up in his mind. His duplicity. The selfish way he treated her. His disdain. His total lack of respect for her. He shouted at her over his muscled shoulder,

'Presently, Sian,' was all he said, 'Presently.'

He waded into the sea, splashing his barrel chest with freezing water, rinsing his arms and thighs, cooling his loins, and swam.

*****

The water never really warms off the Welsh coast. Within minutes of diving in, Martin was on his way back, wading, trudging through the shallows, sand between his toes, an oil blemish staining his right calf. Crude oil.

Enjoying the heat of the sun on his shoulders, drying his torso he padded as far as Sian – who'd stood on her beach mat - and grabbed his towel. Sian wasn't amused by his selfish act. She had a face like thunder. Her face was flushed red and angry, she stormed.

'Enjoy that, did you? Feelin' better now, are you? Get it off your chest, did you?'

Martin dried his hair, 'Sorry? Get what off my chest?'

'Whatever it is that's bugging you.'

'There's nothing bugging me, Sian, okay?' he stressed. Martin was usually stressed these days.

Sian threw her arms about in frustration. She could strangle him when he misbehaved like this. Strangle him!

'Don't give me that tosh. I know when you're upset. I'm supposed to be your best friend, your wife, y'know,' she stared down at her bare feet, wiggling her toes, trying to stay calm, 'Though I wonder sometimes. Wonder about you.'

Her lover slowly drew his beach towel over his back of rippling muscles, back-and-forth, up-and-down. Women adored his back, the hairy-nest small of it, his tightly clenched buttocks. He was handsome, rugged, muscular, manly, attractive, well-built, but possessed the tenderness of a woman's touch, their softness. Women loved that about Martin,

~ 24 ~

'What do you mean, wonder?'

Sian fixed him with her hardest stare, 'You're always so quiet, Martin. Distant. As if you don't love me anymore. Do you, darlin'? Do you love me?'

She pulled her dress off over her head. Martin marvelled at the lift and flop of her ample breasts, her sensitive, distended, rose-tipped nipples.

'Of course, I love you, Sian. You mean the world to me.'

Sian was naturally beautiful, beautiful as the sun, sea, sand, and sky. He choked on his shameful deceit. How could he treat her like this? Martin watched eagerly as his woman arranged herself on the beach mat, her breasts heaving with passion, her soft tuft of pubic hair matt with sand. She opened her thighs for him, her voice took on a husky tone, she arched her body upwards.

Sian made him need her, 'Then give me a little baby.'

Straining hard, bursting, Martin pulled down his wet trunks and went to her. He threw his body on top of hers, crushing her fulsome breasts, her rib cage, loving her moans and sighs of ecstasy as he mounted her, fucking her so hard that she flailed her arms and legs tearing at his buttocks until they bled.

*****

They'd been trying for a baby ever since. He wondered if he was infertile. Overwhelmed by a rush of guilt to the heart, he stooped and kissed her perfect breasts, her twisted lips, tenderly brushing the damp wisps of hair off her cheek. Watching the sleepy-land smile spread over her blushing face. Screwing his eyes shut to stem the tears. Today might be the day that changed her life. His life. He tucked Sian in, whispering his love for her, turning to go, atoning for his guilt,

'I love you, Sian. The last thing in the world I'd ever do is hurt you. But we need the money.'

*****

A vet's overlooked their luxury apartment full of dead or discarded pets, a 15th century inn. Martin took the fire stairs to the secured exit, quit the block, and crossed the road. As he left, he noticed, the entry to the disabled parking bay was blocked - by a makeshift flower bed.

How could someone do that?

Slick's Fiesta was parked in one of the bays reserved for residents, next to his 4x4.

The terracotta-brown fence skirting the pub beer garden had collapsed in last night's storm-force winds. Several branches hung precariously off the trees, reminding him of the tenuous tightrope he trod with Sian, the causeway of deceit that led to his murky life. As if to stress his seedy, dirty existence, the back street was festooned with split clear sacks spewing out soiled plastic boxes, fishy-smelling tin cans, greasy fish and chip papers, winter fodder for the starving foxes.

Martin had been so busy satisfying Sian's libido that he didn't hear the raging wind. Smiling at her memory: how she had got up on all fours for him, 'for better penetration, darlin,' he cut through a dingy alley, past some derelict garages, avoiding the desiccated turds, then jogged downhill to the station.

*****

Amber Slick zipped her sage jersey jacket and pulled on some thick grey woolly gloves. Her quarry felt the wind bite his cheeks as he stepped off the train. The sky was pencil grey; flecks of sleet floated in the air. It was bitterly cold. He walked the length of the platform to the tourist information office. Inside, he was greeted by a blast of warm air, a fat-jolly-hockey-sticks type with a sad squint, green eyes, curly ginger hair, freckles. She spoke cordially in an elocuted old girl accent,

'How can I help you? Do you want to buy a postcard? We don't sell stamps, only cards. Diaries are half price.'

Feeling his bladder protest, Martin ignored her tedious waffle. Instead, he asked for directions to Palisades.

She sounded impressed. 'Palisades?! I have a map!'

Hurry up you stupid old cow, I'm bursting.

Unhurried, she spread out a street plan on the counter, scribbling an x for the station, another x to mark the location of the five-star hotel.

'We're here, your hotel's there,' she said, spreading her webbed fingers, 'It's a thirty-minute walk through the city centre. Are you in a hurry?'

No, I always stand with my bloody legs crossed.

Martin told her he wasn't in any hurry. He had two and a half hours to prepare himself for his client. More than enough time to see the city sights, enjoy some lunch. What did she suggest?

'Why don't you take the sightseeing bus from outside the station? It stops beside the hotel at stop 11. The ticket is valid for twenty-four hours. Can I interest you in one? You do get to see the Roman Baths, the Royal Crescent, Thermae Bath Spa, the Jane Austen Centre…'

'How much?'

She laughed, enjoying his custom, his good looks. If only she were fifty years younger.

'Twelve-pound-thirty. Terrific value if I say so myself.'

'What time's the bus?' he asked, waving his debit card at her.

'There's one on the hour and every half hour.'

He spotted the name badge pinned to her grey lapel, 'Thank you, Juliet, you've been helpful.'

Julia Cavendish flashed him an embarrassed smile, 'A pleasure, young man. Enjoy our city.'

'Where are the Gents?'

'Outside, left, next to the Buffet, you can't…'

Slick waited until he had left before she entered the shop.

'I'm in a hurry. Give me a tour bus ticket.'

She paid the shop assistant in cash, took the pink ticket, pulled on her gloves, and walked out. Slick caught up with him at the ticket barrier. Her man left the station, crossing Dorchester Street at the red lights, then disappeared inside the Southgate Centre.

Prêt was a short walk away. Slick watched enviously as her quarry treated himself to a chicken Caesar salad, a tub of sliced mango with lime, and a steaming hot pot of spicy tomato soup. She made do with an egg mayo sandwich and a cup of milky tea. There was an empty seat by the exit.

Martin took a pew at the back, opposite two chatting students who were busy tucking into an early lunch. He always ate heartily before meeting clients. Working on a full stomach helped to calm his nerves, suppress his guilt. He thought about Sian, waking alone, taking her pregnancy test.

Sian sat up in bed, her tablet open on her naked thighs, duvet round her feet, as her partner took a sip of piping hot soup. She sensed his soup, feeling the steam wet her face as he lifted the lid, feeling the hot liquid blister the roof of his mouth. He spilt vinaigrette down the front of his shirt. She saw the brown oily suspension: all greasy and damp.

'Careful, darlin'! I can feel you, see you.'

He found a vacant toilet and cleaned his teeth using his finger as a brush. Meanwhile, Slick left *Prêt* and hobbled to the bus stop in nearby Manvers St.

The bus was late. Martin checked his *Rolex*: he'd arrive at the hotel just in time. He climbed the spiral stairs, sat on a front seat, clipped on a plastic headset, and dozed. Slick sat downstairs staring vacantly through a window at the flimsy snowflakes, fluttering down, celestial dandruff.

Sian checked a second time, just to be sure, put the pregnancy testing kit on her bedside table, then she rang her man to share the wonderful news.

'Martin! I'm pregnan! I'm goin' to have a little baby!'

There was no answer. She bit her lip. Her heart filled with anguish.

'Why won't you return my call, darlin'?'

She tried again. The call went to voice mail.

'Answer me, won't you? For cryin' out loud, Martin!'

Sian texted:

Call me, Darling. Urgent. Sian xx

His phone was switched off. He left the bus. Slick knew this bus, waiting in the square, giving her quarry a head start. She removed her bobble hat, shaking out her wavy, greasy hair as he vanished through the rotating door into the uninhibited luxury that was Palisades.

*****

Amber Slick was divorced, bereaved. Once a slim, attractive brunette, she'd let herself go after the terrible hit and run accident involving the 4x4. She'd grown jelly belly, a fat bum, chunky thighs. The impact of the collision had hurled the buggy into a stone wall, killing her baby boy instantly. Amber was catapulted under the wheels of an approaching lorry, maimed for life, left a cripple. Her sardonic grin masked her inner pain, an abiding bitterness, a sense of injustice at the outrage.

The driver of the 4x4 didn't stop.

This woman was obsessed. Frightened by her disturbed behaviour, her husband had fled the nest. The infernal voices inside her warped mind spoke to her again last night, creeping into the darkest recesses of her tortured, scrambled brain:

Not going to forgive and forget are you, Amber? Are you listening to me, Amber? Is that bitch with him? The one who watched Timmy die through her rear car window? Is she? Or is he with another slut?

Amber was greeted like an old friend by the trainee manager at Palisades who offered to take her jacket. She walked past her man to the bar where she treated herself to a rare double Bombay gin with Fever Tree tonic. Slick took off her jacket, sitting well out of view, innocuously dressed in a cheap, mint green cardigan, tummy-slimmer slacks by Damart. She swallowed the gin in one, enjoying its biting, piney taste.

Then she waited.

Amber Slick had all the time in the world - to wait.

*****

Minutes later, a smartly dressed, middle-aged, redhead entered the lounge, biting her lip. Other than the inconspicuous woman seated at the bar, the lounge was empty. She saw him slumped in an ornate red velvet armchair, recognizing him from the naked selfie that he sent her on her phone. Her casual playmate for the afternoon,

'My goodness, he's sound asleep!'

She gently shook her toy boy awake, whispering in his ear, so that no-one else could hear her.

'Martin is that you?' she asked in an eloquent, middle-class voice.

Slick surmised that this was her first illicit affair. The sad woman was carrying a smart, tanned, overnight bag.

A change of clothes, love? Satin perhaps?

Mature women preferred the comfort of satin. Amber Slick had witnessed many mature women like her in the company of Braker.

The bastard woke up, 'Yes, and you are?'

The woman introduced herself, 'Angie, my name's Angie. You agreed to sleep with me today?'

'You agreed to sleep with her?' Sian shrank, feeling sick, her worst fears realized, flopping in her bed. His discarded rag doll. She threw the tablet on the floor unable to watch, touch, taste, feel him anymore, and burst into tears.

He appraised his client. He'd never met a woman like her before. She was ageless, evergreen-young, with pure, tanned, perfect skin, roses-in-her-cheeks, melancholy-in-her-eyes, shocks of ginger curls kissing her shoulders. A proud face: high cheeks, piercing shiny grey eyes, cute toffee nose, pursed, thin, rouged lips. A woman of considerable standing and upbringing. A woman to show respect. She was wearing a plain indigo dress, bared arms and legs, poppy red stilettoes. Angie looked fantastic. He tried to age her: late thirties, mid-forties, early fifties? It was impossible to tell. He softened in her presence, becoming more human, loving, caring, than he had felt in his life, finding himself apologizing, sitting up straight for her, like her good boy, her puppy, about to be fed.

'I'm sorry, I'm Martin. Did you bring the...?'

She clumsily unzipped her leather bag, extracting a wad of used banknotes: £500 in £20 notes.

'Mm' she bit her lip, her stomach churned, she felt a hot, burning sensation in her urethra, and badly needed a pee, 'It's all here, would you like to count it?'

He shook his head, sadly, feeling sorry for her. Her first time. She must be absolutely petrified.

'Please, no, there's no need. Let's wait until we're safely inside the bedroom, shall we, Angie?'

She was touched by his surprising consideration for her. His warmth towards her. He'd used her name deliberately. Feeling a warm glow of contentment inside, Angie permitted herself a nervous smile.

'I need the loo, Martin. Can we go, please?'

'Of course, let me carry your bag.'

'Thank you.'

'If you'd like to follow me. Please.'

She wiped her lips with her wrinkled fingers, licking her fingertips with the end of her tongue, biting her rose gloss nails, overwhelming the man with her innocent, sensual allure, her scent.

'Thank you, I'd love to.'

They enjoyed a polite smattering of conversation as they left the bar, taking the grand, spiral, crystal-chandeliered staircase up to the first floor.

Slick maintained a discreet distance, watching them zing-card their way into room 124 from behind a turn in the corridor, then waited patiently in the lift lobby for one of them to leave. Her pent-up fury, her lust to wreak havoc, painful revenge, welled up inside her like a parasite worming its way out of her broken heart, into her distraught, demented mind.

*****

By any modern standard, Helen Carswell-Jones (she insisted upon retaining her maiden name when she was married) was well-off, seriously wealthy. A socialist might say stinking rich. She lived on a stud with her husband Bryn who was big in moulded fittings, flat-pack furniture, her fine young sons, Ollie and Seth, who boarded, several racehorses, and a golden retriever called Sandy. She had a live-in butler-cum-gardener, Sutton, who mucked out the stables, fed the horses, and fed her. She authored books: dark, erotic fantasies like the international best-selling Taut Neck.

Helen owned several acres, horse fields mostly (she had been known to ride), a smattering of apple and pear trees, heated outdoor swimming pool, private tennis court, wine barn, carp pond, and a wild swimming lake that was rumoured to contain trout. Her sons both owned quad bikes, semi-amphibious vehicles which they rode through the shallows when they were at home. Ollie and Seth were away at boarding school. Bryn was in Leeds. Leeds of all places. Away on business.

When the cats were away the kitten would play.

She smiled to herself, sinking inches deeper into the mint green swimming lake, stroking her fat cherry lips with her small brown hand. She was wearing mint white nail varnish, a mint white dress, just the dress.

Doesn't matter, no-one can see me. Only you, Hamish. You can see me, can't you?

'How's it going,' she shouted, with a posh bark, 'Caught any carp yet?'

Helen had agreed with Sutton that his sixteen-year-old nephew could fish for carp today in her murky horse pond before the pond dried up in the summer heatwave. In return for beers with whisky chasers, a swim with her, in the lake. Sutton had served the lad his bevy of drinks from a silver salver and been given the rest of the day off. The boy looked decidedly worse for wear, half-cut, more-than-merry, drunk. Helen was stone-cold sober, scheming, always scheming. The boy replied,

'Caught some, on bread. Put 'em in the far end of the lake, I did. So, they can eat your weed.'

He staggered along the bank so that he could get a better view of her. Mrs Carswell-Jones was very attractive: straight long nut-brown hair, a hint of grey tumbling down her lightly freckled back, nut brown eyes, turned up toffee-nose, fat pouting lips, bushy brows, an all-over toffee suntan,

'Right!' she said, laughing, 'Very good, Hamish. So, they can eat my weed. You look hot, sweetheart. Are you hot?'

'Must say, I am. Just a bit, mind.'

Helen pulled her dress off over her head, nearly drowning herself in the process. She sputtered.

'Do you fancy a swim with me?'

The boy's eye's attempted to grow stalks, 'I didn't bring no trunks.'

'Who said anything about you wearing trunks?'

After she had used the farmer's boy, she let him go, a man now not a boy, home to his grandma. Her thoughts turned to Bryn, her cruel control of him. Play as she would with the farmer's boy, the butcher's boy, the builder's lad, in the pond, the lake, the pool, rolling around in the hay after Sutton had mucked out the stables, Helen, a control freak, would never allow her husband to stray. She thought of the remarkable hi-tech, state-of-the-art, gadget, the intrusive device she had Bryn fitted with. Thought of Sian, poor Sian. Her best friend must be lonely. What with Martin, shame-faced Martin, working (playing?) away from home every night. At their recent dinner party in the wine barn, he couldn't even look Helen in the face.

I wouldn't trust him as far as I can throw him, she thought, Perhaps I should invite Sian over for a swim, a game of tennis.

Helen waded to the bank, leaving her mint white dress, their entrails, floating in the water, and clambered onto the bank. She found her phone in the grass, got a signal, then called Sian. Her call was answered immediately.

'Sian?'

'Yesss,' the voice sounded slurred, dreamy.

Helen was concerned, she knew Sian, knew her moods, her highs, and lows, 'Are you alright?'

'Not feelin so good. Goin' down with a bug or somethin.'

'I was going to invite you over for a swim, a game of tennis…'

'Best not,' Sian said, 'Not while I'm feelin so low.'

'Low?' asked Helen, sounding worried, 'What's the matter, Sian. What's happened?'

'Remember that funny gadget you gave me, to keep an eye on Martin?'

The miniature camera with built-in sound recorder and odorometer made in Japan.

'The fake button with the tracker device, you mean?'

'Yesss, that.'

There was a pregnant pause while Sian pulled herself together, while Sian tried to find the words.

'Well, it worked.'

Helen breathed a sigh of relief, 'Good, I'm pleased it works.'

'You don't understan.' It, I, caught Martin red-handed.'

Oh God! Something's wrong.

'Go on...'

'Martin's about to have sex with some woman for five hundred pounds. Five hundred! Do you believe that?'

I do, no, no...

'I don't believe you.'

'It's true! It's true, I tell you!'

Helen flopped down on the bank, sat on a thistle, jumped back up again, 'Oh Sian, I'm so sorry. What can I do to help?'

'There's more, much more...'

Helen closed her eyes, saying a little prayer, Please God.

'I'm pregnan,' Helen, 'Goin' to have a little baby. Now, I'm sittin' on the carpet with this bottle of sleepin' tablets...'

'Don't Sian! Please don't!' her best friend screamed, scrambling for her clothes, 'I'm coming over. Stay on the line, Sian. Sian? Sian!'

The line went dead.

*****

I'm floating. Floating on air. Floating above the coarse, green grass. I struggle to move my arms, my legs. My bare, pale, broken, arms and legs. Struggling to retain my modesty. Crippled in my black dress. Shorts, I'm wearing tight, black shorts. To protect my modesty. Conceal my injuries. I levitate, rising, high in the sky. I see faces beckoning me upwards. My head turns to face you. My dead eyes open and close. My damp brown hair hangs in drapes off my head. I'm scared: I reach out: I kick out: I scream blue murder:

Help me!

I open my mouth to speak. But it isn't my voice I hear. Isn't Amber's. It's Sian's voice. Calling. In the dark. Fade to black. Sian's voice calling me from the dark. Fade to black. Telling me.

Voices, ringing, in my head:

Amber?

Yes, Sian?

You're goin' on a killin' spree today, darlin'...

I watch and wait.

*****

Angie sat on the loo, her indigo dress hitched as high as her breasts, her beige satin knickers rolled down to her knees, thinking to herself,

What am I doing here? What's got into me all of a sudden? I should be ashamed of myself. For what I am about to do.

She let go of her dress, shut her eyes, and clasped her hands in her lap, as if in silent prayer.

For what I am about to receive may somebody up there, someone who loves me, make me truly thankful.

Prayer over, Angie sighed a long, deep sigh of relief. The luxury braided Palisades toilet roll hung off a brass ring on her left. She pulled off a thick wad wiping herself, enjoying the softness of the tissue against her cleft, the imaginary softness of Michael's fingers rubbing her tenderly, rhythmically, caressing her in the way she used to love being caressed.

Michael used to caress her the way she loved most. Michael made sweet passionate love to her on the sun lounger, on the veranda, in the half-light of dawn, her favourite time of day. Once.

Angie dropped the wad into the lavatory pan, twisted her supple body at the waist, and reached for the tube. She removed the cap, squeezed an ample blob onto her fingertips, and rubbed it in.

'Forgive me Michael,' she said to herself, opening her eyes, imagining his rugged face smiling at her from inside the vanity mirror, 'It's been five long years. I have to move on now, darling.'

He was waiting for her next door, through the bedroom wall. Martin. Waiting to make love to her. One last lingering moment of doubt,

'I'm not sure I can do this.'

'Of course, you can,' she told herself, 'You deserve it. After all you went through caring for Michael.'

Angie shook herself, pulled up her briefs, flushed the toilet, threw the used tube into a bin under the wash hand basin, washed her hands, fluffed up her ginger hair, and opened the bathroom door.

She cast her eyes to the right, seeing the brass latch and chain drawn across, securing her inside.

No sign of a Do Not Disturb notice. Must be hanging on the doorknob.

Angie would hate to be found out. How would she explain to her friends: at the Bridge Club, Aquarobics, Swimming, Zumba, Pilates, Tennis Club for that matter? How could she explain?

I can never tell them. Not in a thousand years. My friends wouldn't understand. Think of all the gossip, the scandal in our village.

She permitted herself a wry smile.

He's gone so far as to stick a blob of blue tack over the spyhole! Martin certainly isn't taking any chances, taking any chances with me. I wonder how many other women he's had, here, in this bedroom. Wonder if he'll be kind, gentle, and tender with me. I wonder if he'll hurt me.

The nerves returned to haunt her. She found herself trembling, shuddering, at the idea of him, his lips kissing hers, his hands caressing her, his body interlocked with hers. Blinking her insidious fears aside, she stepped into the bedroom. Facing her was a full-length, glass-fronted, wardrobe with its doors closed. Next to that, a polished wooden shelf filled with notepads, the hotel guide, two menus, a full tray of cups and saucers, selected fine teas, coffees, shortbread and a kettle. At the far end of the shelf, next to some flutes and Slim Jims, stood an ice bucket filled with bottles of mineral water, a bottle of champagne, sparkling wine, and some miniatures of claret? Angie couldn't tell from where she was standing. There was a narrow mirror over the shelf, a telephone for room service, a wireless internet connection. And, lying beside the ice bucket, a bunch of blood red roses. She thought of the five hundred pounds tucked inside her overnight bag. He had left it on the chair for her, considerately, unopened,

How much has this cost? she asked herself, the champagne, wine, flowers, room, and bed?

The bed itself was sheer unadulterated luxury, a layered wedding cake of a bed: an eiderdown, indigo bedspread, fluffy cream pillows. Cosy and snug. Her heart warmed, she felt herself relax.

Indigo. Cream. My favourite colours.

A bed in which to curl up with her lover.

He lay on top of the bed at the centre. He was naked, well-tanned, with an incredibly muscled physique: barrel chest, taut abs, and extremely well hung. Angie could barely bring herself to look at him. She stood at the far end of the bed, turning away, facing their mirror, murmuring.

'Martin, can you help me unzip my dress, please?'

*****

He didn't respond, didn't answer her. Instead, Martin lay, spreadeagled, on the king-size bed, studying her. Truth be told, he had never encountered a woman so beautiful, fragile as a porcelain doll, so vulnerable, in his life. He found himself intrigued, beguiled by her, the sadness in those big, tired, grey eyes. He desperately wanted to help her.

Neither of them spoke.

Angie glanced up at the hideous plasma screen tv hanging off the wall to her left. There was a slideshow playing shifting images of Palisades: the restaurant, lounge, cocktail bar, a bedroom featuring a luxurious four-poster bed, a table setting for afternoon tea, the rooftop garden, palm tree, indoor heated swimming pool, underground car parking facilities. She found it distracting. Her brief encounter, her fleeting romance, she hoped, with him, her craved-for reawakening, would be testing enough for her without the distraction of an advertorial. She picked up the remote and switched it off.

Martin closed his eyes and pictured Sian asleep in bed, her magnificent breasts cushioned by their duvet, kissing her soft lips before his illicit meeting with Angie. Sian, forever demanding, challenging, insistent that he make love to her until they created her new life, her baby. They'd been trying for so long. He questioned whether she was infertile. How would their lives change if Sian's dreams of motherhood ever came true? Did he want a child at all? How would he cope as the baby's father - with his terrible shame? His mind returned to the fragile porcelain doll.

Was she a mother?

The wall between the bedroom and bathroom was covered in floor-to-ceiling mirror, a hallmark of the lover's suites at Palisades. Angie set down the remote. She suddenly realized they might be being watched. The floor-to-ceiling glass pane looked out over a square, a green space dotted with elm, oaks, a few wrought iron benches clustered round a stone water fountain, a statue of a cherub with a harp, spouting water into a basin. A tramp stretched out over one of the benches enjoying the warm afternoon sunshine. A plump elderly woman with her hair tied in a bun fed a flock of pigeons, titbits, crumbs of stale bread from a paper bag.

Angie thought that will be me one day.

She drew the curtains, plunging the room into darkness. He was afraid of the dark. The shock of the dark brought back vivid memories of the horrid day when Martin and Sian, yes Sian was there, mowed down a young mother and her child, killing her baby instantly, the force of the collision hurling the buggy against a stone wall, her bloodied baby hanging off the straps of the buggy, the poor woman lying, bent, and twisted, under the wheels of their 4x4. How Sian pleaded with him to leave the scene with the maimed woman screaming in agony under their wheels. How Sian forced him to reverse off her mangled body. How Sian insisted that they leave her. Driving off. Their collective guilt: manslaughter.

Miraculously the woman survived, returning to stalk and terrorize them, to endlessly haunt them for their sins.

Angie broke the silence, 'Turn on the lights for me.'

Relieved, his nightmare was over for now, Martin fumbled for the dimmer light switch.

The main bedroom light came on. Angie moved to the other side of the bed, more confident, ready now, for him. She stood facing the full-length mirror, watching him slide across the bed to be with her. He stood behind her, pressing his body against her smart indigo dress, her back. Offering him no resistance, she explained, her classy, articulated voice reduced to a whisper.

'My husband died five years ago, Martin. He was my steadfast pillar of support, my best friend, my lover. I talk to him every morning when I wake and pray for him each night before I go to bed. I think of him every minute of the day. My life is empty, pointless, without him.'

'I'm sorry. How long were you married for?'

'Thirty years.'

Martin felt an overbearing sense of remorse, a compassion for her. Felt sorry for her. He wanted to love her, care for her, make up somehow for the loss that she'd endured, her loneliness, to do something good in his life for once.

Thirty years? She must be fifty, maybe as old as sixty, and yet she didn't look a day over thirty.

'That must be really hard for you, Angie.'

'It is hard. Michael and I were inseparable. We played together, shared the same interests: golf, tennis, swimming, keeping ourselves fit. Even worked together: we set up a successful cleaning company.'

Martin looked surprised, 'Cleaning company?! I thought you might work as a beauty therapist.'

The slightest hint of a smile appeared on Angie's thin, cherry red lips, 'Why do think that?'

'Because you have such a beautiful face.'

~ 44 ~

She blushed, 'You're very kind.

'Not at all. You're a very attractive woman.'

'I try to stay young.'

He changed the subject, 'Do you have any children?'

'No, I couldn't have children.'

'I'm sorry.'

'Please, don't be. Michael and I were perfectly happy without children. We led very busy lives.'

She paused for thought: And you, Martin. Are you married? Do you have children waiting for you at home? Are there women, passing strangers, in your life, rearing your unwanted bastards? Tell me your secrets.

She decided against. The thought of discussing his marriage (surely he wasn't married?) she found distracting, his illegitimate children.

Do I really need to know?

She ran out of small talk. He talked silently, exploring her with his fingertips, his puckered lips.

Angie sighed as her gigolo gently unclasped the hook on her indigo dress, drawing its zip down as far as her bra strap, fluffing her red hair, kissing her earlobes, the tell-tale gingery-red hairs on the nape of her neck, pressing his lips into the soft tanned skin, kissing her tattoos, the hairy down on her upper back. She felt the goosebumps rise on her exposed skin. Felt him pull the zip as far as the small of her back, licking a trace down her spine, savouring her skin, she felt him lick her body, felt a fresh, tingling sensation in her body, one she hadn't felt for years.

God, it's started!

'Martin,' she murmured.

He eased the dress off her shoulders. She slipped her dress down her arms, pulling it down as far as her hips, exposing her shoulders, her slender back, her midriff, her waist, for him to hold to kiss. His lips pressed into the small of her back. He held her by the hips. The dress fell in a crumpled heap round her ankles. She stepped out of her dress showing off her beige underwired bra, her satin briefs. Angie's body was magnificent, perfectly proportioned, well cared for, she had a blemish-free tanned complexion, her skin was well nourished. He leaned into her. His lips brushed her golden skin. Addicted to her intimate body scent, he couldn't stop kissing her divine flesh.

'Mmmn?'

'Be Michael for me.'

*****

There wasn't a moment to lose if Helen were to save her best friend's life. Still wet from her sexy swim, she tousled her damp brown hair with her gym towel, wondering what to do. Should she call 999, ask for emergency services? Ask for who? On what grounds? On the basis of a snatched conversation? Or should she get herself over to Sian's flat as soon as possible?

She procrastinated, unfamiliar with emergencies. Procrastination led to indecision. Indecision led to panic. Her panic brought her out in a thick daub of sweat. She inhaled, sharply, restoring her inner calm. Helen recovered. She wished Bryn were here. He'd know what to do. But Bryn was in Leeds, attending his moulded fittings conference, phone switched off, not to be disturbed. She dried herself, threw on her tracksuit, her soft running shoes, grabbed her phone, and made a beeline for the house.

The imposing Georgian manse overlooked a pink gravel drive. Standing on the forecourt were two muddy quad bikes and a post box red Mini Hatch Classic. The keys were still in the ignition from when dreamy Helen forgot to take them out. She threw open the door, threw her sports socks, towel, and phone on the passenger seat, jumped in, belted up, revved the engine, and shot off down her private driveway, weaving between the opening security gates, out, onto the forest road.

Sian's apartment was three miles away in the suburbs, a ten-minute drive at the best of times, thirty when the schools came out. Helen checked her gold wristwatch: ten-past-two. She sighed with relief. The narrow winding lane took her past the golf and country club, a chain of less-than-well-appointed abodes, to a sharp bend. She glanced at the mirror, applied clutch, selected third, glided round the bend, then had to brake. The queue of traffic stretched into the distance, as far as her eyes could see. There was a bright red sign at the side of the road with faded white lettering:

Road Works

Cars streamed towards her in the opposite direction. Unable to turn round, filled with road rage fuelled by frustration, Helen thumped her fist angrily on the steering wheel, sounding the horn. Just as she was about to pick up the phone and dial 999, the car in front of her edged forward.

Her mind was in a quandary:

Should I stay or should I go?

Helen went. Three red lights, twenty minutes later, she arrived outside Sian's apartment block. She clapped her sticky mitt over her forehead, staring in disbelief. The block had a common entrance, secured door, entry phone. Helen Carswell-Jones stamped her foot on the accelerator pedal, stalling the engine.

Why didn't I remember that?

Unless her luck changed very quickly, she would have to call Sian to enter the building. Assuming Sian was even conscious.

Helen climbed out of the Mini, slammed the door, and rushed up to the entry phones, selecting: Flat 5 - Braker

She held the button down for a full five minutes.

Sian didn't answer.

*****

Roleplay. Martin had engaged in roleplay for clients before as part of their erotic fantasies. But this was the first time that he'd ever performed the role of a woman's dead husband. He found the prospect strangely daunting, detecting a change in Angie who had shaken off her pre-sex jitters, becoming more strident, more dominant. Martin suspected she had a plan, a screenplay, for him, her performing sealion, her captive puppet-on-a-string, to act out. He wasn't far wrong.

'How would you like me to act, to talk to you, Angie?' he asked, gently massaging her shoulders.

She smiled for the first time. The smile lit up her face, 'I'll help you, Michael. Listen to me, carefully. Listen to what I say, what I tell you to do. Pretend you have just come home late after a long, gruelling day at the office. You find me waiting for you in our bedroom, getting undressed for bed. You love to watch me undress. You love me to wear satin for you. I dress in my silky satin slip for you. Pretend for me, please? Then you can let your imagination run wild. Is that any help?'

Martin swallowed hard, 'I think so.'

Angie reached behind her back, unclipping her bra, 'One more thing. Call me Angela, Michael. My husband always used to call me Angela when we made love.'

Made love. Such an old-fashioned expression. We're about to fuck, and she wants me to make love to her, as her dead husband, he mused.

He remembered her five-hundred-pound payment, the cost of hiring the lover's suite for the night, the cost of *Moet & Chandon*, his train tickets. Sian, awaiting his return, none the wiser. What would she do to him, to herself if she ever found out? The consequences of his infidelity, his fake life, didn't bear thinking about. Martin re-focussed, checking his watch. If he got his skates on, he might just catch the 16:43 back to Paddington. He could be home with Sian by eight, pretending he'd had another tiresome day, selling financial investment proposals to recently bereaved widows. He heard Angie's refined voice, articulating in the background. She hadn't paid yet.

'Shall we make a start?'

She had his full, undivided attention. He held her slender waist, 'Yes, where do we begin?'

His client was sweating profusely. She commenced, 'You're home late tonight, darling.'

'I had a hard day at the office, Angie.'

'No, not Angie,' she chided, 'Angela.'

Martin removed his hands from her midriff realizing that he shouldn't be touching her there yet, 'Sorry, I meant Angela.'

She unclipped her bra, 'There's no need to apologize. Being so in love means never having to say sorry to each other, doesn't it?'

He nodded his understanding, as the truth finally dawned on him: this fantasy, this roleplay of hers, isn't just make-believe. This is for real! She thinks I'm him!

He watched dry-mouthed in the mirror as she casually slipped the bra straps over her shoulders, let the straps hang off her elbows, easing the cups off her breasts. She let her bra fall on the carpet, reaching for him, wanting him to touch her. He gasped at the sight of her buoyant, busty, buxom, breasts, her round cherry red nipples, speckled with sweat. She craned her head. They kissed, deeply, pausing for breath.

She spoke, her voice was hushed, 'You can rub my breasts, if you like, Michael. Would you like to rub my breasts?'

He cupped her breasts in his hands, loving the feeling of the soft undersides, her sore bra weals, kneading her rounded, doughy breasts, flicking, rubbing her nipples, until her teats stood erect.

'Love that, don't you? Love it when you rub my breasts. I love you, Michael. Do you love me?'

He gulped, lost for words: he'd never felt, touched, caressed, loved, a woman like this before - a mature woman like Angie. Her allure erased Sian from his mind, obliterating her completely. After several tense silent moments her gigolo found his voice hissing the fatal words in her ear, his voice slurred, dreamy, happy, held in a magic trance, her trance.

'I do, Angela, I love you so much, I worship the ground you walk on.'

The sad truth was he really meant it.

*****

Getting the shakes. Struggling to control myself. Angry, feel angry. Frustrated. How long do I have to wait…

Not much longer, darlin, Sian's subliminal voice reassured her, Now have you remembered everythin'?

Amber Slick steadied herself, pressing the flat of her hand, feeling the vintage mural wallpaper. She surveyed the corridor, the ornate passageway to their luxurious love-nest. Lucky them.

She felt the hatred boil up inside her, threatening to spew out of her face like hot bloody vomit. Clenching her fists, she brought her deadly rage under control. The lift lobby was empty, there was no-one coming,

Thank God! she sighed, inside her warped mind, can't catch me, can you? Ha! Wait a minute…

One of four sets of lift lights changed, a red light moved: basement, ground floor, first floor…

Amber held her breath…

…second, third, fourth…

She sagged at the knees crouching like a leopard poised, ready to pounce on her unsuspecting prey, then checked the bucket bag wedged between her knees. Still there. Her lethal weapons were still there. Relieved, content to wait, Amber shut her eyes, swimming in an imaginary tide of blood, her black dress clinging to her body as she turned scarlet, puce, crimson, purpled with pent up rage, to Sian, for comfort.

Nearly there, darlin,' nearly there, shut your eyes, Amber, shut your eyes an' I'll take you there.

*****

Helen reasoned, since the summer holidays had just begun and she knew from Sian that several of the apartments were occupied by wealthy students, there was a good chance that some of them might still be in bed, sleeping off the excess of the night before.

She pressed: Flat 6: Smart, there was no reply.

She pressed: Flat 4: Gelding and struck it lucky.

A knackered voice replied, 'Hello?'

'Please help me. I need to see Sian Braker in Flat 5 urgently. My name's Helen,' she explained, 'I'm her best friend. Please let me in!'

The voice sounded agitated, 'I know who Sian is. She lives next door with the weird guy. Martin, I think his name is. Not that he's ever here. Anyway,' he asserted, 'how do I know you're who you say you are? How do I know you're not the crank?'

'Sorry, I don't understand. What crank?'

'Sian's being stalked by some mad woman. Stands in the car park most days, staring at her flat. Funny, haven't seen her today. Must be having a day off.'

'Stalked! By a woman?!'

'You heard,' the young male voice faded, 'If you don't mind I need to snatch some sleep.'

Helen shouted, 'Wait! Sian told me she's taken a bottle of sleeping tablets. She needs urgent medical assistance!'

She heard the click of the door, a sudden alarm in the young man's speech, 'Come to the first floor. Meet me by the lift. I have a key. To her flat.'

Helen couldn't believe her luck had changed, 'A key?'

'Yeah, Sian's always losing hers. Asked me to keep a spare. Come up.'

He was waiting for her in the lift lobby, the most beautiful young man she had ever seen. Wild staring eyes, scruff of teak hair, fat cracked strawberry lips, a long melonic face smattered with freckles, black tee-shirt, boxer shorts. A little bit old for her liking, student, eighteen, nineteen? Still, on another occasion. She shook the wicked thoughts from her mind, tried to take his hand.

'Helen,' she said, pleasantly.

'Tom. Come on!'

He hurled open the lobby doors, sprinting down the corridor, closely followed by Helen. Sian's flat was at the far end of the corridor. There was a sisal doormat outside that read: Step Inside, Love

Helen felt sick, had no desire at all to go inside, dreading what she would find. Tom unlocked the door. They entered Sian's flat to find her lying sprawled on the bedroom carpet clutching an empty phial. Tom closed his eyes out of respect for her - the young woman was naked – he knelt beside her, feeling her neck, struggling to find her pulse. Helen rued her best friend. She was barely breathing.

'Cover her with the duvet,' Tom yelled, 'We must keep her warm. Are you trained in first aid?'

Helen shook her head, pulling the duvet off the crumpled bed, covering Sian to keep her warm, 'I'm sorry, Tom, I'm not.'

'Me neither,' he mumbled, standing, remembering the phone in the hall. He left Helen to watch over her stricken friend, 'I'm calling an ambulance. Stay with her, Helen. Stay with her.'

'Is she going to be alright?' she asked out of desperation.

Tom looked away. He couldn't bring himself to tell her the shocking truth.

*****

He moulded his body round hers freeing her, releasing pent-up inhibitions, mournful grief. Languishing under his forceful pressure, relishing the rub of his cusps of muscle against her back, the divine sensation of his proud flesh: erect, turgid, pressed into the crevice between her fleshy buttocks, she relented, capitulating. Angie lost control, gasping as he kneaded her breasts.

She reached behind her, and drew his hungry mouth to hers, kissing-him-some-more. She covered his hands with hers, sliding his palms over her tummy, pausing to explore her deep navel, her pearl charm, her neatly concealed belly button, his rough hands, caressing her belly as she slipped his fingers inside her satin briefs. She tantalised him, allowing him to fondle her soft, hairy mound.

'Pull down my pants,' she croaked, her voice hoarse, husky with sex.

Martin obliged her, stripping Angie's satin briefs off as far as her knees. Mesmerized by her explicit nudity, her daring, final exposure in the mirror, he let her go. She dropped her pants, stepped aside, reaching for her bag, breathing sharply, struggling to speak, she was so aroused.

'Fetch the chair, Michael. Sit facing the mirror. Close your eyes. And wait.'

Angie went to the bathroom. Martin fetched the padded chair. Sat, shut his eyes, and waited…

'You can open your eyes now.'

He opened his eyes. Angie knelt between him and the mirror, sipping a glass of red wine. She'd applied fresh lipstick, make-up, he noticed: a bold slash of blusher, primal warpaint scarred her cheeks. She downed her glass of wine, and moved in, closer. Angie reeked of statement-making sexy perfume. Martin had only smelled it once before, at an exclusive perfumery in Paris. The unmistakable fragrance of chocolates, red berries, with caramel: Angel, the twenty-three-year-old cult fragrance by *Thierry Mugler*, the sexiest scent in the world. He was impressed. Her sharp aroma, her irresistible masque, her satin fetish panties, took his breath away. Overcome with pride for her, he wanted to fuck her, hard,

Angie. Angela. Angel. My Angel. My Angela. My Angie.

'Well, Michael?' she asked, posing for him with one hand on her hip, 'Will I do?'

She was wearing single chain diamond dangle earrings that accentuated her tired face, gilding her swan neck. She stroked the base of her throat with her wrinkly fingers. Her lips were sealed. Her eyes shone with tears. For one sacred moment, he was lost for words. His heart went out to her.

'You look beautiful, Angie, just beautiful.'

She sat on his lap, facing him, her arms wrapped around his neck, kissing him. With just one secret left to share, she showed him her intimate tattoo.

He protested, 'Angie, I'm not wearing a...'

She pressed her fingertips to his lips, 'It's alright. I've had my menopause.'

They kissed-some-more. She impaled herself on him hungrily, feeding him inside her lubricious cleft, sliding up and down his slippery shaft. He bore her body weight, grasping her small buttocks, stimulating her naughtily with his stubby middle finger. She shuddered at his intervention, writhing in ecstasy on his glorious spear, cupping her breasts, forcing her stiff nipples between his dry lips, suckling the baby she couldn't birth. They ascended, flashing pinpricks of light, glowing scarlet fireflies pervading their ruptured minds. They bonded, their bodies melded, locked-together-tight, they gripped, clawed, clenched, tore, and fought each other.

Soaring to her climax, she screamed out loud, 'Miss you, Michael! Love you!'

Spent, shattered, a tarnished doll, she flopped against Martin's slumped body, whispering softly, lovingly,

'Do you love me, Michael? Please tell me you do.'

'Yes, I love you, Angela, very much,' he groaned.

Tenderly, she slipped him out of her, kissed him on the forehead, and stood.

'You made me all sticky, darling. I think I need a shower.'

He smiled, genuinely happy, truly content for the first time in his life, 'I think you do!'

He shut his bleary eyes, fell asleep, dreaming of her, the craving love she just made to him.

Angie said a fond, 'Goodbye Michael' - under her breath.

She gathered her clothes, grabbed her bag, spread five hundred pounds over the bed, had a shower, dried herself, did her hair, put on some fresh make-up, got dressed, then left him, slumped on the chair.

*****

His routine was always the same. Martin met his client in the bar, went to the room, had paid sex with her, kissed her goodbye, then, exhausted, he took a rest. Later, he would bathe, shower, and sanitize, removing all traces of her sediment from his body, dress in fresh clothes, take the early evening train to London.

Angie, still red-faced, feeling ashamed of herself, was in a hurry to leave. Unaware of the threat posed by the crippled woman, she passed Slick in the lift lobby. Slick followed her to the dingy, oily, smelly, underground garage where she attacked her from behind. She strangled her victim gracefully, silently, drawing the garotte tightly round her neck. The woman thrashed her head from side to side. Her brittle nails tore out her assailant's hair. Her elbows pummelled her ribs. The victim strained and stretched, kicked, and bit. But Slick clung on. Until her death. Calmed, the woman relaxed onto Amber's flat chest. Angie fell asleep one last time dreaming of the time when a gigolo made love to her, pretending to be her dead husband. Her neck still in twine, her sad head flopped forward, her dead eyes rolling up, staring into empty garage space.

Amber carefully unwound the sacrificial wire, with its carved acorn handles, from the corpse's neck, as if she were peeling nylon sea fishing line off a reel-spool, stowing it in her bucket bag. She locked Angie's corpse into its new 4x4 jeep casually dropping the keys down a storm drain, left the garage, and took the staff lift to the first floor.

Martin stirred from his slumber thinking of her, playing out her fantasy. How she'd left him asleep, left his fee on the bed, then bolted like a frightened deer. He wasn't surprised. No matter how promising their intentions, clients never stayed long once their sex was over. And yet, she found a kind of love with him. He felt sorry for her, more than sorrow he felt he loved her. He reflected forlornly on their brief encounter.

At least, he made her happy.

He heard a gentle knocking on the door, the charming, feminine, squeaking of a stalking bird.

'Room Service.'

He stared at the bottle of champagne lying unopened in the wine cooler. Her empty glass, the crimson stain on the carpet. He didn't recall ordering food. He eyed the door, recalling the Do Not Disturb sign hanging on the doorknob outside.

'Room Service,' the high-pitched voice repeated, 'Fresh supply, coffee, tea, milk, biscuits for your bedroom.'

Martin checked the beverage tray on the sideboard. It hadn't been touched.

He shrugged his shoulders, 'Just a minute.'

He went to the wardrobe, took out his fluffy white gown, put it on, tied the cord at his waist

… and opened the door,

'No! Please! No!'

Martin Braker puts up his fists, boxer-style, in a vain bid to defend himself.

Slick was insane. She went berserk. She swung the meat cleaver at him with all her might, slicing a deep red gash in the man's forearm. Horrified by the sight of his blood soaking the white gown red, he recoiled, collapsing, falling to his knees in prayer, praying for his life. Slick swung the cleaver, slicing into his neck, again and again and again. He keeled over and toppled forward.

His final act was to kiss a cripple's feet.

Jess

JESS LOVES TO DRIVE AT NIGHT, the thrill of the chase, the glowing array of lights on her dashboard. She feels dark: deep suntan, ripe plum lips, dark mascara, leather jacket, driving gloves. Feels in the mood: the girl who loves to kill, chasing her love to die for. Gripping the steering wheel, one-handed, lifting her soft camisole, rubbing the scarlet weal a man gave her fighting to the death. She feels hurt-in-her-heart, vengeful, shows no remorse for the unforgiven sex.

Her unsuspecting quarry joins the motorway. Entering the loneliest stretch, he accelerates his Tesla to eighty, ninety, one hundred miles an hour. Torn jeans, torn name, torn heart, torn flesh, she struggles to keep him in her sights. Just in time, the highway narrows to two lanes, chevrons keep them apart. Jess checks her clock radio: almost midnight. Time for the news. She will hit the headlines, dominate the traffic report: reports are just coming in of an...

Lights on her dashboard flicker red, amber, green. She takes her foot off the accelerator, selects fifth, moves herself clear of him, slowing till they're chevrons apart. Jess turns on the radio, the DJ plays his final song of the night: his final song. Jess selects fourth, third, second, stops the car. *Drive* ends. The DJ says goodnight. She turns up the heat. The car in front explodes in a fireball: hell, hath no fury like a woman scorned.

*****

Imagine an arena, a natural coliseum offering every type of fight for which you could wish. Whatever his dream, this is where she'll make it come true.

The murky hollow, nestled in the bowels of the downs, isn't his idea of paradise. Their clandestine liaison, reason for her to appear, is her idea - not his.

Koch drives carefully over the speed bumps on the drive thru the woods, her secret enclosed like velvet baize on a card table. His rank precludes him from privileges such as his hero's jetpack, shared use of a modified Aston Martin DB6. After a hell of an uphill struggle, the winding lane dips. He kills the engine, saving petrol, coasts downhill to the car park, arriving at the break of dawn, their designated time of rendezvous.

There is a hut converted into an angling tackle shop. Signs indicate his and her toilets. Her toilet sign refers to baby changing facilities. This strikes him as odd given men are deemed as capable of changing nappies, playing parent, as women. Koch enters the cabin, slips the latch, switches on the sea-blue pump-action gravitational suction system for human waste. Stands over the toilet, drops his jeans, his jockstrap, and relieves himself. To his horror, the hand basin is bereft of bactericidal handwash. There is no hand-dryer. Dismayed by the poor standard of hygiene, he shakes his hands dry as he steps outside. A sign explaining the venue is closed for holidays clings to the shop's roller shutter blind.

He traipses thru the teeming rain to his van, loading his well-honed, muscular body with creel, lounger, telescopic fishing rod, umbrella, landing net, and a body-sized unhooking mat, for her.

She's late. Where is she? He needs to fight her.

Koch likes his action fast, furious. His arms to ache with pleasure. A steady stream of hand-to-hand fighting to leave him exhausted, happy in a way only hard-fighting women like her can. He thinks of his wife, her unborn child.

Thinks he hears a voice call him. Her? No, the call of the wild. He feels sad. His heavily pregnant wife waits anxiously for his return. Reflections on his family life are rudely interrupted by a woman's voice,

'Ready to fight me?'

He bows his head in shame. Jess dismounts from her pink hybrid mountain bicycle. Her face, bum, thighs and calves are spattered with orange mud, caked on by the gruelling uphill climb. Her chiselled cheeks are taut with strain. Under the grime lies a simple slick of make-up. Her lips are plump with pout. Her eyes shine with the tears of one who faces an unknown fate at the hands of her foe. She takes off her helmet. Her hair is thin, wispy. She extends a manicured hand, slim fingers, no ring.

'I'm ready to fight you,' she says, casually undressing for combat, 'Shall we get it over with?'

It is a twisted game, she plays. A necro-sexual foreplay, climaxing in death. She hides behind masques. Trades futures on the dark web. Leaves no trace of human waste, corpse, or detritus. The halcyon days of illicit drop-offs coded tell-tale slips of rice paper are long gone. She traces, tracks, shuts down, then kills. The foe has changed her motives remain the same: disrupt, disturb, destroy. Jess mirrors the cruel, dispassionate society we live in. Owes no allegiances. Holds no respect, no morals. Recognizes no authority except the hand that feeds her. Officially, she doesn't exist.

*****

Neath stands on the right-hand side of the escalator when she passes, wiggling her bum at him, swaying her hips. The central aisle between the escalators is littered with paper flapping in the breeze. How long will it take commuters to create a firetrap as a result of their laziness? He dismisses the notion from his mind as he alights in the ticket hall, following her thru the ticket barrier.

Jess is wearing an unzipped black leather bomber jacket, a clingy cream camisole, skin-tight faded denims, slashed at the thighs, sneakers, a clootie bobble hat to keep her head warm. She lifts her camisole and rubs the nasty gash under her full left breast: a flesh wound from her mud-wrestling fight when she killed a man with her bare hands. Death is no stranger to this woman. She's tough. She'll survive as long as she stays fit, beautiful. She drops her camisole, zips her jacket, walks out of the station into the sleet-flecked fresh air, turning right onto the high street.

Neath follows her at a discreet distance, stopping to buy a paper from a kiosk. An old man with a glass eye stares over him at the white vellum sky, taking money in his gloved hand, his fingers cyan blue with cold where they poke thru holes in the leather.

The sleet turns to snow too light to settle. Flakes flicker on his eyelashes. He sees her cross the street at a pelican crossing, turn right by an arcade: greengrocer, halal butcher, pawnbrokers, chemist, walk under a railway bridge. Neath crosses the road at a break in the rush hour traffic, wary of the pigeon shit smearing the wrought ironwork, cowering in case the vermin's mess falls on him, ruining his smart navy Crombie coat.

Jess stops at a left-hand turn while an HGV draws into the goods entrance of a DIY superstore, crossing the road when it is safe. Trust to no-one: the lorry might reverse, flatten her, squash her supple body in one long red blood-trail underneath its heavy wheels. Trust to no-one, except herself: rule number one in her survival manual. She glances over her shoulder at him, her snub nose red with cold, cheeks pallid. Neath knows her pre-ordained fate. He feels for her.

The rundown industrial estate is at the next turning on the left. Jess waits outside a three-storey ruin. A 4x4, Merx, and Lexus pull in, parking on the puddled yellow line in front of a disused soap factory with a redbrick chimney. Each car deposits a woman. Doors are slammed. Kisses are blown. The partners go off to work. Their women gather in the snow outside the converted workshop stamping their feet, waiting for him to unlock the cast-iron door, let them into the warm: two Caribbeans, an Indian, an Arab, Essex Girl, and Jess.

For Christmas she received an unusual present from him: a voucher to attend a one-day course where she can learn to make a dress in a day. Neath knows her vital statistics, had her examined head to toe, even the raised dark chocolate mole in her left groin. Knows all there is to know about Jess: her medical history, illnesses, injuries, mental health, diet, her sexual preferences, on the basis that he has a need to know.

He grins as she undresses in front of the other, shocked, women, and tries on a sample dress. It fits her perfectly. Each woman sits by their assigned sewing machine. Neath explains how to sew a dress. They cut out material from a pattern, then started to sew. He is patient with them, very understanding. At noon they put on their snug winter coats and buy lunch in the local café. All, except Jess. She just sits, staring nervously at him, wondering what is to become of her as he scoffs his bland feta sandwich. They don't speak. They don't need to.

After lunch, the women return, finish their dresses, stand behind a screen and try them on. They are delighted, parading their hand-made frocks around the cutting room, flaunting themselves, tipping, handsomely. They promise to attend his next course. Neath leads his happy flock down six flights of stairs to a tiny lobby by the factory exit, waiting with them until their mates pull in to collect them. The dilapidated industrial estate is dangerous after dark: drug addicts, rapists, beggars, rats-the-size-of-cats frequent the foetid-piddled streets.

He returns upstairs. Jess waits until he is seated. He watches, avidly, as she wriggles out of her jeans, pulls the loose camisole over her head. She is wearing her ruby red bra, soft pink cotton panties. He knows she feels apprehensive about the colour, his reasons for choosing pink. He beckons her to put on the dress. Jess pulls it over her head, rolling the material over her breasts and tummy, pressing the creased material close to her skin.

She looks pleased. Jess has a pretty pink dress with a red flower on it to take home: a summer dress, sleeveless, cut above her knees. The dress is fashionable. She is happy with her dress. He loves her when she is happy like this, his heart sinks at the thought of how he lost her love.

'I'm sending you back,' he says, passing her a folder stapled with a colour print: a ruddy-faced, chubby-cheeked man with a beard, 'You're to wear the dress for him. He likes his women in pink. Our agent, Hans, will contact you,' Neath hands her a shot of a bearded blonde athlete, high cheeks, scowl, 'Meet him tomorrow night at six beside the Four Acts of Love. He'll be riding an ice cream tricycle. You can't miss him.'

Jess smiles, her lips, plump with pout, 'Acts of Love? Ice cream in January? It's minus seven, snowing hard in Nuremberg. What is this, Neath? One of your sick jokes?'

'No, this is for real. Read the instructions. He will issue you with a firearm. You are to acquire the target as he leaves The Old Boar opposite Oude Kirk, take him to Hotel Elk, despatch. Your expenses are pre-paid: train, flight, metro tickets, meals, hotel. You'll pose as Spitz. Your flight departs Stansted tonight at eight-thirty. Are there any questions?'

Her eyes shine with the tears of a woman who faces an unknown fate at the hands of her foe. Jess puts out her left hand. The nail has been ripped off of her ring finger. She has no pinkie,

'If they catch me,' she pleads, 'will they tear off another nail, or saw off my little finger?'

Neath can't stare her in the face: the deceit. She looks beautiful in pink. Such a terrible waste. He feels ashamed of himself.

'Shall we get it over with?' she says, bravely.

She knows something's wrong. Call it woman's intuition.

He stares at his feet, can't bring himself to tell her the dreadful truth.

Let her go, he decides, let her go.

*****

Heist's initial reaction, when he reads the WhatsApp, is one of intrigue. He can't believe they're sending her back after the pain he inflicted on her last time.

He slumps on the seat of the shoulder press having lifted 115kg, watching a young frau perform on the treadmill opposite. She isn't wearing her sports bra today, just a loose vest, tight-fitting shorts. He hopes she had warm clothes to change into when she ventures out into the snow. On another occasion he might test her. Today, he has more important priorities. Heist rubs the ugly black and red tattoos of death and hate etched into his massive biceps. The girl slows to a walk, checks her app, removes her earplugs, halts, turns to walk off the belt, stands perfectly still, and admires his animal physique.

'What are you looking at, liebe?' he taunts. His withering look makes her wilt in her trainers.

'I am sorry, I saw you smile at me,' she tells him, 'I thought you might like to fuck me?'

'You didn't see me,' he hisses, menacingly, 'Get out of here!'

'If you say so. Auf wiedersehen.'

Frightened, the blonde grabs her towel and hurries out of the gym.

He seeks further clarification:

How will I recognize her?

She will be wearing a zipped black leather bomber jacket, over a pretty pink dress with a red flower on it: a summer dress, sleeveless, cut just above the knee. The dress looks fashionable. Bare legs, pink sneakers, a white clootie bobble hat to keep her head warm.

Why does she need to keep her head warm?

Because her hair is thinning, balding.

Why is she balding?

She suffers from alopecia.

What is the password?

Christmas Dream.

The song by Perry Como, right?

Correct.

Ha! I have the music as a jingle for my tricycle!

Then you can play it to your heart's content, can't you? I have to go. Danka!

Ich dien!

What was that?

I serve!

Ah, of course! Don't we all? Auf wiedersehen.

Auf wiedersehen.

He grabs his towel, leaves the gym, goes to the men's changing room. The room is full of steam - a Turkish Bath: the stench of sweat from the fat swine who shower there after their vain efforts to work off their potbellies. Heist opens his locker, retrieving his warm hoodie, baggy tracksuit bottoms, avoiding staring at the sumo-bellied double-breasted baldies. They disgust him, gone to fat on their sausages and beer, a disgrace to the land their fathers and grandfathers fought for. They should be ashamed. He quickly dresses and leaves. Outside, it stops snowing.

His cosy furnished apartment is a short walk away in Alstadt the historic city centre. Alstadt is divided into Sebald, north of the River Pegnitz, and Lorenz to the south. The old town was completely destroyed by the allied bombing raids during the war and had to be rebuilt. He will never forget what they did to his beloved mediaeval city. Heist enters his student apartment in Sebald, a bargain rental: only 595 euros a month. There is a bedroom, kitchen, and bathroom.

He runs himself a hot bath, strips beside the pink bathtub, sliding under the water, dreaming of her: wearing only her pink dress, floating face down in the muddy waters of the swollen river. Heist sleeps in the bath until the water turns cold, climbs out, shaves off his beard, brushes his teeth, then he goes to bed.

When he wakes up it is dark, time for his injection. He keeps his insulin cold in the fridge with the drug. His thighs and buttocks are covered in pinpricks, hollowed out by the countless jabs he has endured since he was diagnosed as Type 1 diabetic at the age of four. He learnt to inject himself using an orange until he felt confident enough to slide the needle into his flesh at the correct angle. They say pain is something you get used to, but each jab hurts him just as much as the last. Heist rests his foot on the bedroom chair and stabs himself in the thigh imagining it is her thigh. He sterilizes the needle with a swab, returning the syringe to a metal casing that he stores in the kitchen cupboard.

The drug comes in a small bottle with a rubber cap, sealed with a metal ring. Heist takes one out of the fridge, unwraps a fresh disposable syringe, and sticks the needle in the cap, drawing off fluid till the syringe is half-full. There is an air bubble. Air trapped inside a syringe can, if injected into the human body, induce an embolism, a bubble of air in the bloodstream, fatal if it reaches the brain. He doesn't bother to expel the air. She is going to die anyway, what's the point?

Unusually for him, he feels uncomfortable about this assignment. Guilty about his act of deceit towards her, the danger his despicable act could cause. Heist feels for her standing, waiting for him in the freezing cold by the ice fountain overlooked by the white tower of death. This is the choice he made when he was acquired. To kill men and women, despatching them mercilessly, without love. To exist as lowlife in his squalid hovel inside the mediaeval city wall, a sleeper waiting to be activated by some faceless clown in an alien country he'll never visit, a superior authority he cannot trust.

Rule number one: trust to no-one.

Heist must comply with his instructions or risk being exposed. Risk having his extreme political convictions broadcast to a disparaging world. He believes in the sanctity of the Aryan race, the blue-eyed, blonde-haired boys and girls who march with him in khaki-uniformed legions thru the pine forest on Sunday mornings waiting for their time to come. He is convinced, they will rise again. Until then, he'll lie low in his hole, a slug of contempt waiting for the rain of anarchy to fall on the unsuspecting heads of civilisation.

He walks slowly but steadily along the icy streets, crossing the flooded grey river at Maxbrüke by the ancient Weinstadel passing Unschlift Platz to Karl-Grillenberg Strasse. Soon, he reaches the frozen fountain. She will have taken a U1 transit from Hauptbanhof central railway terminal to Weisser Turm, having arrived at Hotel Elk late last night. He hopes she speaks German. Her journey to the city by U2 transit from the airport is easy enough. Finding her hotel at night-time in the knot of narrow backstreets beside the river? Impossible!

He loiters by the mis-named Four Acts of Love. It is actually called The Marriage Merry-Go-Round: four hilarious, vulgar bronzes of wedded bliss, from courtship to skeletons, one of the largest figure fountains of the 20th Century.

Despite his balaclava helmet, warm winter fleece, and tracksuit bottoms, Heist is chilled to the bone. He stamps his feet on the pavement, removes his leather gloves, blows into his hands. It starts to snow. A small group of forlorn tourists appear at the top of an ornate tiled staircase, step out of the transit station, stop, and take a photo of him by Death, the fourth bronze. They laugh at him.

They will laugh on the other sides of their smug faces when we march again, he broods.

The group disappears in the direction of the beautiful Lorenzkirche church, a warm hostelry, a stein of blonde beer, to wait for his signal.

Heist checks his watch. The icy street is deserted. She is late. Where is she? A slim figure appears briefly at the top of the staircase, disappears from view. He walks slowly around the fountain. She is standing by the second bronze, Family a sculpture of a mama and papa withered by their screaming infant son and baby girl. He sends a text. Jess is wearing her black leather bomber jacket, a skimpy pink dress. Her legs are bare. Sneakers. Bobble hat.

'Mein Gott!' he swears, under his breath, 'She must be fucking freezing!'

He listens to her sing: his sweet, lilting songbird. She smiles for him, the smile that disarmed a thousand men. He can't help himself, can't help but sing with her. Jess overwhelms him with guilt. Guilt resonates in his hoarse voice. They stare up at the starry night sky, white tickertape fluttering down onto their frozen cheeks and lashes. Tears of pride glisten in their eyes, masking their true feelings, real expectations. The tourists reappear beyond the fountain of Death. A taxi creeps off its rank in Jacobs Platz.

Jess smiles at him.

'Come to me,' he tells her, excitedly, 'I have a present for you.'

She takes his hand. He holds her to his face. Her ring finger has no nail. Her hand has no little finger. They walk beyond the fountain of Death, footprints covered with snow, still she sings.

The tourists close in on her, dragging her from him. One thug pulls her arms behind her back. One kicks her hard in the calf, forcing her to slump to the frozen ground. Another tears off her warm hat, holding her head, twisting her confused face away from him, baring her gilded neck. Heist removes the metal case from his fleece, a syringe primed to inject her. Holds her smooth, soft chin still, smudging her cherry red lipstick with his gloved thumb.

'Hans?' she pleads her teak eyes shining with icy droplets of fear.

'Hans is dead!' he jeers, 'Hans is lying in the silt, rotting in the Pegnitz!'

'Then who are you?'

Jess starts to whimper, tremble. He feels her teeth chatter against his face. The taxi arrives. Her time is over. He stabs the needle in her neck, depressing the plunger, feels her body flop, a soft, soggy, sponge rubbing his thighs. The thugs let her flaccid torso sink to the ground.

'Go easy with the manicure,' she says, sexily, as she lapses into unconsciousness.

*****

From what Jess can see and feel, she is lying on a bed, incarcerated in a dungeon. The cell is hot, humid, claustrophobic as a sauna. Women are meant to perspire, but her body is spurting out sweat in a human geyser. The crumpled sheet beneath her back is saturated, leaving her restless, uncomfortable. She has no idea of the time, desperately needs to piss. It's hard to hold it in when your limbs are under full restraint.

She wants to rub the sore gash under her breast, a flesh wound from her mud-wrestling fight in the pissing rain when she killed a man, snapping his neck like dry matchwood with her bare hands. But her wrists are firmly manacled to the bed. The bruised creases in her elbows hurt where the leather straps rub her needle-holes, punctures made by an evil foe determined to pump her full of truth drug - until she breaks.

Her neck is stiff from staring at the bare light bulb hanging from the craggy rock ceiling. She cranes her head to the left. Her captors have gone to considerable lengths to install a coat rail, plastic hangars beside her bed, confirming her worst suspicions. There, displayed in order of their removal, are her pink dress, ruby red bra, and soft pink cotton panties. Jess shivers and shudders - despite the cell's heat.

A zephyr blows over her hair making her skin wrinkle. She misses her clootie bobble, sneakers, dress, her underwear for that matter. Jess feels, smells, senses, him approaching her, sprawled over the bed. She cranes her neck, her chin hugging her chest, watching him take up position at her feet: her perpetrator of fear. She fears he will torment her, extract her intimate knowledge, then kill her.

He is tall, skeletal to look at: thin blanched face, ice-blue eyes, straggly hair. He wears pebble-glassed bifocals, full-length leather trench coat: a crossbreed hybrid of Satan and Goebbels. He bows from the waist for her, then looks away, clearly embarrassed by her nakedness. Jess tries to close her legs for him. The leather straps wrapped round her thighs, steel chains binding her ankles, prevent her from doing so. He looks like fun, not. A failed family man, divorcee? His worried face tells her he doesn't want to be there any more than she does - reassuring to know.

His colleague walks out of the shadows: short, well-built, ruddy-faced, chubby-cheeked, Balbo beard. His gold fillings shine in the lamplight when he leers at her, which is far too often. He paces around her, examining her: head to toe, pausing to feel her raised dark chocolate mole. She winces as he touches her wound. He runs his stubby fingers over her body, caressing her until he feels he knows every inch of her. He admires her dress. Jess feels a rush of adrenalin. It's him, the man she came to kill! Without warning, the slob grips her petrified face and presses his thumb into her soft cheek, holding her deformed hand aloft, his trophy. He has bad halitosis. She wets herself.

He kneels between her open thighs and asks her name.

'My name is Spitz,' she says, groaning, 'Spitz.'

He slaps her, bending her face, screaming blue murder at her, 'Your real name! Tell me your real name!'

Jess vows not to speak to him for as long as she lives. Feels him being pulled off her by the tall man. At least, he has a heart.

As soon as her captors have left the room, she bursts into tears of relief, straining against the shackles that bind her.

*****

'You won't let him hurt me again, will you Daddy?'

'No, child, I won't let him hurt you. He has gone away. He has been sent far away.'

'To where the faeries live?'

'Ya, to where the faeries live.'

'Good! He was horrid to me! Horrid! I hate him! Hate him!'

'Calm down, child. He has gone. Did you like Heidi?'

'Mm! Heidi made me feel all nice inside!'

'Did you tell her about him?'

Jessie shakes her head, left to right, 'Oh, no,' she says, looking very grown-up, 'I wouldn't do *that*.'

Her body is dripping sweat. The crinkled sheet under her bum is soaking wet, leaving her sore.

The strange man with the female voice has a heart, feels sorry for her, doesn't know where to rest his hand: on her thigh, her tummy, her breast? In the end he settles for her cheek, brushing her face affectionately with the back of his hand. Jessie likes him, always liked him. He looks years younger without the bifocals and trench coat. He reminds her of her daddy.

Patiently injecting her thigh with truth drug, listening, mostly listening, he empties her mind of memories. The heavy lump inside her bowel. A coloured imprint of the man she came to kill.

She can tell he is embarrassed by her. They don't speak for minutes on end,

'I am sorry,' the strange man sats, patting her thigh, 'So sorry.'

Jessie shuts her eyes, squeezing out more tears, trying to stay alert, to battle the drug. Sealing her lips closed to his questioning,

'Tell me his name and I can send you home.'

She vowed not to betray him for as long as she lived. She shakes her head from side to side.

'Tell me his name.'

She bursts into tears.

Turning her head to face her interrogator, she asks him, 'Will it hurt?'

His face pales, lips quiver, 'No, child, it won't hurt.'

The syringe lies in a kidney dish at her feet. She cranes her neck as her medical expert holds it up to the light, expelling a bubble of air. There is a brief respite as he dabs her right thigh with a sterile swab. She lies back, can't bear to watch. He slides the tip of the needle under her skin.

Jessie shuts her eyes feeling the heavy lump inside her bowel. Some agents put up a lot of resistance. She is one of them. Her limbs are weary. Her joints are stiff. Her muscles ache. She braces herself, tenses the muscles in her legs, then arches her body upwards.

The needle snaps! Its tip is lodged in her thigh. Jessie relaxes, sinking into the soft bed. Bliss!

She opens her eyes, craning her neck, watching her executioner hold the syringe up to the light, examining the break. To her surprise, he totters to the end of her legs, takes a fresh needle out of the kidney dish, and attaches it to the hypodermic. The man at her right thigh prepares to re-inject. Is Jess about to become the first woman to be put to sleep by lethal injection since the end of the war?

She senses her lucidity return. Her pathetic host turns to face her, in his hound dog expression,

'I'm sorry. I carry spares.'

He slides the needle deep into her thigh. Jess winces, raising her eyebrows, humming a trendy tune inside her head. Concerned, he might not have put a woman to sleep before. Worried, he doesn't have a clue of what he's doing. She didn't bleed when the needle snapped. Why didn't he find her vein?

'My groin.'

'I am sorry, child?'

'My groin. You'll find a good vein in my groin? Next to my mole?'

Jess feels the needle pull out of her thigh, watching intently as he holds the hypo up to the light and squeezes out an air bubble. His incompetence prompts her to focus on her impending death. Depending on the serum or cocktail in the syringe, her death could be prolonged, painful, or pleasurable just like falling asleep. The most efficient method would be for him to increase the concentration of the truth drug, sodium thiopental, administer a single dose. Her expiry could be expected to take as little as one and a half minutes. She much prefers quick and painless.

The alternative three-stage solution doesn't bear thinking about. An initial shot of pentobarbital to render her unconscious. Followed by the neuromuscular blocking drug, neat pancuronium bromide, to paralyse all of her muscles except her heart, stop her breathing. Then a lethal dose of potassium chloride to arrest her heart. With luck she might be dead in ten minutes. The potassium irks her. Given alone it causes terrible pain akin to fire, electricity coursing through her veins.

She weighs up the advantages of dying. She'll no longer be in pain. They won't be able to hurt her anymore. Jess supposes that constitutes some kind of happy conclusion, gazing deeply into her assailant's eyes: cold, dispassionate, ruthless,

'How will I die?'

He sucks in his cheeks, palpates her vein, looks away, and jabs the needle into her groin, his forehead sweating beads of concentration, 'I am injecting you with three different serums: a sedative, a neuromuscular blocker, then potassium chloride to arrest your heart.'

Jess shakes her head sadly, speaking from the heart, 'I want you to know, I don't blame you.'

He seems relieved: 'Thank you.'

She thinks of the young frau who wasn't wearing a bra or panties, just a loose white vest, who took out her plastic earplugs, and washed her clean.

'What are you looking at?' she asked.

'I saw you smiling at me, thought you might like to fuck me?'

The young frau who kissed her breasts, caressed her moist cleft, then asked her for his name.

'Get out!' she cried.

'If you say so. Auf wiedersehen.'

The frightened blonde who grabbed her wet flannels and towels and hurried from the cell.

Jess is ready to die, 'Can we get it over with, please?'

Her captor looks at her as if she's mad. He feels sorry for her, she knows he does, he wants to be somewhere else. Jess feels the needle lying in her groin. He is about to depress the plunger. It occurs to her that it is illogical for the enemy to kill an agent before they extract the necessary information. She scans her assailant's bovine face, teary, pleading,

'Why now?'

'I am sorry, child. So sorry.'

'For fucks sake! I get that! Why kill me now?'

'He's waiting for you outside the door. He wants your body.'

She pleads with him to kill her. Stares at the syringe. Closes her eyes. Feels the twinge, as he depresses the plunger.

*****

The wheels on the train go round and round all night long. Or so it seems. The ride to the pebble-dashed, unmanned halt seems to take forever. Neath stares at his worried expression in the dark window, guilt coursing like treacle through his arteries. Only matched by the yellow, dirty sea fog pervading the vale as the train squeaks its way round the home curve towards his destination.

His chin is stubbled from where he didn't sleep last night. He hasn't heard from Jess for forty-eight hours. If she bleats, squeals, if she sings… The train slows at the home signal. He seeks relief, urgent clarification, before he dines with his control. He scrolls thru his phone screens and sends a coded message. The response is instant, frighteningly instant,

Where is she?

She is dead! Dead!

What? That's not possible.

She is dead! Hans is dead also!

Who are you?

Ich dien!

Who are you?

I serve!

Auf wiedersehen.

He feels sick in his gut. The wet squad is a blame culture, deliberately perpetrated by his control to keep underlings on their toes. If she is dead, he'll have the blood of his best covert agent on his hands, not to mention her. Neath can't believe she is dead. She bore his child. Had his baby. Now he will have to care for him, collect him from school at exeat, cope with his grief, take him back to the Broads, the country haven, she treasured so much when she was alive. He loved her once, before he came out.

Neath climbs down from the train, his clean white trainers scudding grit on the platform as the door slides shut behind him. The train meanders off past the distant signal towards the sea, its final resting place. His lungs suck in the chill of thick mist. The smack of salt tests his lips. He pulls his old school scarf tight round his neck, lifting his collar to warm his ears. As he huddles into his coat and edges towards the exit, he sees a delicious manly figure, moving towards him.

The man descends on him, a bat flitting out of the lamplight. He draws him close. They hug. He opens his mouth to him letting his langue tumble down his throat. They kiss deeply, longing, yearning, for each other. It has been so long. Neath feels him harden through his crisp, stretch-cotton, khaki sharps. Pushes his hands inside the dark navy bullet-proofs, feels him throb. They stop kissing.

He regards his control pleadingly, wants to share his bed, his passion. Wonders at the devious expression spread over his man's bearded face. He's wearing a bobble hat, olive green, red fish emblazon. He thinks of her is she alive, warm? Her head gets so cold without her clootie bobble. Or is her body cold? Neath decides to play his ace of hearts with his control over dinner, risking all: promotion, position, career. He has to, for her. His boss seems more preoccupied with his new underpants than the fate of the brave, dead, woman,

'Love my new chuddies?' he hoots, 'Absolute ripper of a product! Like 'em?'

'Suit you, suit you down to the groin,' they kiss-some-more, 'My perfect man. Do they...?'

'No, they don't deflect bullets. We're not that advanced. Take my arm, boy.'

Neath relaxes. He loves this man: his humour, his smooth body, his sophistication, his taste, his sex. They move off of the platform to the booking hall: appreciating the glowing embers of the fireplace, tattered seaside posters from last summer's heatwave.

He recalls her mudwrestling with the enemy, snapping his neck, as the rain poured down, as he watched him die in her hands from the safety of a birdwatching hut. Neath loves birds. Birds that kill. The dead man was a closet gay. He left behind a broken heart. The notion strikes an inner chord, a connection.

His love wheels him up a country lane, past a malt house, the dark stacks of a brewery chimney. A broad estuary stretches into the distance. He shivers as his companion, lover, direct report, controller, grips his elbow, taking him to one side, like a naughty little boy in his middle class,

'We're here. Step inside.'

They step into the empty restaurant with rooms, stamp their feet, wait patiently by the till. A smart young girl in black shirt and trousers is busy setting a polished wine goblet on the only laid table in the house. She flicks her service cloth over her arm, comes over and greets them.

'Hello!' she says, cheering them with a lovely smile, 'Is it Mr Michael Hadleigh, double room, breakfast, dinner for two at seven-thirty?'

'It is, indeed, dear,' his control replies, giving his whipping boy a sly wink.

'If you would like to follow me, I'll show you to your room?'

She is wearing a gold name badge. They follow her upstairs.

*****

Neath goes to speak to him about Jess - just as the server arrives at their table with the menus.

The place is empty.

'Tonight's special is Dover Sole,' she announces confidently, 'Afraid the Halibut's finished.'

'Finished, dear? But we haven't started yet!'

Neath raises his brows at the server:

Don't worry, girl, he's always like this: showy and posh.

She looks glum, having disappointed her only guests tonight. He thinks of her, lying cold. The girl speaks, wanting to be of service. Neath encourages his glum rag doll. She fakes a face:

'I'm sorree,' she panders, 'Can I fetch you a drink?'

Fetch! He likes that! Fetch! As in fetch my slippers, girl. He smiles genially, he likes that!

'Tanqueray. Double. Fever Tree. No Ice. Mixed. Think you can manage that?'

Oh, dear, we are in a funny mood tonight, aren't we?

Neath beams at her. She blushes.

'I'm sure I can!' she crows, looking daggers at him, 'What can I get you to drink, Sir?'

'Scotch.'

'Ice?'

'No, Scotch.'

'Thanks.'

She trots over to the bar. They browse the menu. Neath goes to speak. His man places his hairy hand over his fist, pressing it to the table. His glass wobbles. His fish knife moves to the right,

'A little bird tells me your girl has gone missing. She is yours, isn't she, dear? Had your bastard I hear. You never told me you were straight? One *is* disappointed.'

Neath slumps in his chair, his jaw flaps into his neck, stunned, speechless. He isn't hungry.

'Won't sing, will she, your pretty nightingale? Won't blow the whole show?' his control asks.

He struggles to speak, reeling, still in shock. Her. Her son. His dearest man. His acid. His spite.

'Think we should let sleeping birds lie, don't you? No point stirring up a hornet's nest with our new friends is there? Not with all this wretched Brexit business. Don't think the new PM would take kindly to a cock-up in our backyard, do you?'

He shakes his head at the hypocrisy, the incredible C-Y-A of his superior. He loves this man!

'Now, can I suggest the Dover Sole?' his lover says, unfurling his spotless pink cloth napkin, 'I hear the local fish is exceptionally good.'

*****

Jess hears a loud thud. A second thud. A jackhammer! She closes her eyes. Feels the twinge. A creaking noise! The door opens. She cranes her neck to watch. He looks up. At her. Standing over him. The girl, shouting at him,

'Gerd, no!'

He lets go of the syringe. It lies between her thighs. The girl fires twice, shooting him between the eyes with a .22 calibre semi-automatic. Jess is spattered with his blood, brains, shattered bits of bones. She shuts her eyes, relaxing as the girl gently unshackles the straps that bind her.

'You are in a bit of a mess,' the blonde young-frau observes, 'I must wash you. Please, do not move.'

Jess flexes her muscles, clenches her fists, wiggles her toes. It feels good to be alive. She tries to sit up, can't, isn't going anywhere in a hurry. She focuses on the now. Her mind comes alive. She asks the girl, 'What day is it?'

The young frau checks her digital watch, 'The time is almost twenty-one hours on Thursday.'

Thursday? Her mind swims. Monday: dress-making course. Jess stares at her clothes on the rail covered in blood, her pink dress ruined. Tuesday: my abduction by the frozen fountain. She shuts out the carnage of her captivity. Tonight: liberation. Tomorrow: the man is coming to fix the dishwasher. Saturday: collect my darling boy.

She stares at her liberator, bewildered.

~ 85 ~

'Don't worry,' the girl soothes, 'You are safe now. I have checked you out of the Elk, brought all your things: passport, handbag, case.'

'Thank you!' she cries, finally breaking down 'Thank you! Thank you!'

Heidi takes her in her arms, cradling her sobbing head to her breasts, rocking her like her baby, 'It's alright. It's over, darling.'

'Why?' Jess asks her, loving her warm caress, her soft hugs, the sweet kisses on her lips, 'Why did you save me?'

They both know why.

They share a love to die for.

Knight

CHANTAL STRUTTED ONTO THE PATIO, glided down the stone steps, threw her lady-bundle onto the sun lounger, and faced the camera. The sun lit up her burnt sienna hair, accentuating her crème caramel extensions. She raised her arms and clawed at her shocking mane. A stray kiss-curl brushed her lips.

Raising her brows, fluttering her lashes, she let an arm hang around the full curve of her bum, her slim fingers scratching the backs of her greatest assets, her faintly tanned thighs. Chantal was modelling sexy lingerie: a candy apple red bra, a crotch-hugging red thong, sheer black tights fringed with delicate lacy bits, classic rhubarb stilettoes. She purred like a contented cat,

'What do you think, Dani, good?'

'Very good, Chantal. Can you just turn to face me? That's it. Legs slightly apart. Lovely.'

Dani took five consecutive shots of her muse, then nodded, watching avidly as she stripped off her bra and thong.

Beautiful, quite beautiful.

Chantal squatted on her tummy. Dani felt her smooth skin as she reclined on the sun lounger sipping pink gin, closing her eyes, gently caressing her muse's breasts, the dimples in the small of her back, her pert buttocks. Finding the girl's intimacy overwhelming. Barely able to contain her excitement. The divine thrill of Chantal's naked body, rubbing, gently, against hers in the heat of the torrid afternoon.

She wiped the sun-tears from her eyes. The sea's glare made her cry. Her muse raked her shock of caramel in a thick drape, so that her bulk hung heavily down one side of her blushing face.

Fascinating, the way Chantal's act of facial exposure made her blush in a rash over her cheeks, neck, chest, breasts, tummy, thighs, heightening the delicate fawn in her freckles. Fascinating, how her intimate exposé gave her face colour, her thin neck, the gilded look of a swan.

Dani fantasized, feeling her girl's tongue probe her mouth, gagging her with an obscene desire. Chantal stopped rubbing herself on her lady's tummy, stood up, and put on her swimsuit.

The hooped bullring, crudely torn through her left earlobe, gave her the appearance of a gypsy, a sultry private dancer in the closed court of her lady. She bared her teeth, her cheeky gap, gave Dani a fierce snarl, breathed in at her midriff, let her arms hang freely, flaunting her bold egg yolk yellow swimsuit, its plunging neckline, swivelling her hips to the left. Crying out for her.

'Chanteuse!'

She heard the camera click.

'How was that Dani?' she cooed.

Chantal knew full well that she was picture-perfect, an undiscovered talent about to go viral. Picardie had her fame arranged at a grand internet auction of Chantal Merlin to fashion houses, modelling agencies, journals, magazines, webcams, individual clients around the world. Such was the promise of stardom, the share of the spoils, that she never thought to question Dani's background, or motives.

Her cot was an insult, the room tiny, but she could live with her minor discomforts in the pursuit of wealth. There was little else for her to do at the beach house but clean, launder, serve food, and shop. Other than please her.

'Perfect!' Dani affirmed, 'Have you prepared our picnic for this afternoon?'

Chantal crossed her arms behind her back and counted her fingers.

Ham, brie, fromage bleu, pâte, anchovies, eggs, baguette, olives, vine tomatoes, grapes. Oh, and champagne! Mustn't forget the champagne!

'Yes! Everything is ready.'

'I think I shall wear a dress today, Dani,' she added, pronouncing her name darn-e as in a curse or mend in a holed sock, 'If I may? Please? It would be so lovely to wear my dress.'

Dani's cheeks sagged, like the cheeks of a face struck with severe Bell's Palsy.

'Of course, Cheri, but be careful not to get your hem wet when we go rowing.'

After she had changed out of her swimsuit, Chantal assembled the picnic hamper and loaded it into the boot of the artist's splendid pea-green, yellow-wheeled, Citroën 2CV. They set off in high spirits, Dani driving carefully round the hairpin bends, taking a narrow, winding track, high up into the vertiginous no-man's land.

Every so often, they spotted a memorial headstone standing in the straw-dry grass by the roadside; marking the place where unsuspecting tourists inadvertently motored too close to the edge and tumbled down the steep slope. Occasionally, when the road veered to the right, Chantal caught sight of the acres of charcoaled trees decimated by the frequent forest fires. She thought of the flume Dani pointed out to her, burning on the inaccessible mountainside, their eternal burning flame.

After an hour, the road widened and wound downhill, through shady olive and lemon groves, to a line of pine trees. Dani pulled over, drove down a dusty track, and parked the 2CV in the shade. Chantal carried the hamper down to a short strip of brown sand, punctuated with dead cones, and spread the blanket. They picnicked under the pines dressed in wide-brim straw hats to keep the sun out of their eyes. The artist didn't drink.

'Drinking, rowing and driving don't mix,' she opined, eating sparingly: a few vine tomatoes, some olives, a sprig of grapes.

It was left to Chantal to eat the lion's share. Her hostess showed her the dregs of the champagne.

'Come on, Cheri. Such a shame to waste it.'

After Chantal had finished quaffing and packing the hamper, they went off to find the boat.

'I think I may have drunk too much champers,' she slurred dreamily. 'It's so calm and peaceful out here on the lake, don't you think Dani?'

'I do! The glare of the sun off the water, the slop of water against our little boat, the stir of my oars in the cool, clear lake. I find it all so soporific. See how clear the water is! Can you see the carp, grazing in the streamer weeds?'

Dani stopped rowing, letting the boat glide to a halt in one of the secluded bays that gave the grand lake its irregular shape. It was impossible to see all of the bays from one vantage point, or, indeed, to be seen. They were alone where no-one could find them. Dani had planned the day, Tuesday, and time:

siesta time, to perfection. There were no other boaters. They wouldn't be disturbed.

Chantal leaned against the side of the boat, peering into the crystal-clear water. She could see right down to the streamer weed, huge fish grazing, heads down. The view reminded her of an aquarium. She blinked her stiffened eyelashes, turning her head away: the transparency made her feel queasy. Her head span.

The water must be at least five metres deep here, she estimated.

'You must be tired out, after your labours this morning,' Dani observed, 'Why don't you have a cat nap, Cheri? I am happy to stay here and rest awhile, to sit, and dream.'

'Mm!' Chantal stretched her arms and sighed. 'You make the lake sound so romantic. I shall! I shall sleep while you rest on the lake, watching over me.'

She closed her eyes, bowed her head, her chin flopping onto her chest, and fell asleep.

'Sweet dreams, Chantal,' whispered Dani, 'Sweet dreams.'

She couldn't take her eyes off of her muse, slumped on the seat facing her, dozing in her boat. The sun lit up her burnt sienna hair. She wiped a wisp of gold off of her brow, letting her fingers brush her lips. Chantal smiled, resting her arms on her legs, her slim hands drawing up the hem of her navy floral print dress, revealing her lightly tanned thighs, holding her legs slightly apart.

Dani gasped at the sight of her blueberry-patterned cotton briefs, her well-moulded shape. She reached forward and pushed both her hands firmly up the soft insides of the girl's thighs, her fingertips, placed, within easy touching distance.

'What do you think, Dani, good?' the girl murmured.

'Very good. Can you come a little closer? That's it. Legs apart. Lovely.'

She leaned forward and slipped her fingers inside Chantal's damp briefs, relishing the lush feel of her fine hair. Chantal gasped pleasurably, surprised by the intimacy of her lady's inspection.

'Perhaps I should take my dress off for you,' she purred, 'Would you like me to take off my dress?'

Dani inhaled deeply and nodded, watching her muse stand unsteadily and strip in front of her.

Beautiful, quite beautiful.

Chantal gave her a fierce snarl, letting her arms hang freely, woozily flaunting her small breasts, swivelling her bare hips to the left. She brushed her lips against her lady's face, relishing the sensation of her tingle-touch, her lambent tongue licking her out as if she were the residue of a pink ice cream coupe glace. She felt the boat rock. Felt the boat tilt.

'Dani!'

Then she was floating in the ice-cold water. The crystal-clear water. Staring at the carp. Kicking and screaming. Her burnt sienna hair splayed. Her liquid mane of caramel wrapped around her frozen face.

Beautiful, quite beautiful.

Floating, like a freefall foetus, drifting in her full womb.

Dani relaxed, slitting her eyes, barely able to contain her excitement at the sight of Chantal, drowning in the ice-cold water. In the scalding heat of the afternoon. Her muse, rolling on her front, a Nyad, a nude mermaid without a tail. Turning barrel-shapes like a pared woman-carrot, for her, in the water.

Look at the froth coming out of her pink mouth! See her body, roll, wash and tumble!

'Oh, my dear, you can doggy-paddle, can you.' she remarked, 'swim to me, that's a good girl.'

'Huurgh! Help me! I can't swim! Huurgh!'

'What a shame, Cheri. Neither can I.'

Desperate to stay alive, Chantal clawed the rim of Dani's little rowing boat. Gripping the side with her white digits. Breaking her fingernails. Chantal was tipping her boat over!

Can't have that!

'Huurgh! Help me into the boat!'

'I'm sorry, Chantal. I can't help you. You'll tip the boat over, you see. Then what'll I do?'

Chantal gawped in horror as Dani forcibly prised her fingers from the rim of the boat, then pushed her startled head underwater with her bare hands, launching her, like the world's first woman torpedo. Her blue head bobbed up, barely an oar's length out.

An oar's length?

Dani wielded, brandished, the oar like a sword, like King Slayer in Game of Thrones! Chantal's eyes bulged, salted, red, with horror. Her mouth frothed and screamed. Dani pushed the blade of the oar into her navel, the sexy bull's eye in Chantal's slim tummy, forcing her arms and legs to pump like a jellyfish. Chantal wouldn't drown! Pumping and pulsing, a jellyfish in the clear water. Dani freed her, let her blurt, and spurt, and spew out water so that she could scream. On the grand lake where no-one can hear you scream.

'Huurgh! No!'

Then, she raised the blade of the oar and spliced her muse's beautiful neck,

'Au Revoir Chantal!'

*****

Faith's fuzzy features appeared behind the frosted partition to the bedroom. As it was her first day as Dani's muse, she was reluctant to disturb her. She tapped sharply on the rough plate glass.

'It's only me, Faith? Please may I come in?'

Dani looked up from her painting. She was having difficulty with the cloudy grey sky. Grey skies presented her with turmoil, a conflict between the dark and light. It was raining heavily outside, tiny meteorites of distilled water splashed and fractured on the four stone steps that led to the churning sea.

She had set her easel on a spattered groundsheet in front of the window on the pink tiled floor, not wishing to soil her bobble rug. The art was her landscape: the sky, the mountains and sea, her patio, the grey divan.

Faith had arrived in the middle of the night, bedraggled after a lengthy hike from the nearest village, unable to find a taxi. Dani had undressed her, put her to bed, and let her sleep on in the morning before she officially became her companion. It was nearly lunch time.

'Of course, you can come in. You don't have to ask. My poor girl, you must be exhausted.'

Faith slid the door open, padded barefoot up to the artist, and stood at her shoulder, admiring the watercolour, its drab, dull scene matching perfectly the gloomy vista outside.

'I am exhausted,' she stated, throwing an arm, 'A joker launched a drone over Stansted.'

'Oh dear! Well, you're here with me now, and that's all that matters. Did you sleep well in your cot?'

'Yes, thank you. I made you a tuna fish salad and freshly baked cob with iced mineral water.'

Dani glanced over her shoulder, 'You have it Faith.'

'I'm sorry?'

'I said: you have it. I seldom eat.'

You must eat, Faith thought but didn't say, you'll fade away. 'At least drink some water?'

Dani placed her brush on the palette and twisted upon her pow wow to face her,

'I never drink water. It makes me ill. Please, take it away.'

Faith tutted, turned on her heels, and marched off to the kitchen. When she returned, the artist was painting the olive-green mountains. She spotted a void at the centre of the canvas,

'You haven't painted in the sea?'

Dani shied away from her, 'I never do. The thought of water appals me.'

'I've cleaned the bath, toilet, hall and kitchen,' Faith confirmed, 'I think I'll go and rest in my cot now, and read my book, if that's alright?'

Dani leered at her, 'Of course, dear, mustn't let those bleary eyes spoil your looks, must we?'

Faith nodded, curtsied, tried to think of something to say, but couldn't. She left the room.

The hall was dark and dingy, lit only by the half-light dulling through the frosted front door. A whole wall was devoted to paintings of rainy scenes in Paris: a drab street in Montmartre, a crowded flea market near Notre Dame, a packed river boat gliding under Pont Neuf, shoppers braving the rain outside the Moulin Rouge.

She studied the prints more carefully, a restaurant: Le Consulat, a patisserie, a brasserie: Le Palmier. An artists' market was closing down: the artists were covering their art, folding their wooden easels, scurrying to the nearest shelter. The art came to life before her eyes. Faith heard mothers scolding their children for splashing in puddles. Shoppers groaning as their brollies were blown inside-out by gusty winds. Old men greeting each other in rain-soaked streets. Everybody huddled under shelter, fleeing the pouring, driving rain, the seeping spouts of water.

The prints were framed in olive-green: the colour of the mountains, or flame-red: the burning flume, the eternal flame. She thought of the woman fading away, shrinking, dying. Her urgent message:

You must come now, Faith.

Each painting bore an inscription:

Paris: Il va pleuvoir! Daniela Picardie.

There was no upstairs at the beach house. Other than the entrance, which opened onto a narrow country lane, and the door to her lady's boudoir, the hall had two solid oak doors with wrought-iron handles.

The door on the right led to the kitchen, a throwback to the Fifties with an enamelled cooker, deep marbled sink, draining board, and old-fashioned larder. No mod cons. Propped against one white-washed wall was a wonky wooden chair and pine table. A table for one: Faith. The kitchen ended in a dark cubby-hole crammed with pails, mops, bric-a-brac from the patio, pots, pans, more paintings of Paris in the rain. Daniela's obsession with water: negative, depressing, images of water, bordered on the bizarre.

Faith shook herself out of the daze. To the left of the hall a half-sized door led to her room. She stooped, bent double at the waist, and stumbled inside. Her bedroom was like a cupboard. There was barely enough room for the small chest of drawers, a little basket-weave corner chair, and her cot. She slid down the wooden frame, climbed atop the mattress, snuggled her head in the soft child's pillow, curled up in the foetal position, and fell asleep. Faith dreamed of her knight in shining armour, galloping to her side on his gleaming white charger, gathering her up in his strong arms, rescuing her. Felt her body lift towards a distant beacon of white light. Read the kindly look on the knight's face.

Faith woke with a shock, pouring with sweat. She checked the Tom & Jerry clock on her pillow. No time had passed at all. She rolled her head to the left.

Saw her phone by her face. Faith had a new message, from him. He'd be here for her, to rescue her one fine day in time. She fell into a dreamless sleep.

Falling asleep, hunched up in a baby's cot inside a hot cupboard, dressed in tee-shirt and shorts was a daft idea. She woke drenched in sweat. They say men sweat and women perspire. Faith sweated because she had the physique of a man built through her sheer graft and persistence into the body of an eighteen-year-old gymnast, the antithesis of the debilitated Dani.

She swung her legs out of the bed and tried to stand up straight, feeling the warmth of the bare wood floor percolate through the soles of her feet, finding that she couldn't. The white-washed ceiling was too low. To her intense irritation, she realised she would have to dress in the hall.

Her clothing was strewn over the basket-chair after her stressful arrival. Faith had literally crashed out in the cot, woken, and started her unusual role as artist's companion. She reflected on how far she had come in her troubled life.

Faith Geatish was abandoned as a baby, wrapped in swaddling clothes, and dumped next to the food bank behind Haughton supermarket. She had never managed to trace her mum. Or her dad, who was rumoured by the locals to have run off with a part-time cleaning supervisor from Aigburth. In her heart she knew her mum died that snowy night in January.

Her loving foster parents, Esther and Jonas, raised the little girl like their real daughter, Claire. The girls attended the local infant, junior, and secondary modern schools. Claire was a bright spark, always top of the class at maths, physics, chemistry and biology: subjects Faith couldn't understand. She preferred sport, winning the school cross country race three years running, excelling at field and track events, joining the nearest running club, Myrtlesham AC.

Opposites attract. The teenage girls became lifelong friends. Or so Faith thought. At the age of sixteen, Claire won an academic scholarship to a boarding school, East Dene High in Sussex. They drifted apart. Claire changed; became distant, aloof. She mixed with a different social clique, dare she say, different class of girl. Her life was transformed. She rarely came home to see her parents, preferring to while her time away at all-nighters, rock festivals, wild parties.

Faith felt confused, insecure, worthless. She began to binge eat and put on excessive weight. She hated herself every time she stared in the bedroom mirror at her folds of flab, her drooping boobs, her fat bum, the bloated tummy, her chef's arms, and pig's thighs.

The atomic bomb dropped on her seventeenth birthday when Esther and Jonas sat down with her on the threadbare sofa and broke the news. She wasn't their daughter. Faith burst into tears, fled the room, went upstairs, locked herself in and stayed there, refusing food or drink, swearing at her false mum, wishing her crazy world would go away.

On the third night, she self-harmed, trying to cut out her puppy fat with a carpet knife. Jonas burst in just in time to save his daughter's life. There was blood everywhere: thick, congealed, soaking, steaming blood, saturating the candy-striped duvet, the crimson bedsheet, her pillows.

Need-to-buy-my-princess-new-bed, Jonas's brain check-listed, his mind's default method for coping with the abject bloody horror. He swept up his blonde-haired girl, patching her up as best he could with torn strips of bloodied sheet, gathered her in his loving arms, and ran past Esther. She was screaming, dialling 999. He bundled his girl's limp body into his sidecar, then shot off down the A414 towards Princess Alexandra Hospital on his Harley motorcycle, a bat out of hell.

Dad, guardian dad: who cared who he was, or what he was? Jonas saved his just-as-loved, just-as-precious-as-Claire, just-as I love you, kid, now don't you die on me, hold on, kid, as Claire. He and the A&E Superstars saved Faith's life that night.

The wasted young adult spent the next six months in and out of a psychiatric ward. Some bright spark had the common sense, the human decency, to keep the poor girl off Lithium, ECT and Risperidone. To give her half a chance to rehabilitate and help her start afresh.

Claire came home. Fuck her academic career. Claire came home to be with her kid sister.

At the age of seventeen years and nine months, Faith Geatish accompanied her doting dad to the gym. There she met a stunning brunette with a big heart and can-do attitude, who burned her out till her bones ached, who worked the gross slabs of fat off her gym-flailed body until the muscles bled out of her torso. They became best friends and fell in love.

From the day she met Kirsty, Faith Geatish never looked back.

*****

The beach house was stifling hot, humid. The rain stopped falling. Images of wisps of steam, rising off a warm patio, came to mind. Faith scooped up her sports bra, red fitness pants, towel, postcards and pen, and bolted for the kitchen.

There was no sign of Dani, she must be having a catnap. The wasting caused intense wearying in the artist's joints. She routinely took three hours sleep in the morning on her divan, four hours siesta in the afternoon, and liked to be in bed by dusk.

Faith suddenly felt guilty, arriving in the early hours: the drone at Stansted: her feeble excuse for missing the flight. Truth be told, she was in the gym pumping iron and just forgot the time. Dani's face was a picture, drained of all colours, blanc like the sea in her paintings, when she arrived. What was that all about?

She changed and left her dirty clothes in a neat pile on the floor for handwashing after the lady retired for the night. There was no washing powder under the sink, no linen basket, or pegs. Even the stale, damp atmosphere felt temporary, as if time were running out.

Her informal au pair agreement expired in mid-September when she hoped to return home and commence training as a PE instructor with Kirsty. Faith doubted Dani would last that long; the woman hardly ate or drank. She went to the larder, found a beaker, poured herself some water.

The gymnast sat at the kitchen table and stared at the picture on the first postcard: a panoramic beach scene from Port Grimaud. She had camped in a tent a shell's throw from the sandy beach when she was sixteen with Claire, Esther and Jonas. Her first and only holiday abroad. The happiest time of her life.

She recognised the grade II listed players, as Esther laughingly called them, at leisure. The Germans in their power boats. The French on water skis, jet-skis, windsurfing. Les Anglais squatting in the sand. Basting their roasted fat. Stuffing their faces: beignets de pommes, glâces de citron, frites.

Succumbing to the charms, necklaces, and bracelets of the tall lookie-lookie men who arrived in droves from northern Africa to sell their wares. The jet-set on the other hand, Esther elaborated, lived on floating gin palaces off St Tropez, dancing the night away in exclusive clubs, dining in the Michelin-starred restaurants scattered around the harbour. Faith turned the card over, filled in the address, and wrote:

Dear Esther, Jonas and Claire, arrived late last night, my fault! Beach house is beautiful, overlooks a pretty bay, surrounded by mountains? Room's a bit small! I'll get used to it! Guess what? It rained today! Mme Picardie seems like a nice lady. Think I'll enjoy my stay. Wish you were here? Ha! Ha! Miss you lots. Faith x

She made a note to visit the village in the morning to buy baguettes, brie, pâte, olives, wine, and stamps. She checked her phone. There was only 2% power remaining. She hadn't brought a charger. Perhaps she would find one in the village.

Dani didn't appear to communicate. There was no telephone or tv set, not even a radio in the kitchen. Faith picked up the other card, a seedy-looking print of a mermaid, and wrote:

Darling Kirsty, dreamed of you last night, lying in my arms. Miss you beyond words! Beach house is beautiful, overlooks a pretty bay, surrounded by mountains. Room's a shithole. I'll get used to it. Guess what? It rained, yay! Picardie's weird, clingy, makes my flesh creep. Still, I haven't been forced to pose yet. Miss you so much, you're in my heart, I love you, Faith xxx

Faith left the postcards on the kitchen table, took her towel, and padded over to the larder. One of the cold stone shelves was filled with stoppered bottles of mineral water. She grabbed a neck and entered the hall, surprised to see a framed picture of a young woman resting against a beige stone wall, in the shade of an olive tree, among the paintings.

She inspected the photo. The hair was definitely different: a cascade of lush burnt sienna flowed from her harsh central rift, over her shoulders, and kissed her pancake-flat chest. But there was no mistaking the gaunt facial features: the pallid complexion, hollow cheeks, dry-chapped lips, or the tiny head. Her arms and legs were bone-thin, her joints jutting through the parchment skin of her elbows and knees. The unflattering iris print dress, its tight red sash and knee-length hem, bore testimony to the skeletal figure that barely lived inside.

Faith gasped at the signature, scrawled recklessly across the portrait:

Dani, June 2018.

Last month! The woman's inked-in irises had been gouged with the tip of a biro? What kind of sick mind did that? Her body shivered, involuntarily, as she approached the frosted glass door.

'Dani? May I come in, please? It's only me?'

There was no answer.

Faith let out a long sigh of relief and slid back the heavy partition. The artist was lying huddled one side of the Joelle facing the mirror. She made out her tiny face, hooked nose, sleeping eyes.

Ah, she's away with the fairies! You sleep on, Dani!

She tip-toed to the sliding glass, inched it open, held her breath, praying she wouldn't conjure up a draught, and glanced backwards. The skeleton stirred, rolled over, and went back to sleep.

Faith exhaled as her feet hit the hot flagstones chiding herself for her own stupidity.

Geatish! What's got into you?

She examined her nails. They were chewed to the quick. Carefully, Faith slid the door closed, sat on the divan, and guzzled down half a litre of water. Her left eye wandered, squinting to the right; she was nervous. She brought it under control. She slid her fingers inside her fitness pants and scratched the irritating itch in her groin.

Stop it, girl! Pull yourself together. Why the stress all of a sudden?

Faith looked out across the bay. The sea was royal blue spattered with olive green where the trees reflected off the clear water. Far away in the distance she saw a yacht in full sail.

Her knight in shining armour, come to save her?

She snapped out of her dream and hit the deck. Working her body to the limit Faith completed a hundred press-ups, squat thrusts, cobras, planks, half-planks, pelvic thrusts, more press-ups. Jogging-on-the-spot. Pushing her muscles until they ached. Thrilling to her rush of adrenalin under the hazy sun. She collapsed on the divan exhausted, mopped off her slick body sweat with her towel, sipped lukewarm water, until she relaxed, and felt herself cool, slightly,

Stupid! Stupid! Stupid!

Faith felt her scalp burning under her thin blonde hair, her pale beige skin blistering sore, blood-blush red. Hot, sticky and sunburnt, she crept as far as the glass, and looked inside. Dani was still asleep. Relieved, Faith crossed the bedroom, turned a ceramic door knob, stepped inside, and locked the door securely behind her.

If her cot room was small, the toilet-come-washroom was miniscule. Its white-washed roof, complete with dusty cobwebs and garden spiders, sloped in a similar slant to her cage, making it impossible for her to stand up. There was a grubby portal high up on the outer wall, covered in mould. No daylight. A snarled-up wall fan. No air.

She switched on the light to the doll's house room, instantly struck by the stench of stale sweat, urine, faeces. The previous occupant, none other than charming Dani, hadn't flushed the loo which gaped like a black hole in front of her. The left wall was bare, devoid of features. To the right there was a dirty wash basin with a pine shelf hung under a smeared cracked glass mirror.

Cracked! Seven years bad luck!

Coo, sarked Faith, this is nice!

She flushed the toilet. Ugh!

Faith turned to study the fascinating collection of face flannels that her host had laid on for her, to cats lick herself clean with. Picked them up, one at a time. Inspected them. Sniffed them. She even came up with a rhyme to describe them:

This little flannel has curled hairs, this little flannel has one, this little flannel has stale sweat, this little flannel has none, and this little flannel went wee, wee, wee, wee, all the way home.

She giggled. On the pine shelf, between the pink toothbrush and the red toothbrush, stood a sensitive male roll-on deodorant.

No way!

Other than a rolled-up tube of toothpaste, that was the washroom.

The shithole from hell, Faith opined. She'd come across worse, not.

She struggled for breath, dreading the approaching wodge of claustrophobia that pressed at her nostrils. Her hair was soaking wet, her head and body bubbling, oozing sweat. She felt heavy, felt the urge, pulled down her fitness pants and undies, crouched and peed, sighing with relief as she emptied her bladder. Faith fumbled with the empty cardboard loo roll, gave up, then waddled across to the wash basin. Now, which flannel? Her ears popped at the sound of a gentle knock. She heard her mouth rasp against the door.

Dani!

'Are you alright in there, Cheri?'

Faith squirmed, 'I'll be fine, thank you.'

If I can find a clean flannel to wipe my arse with.

'Why?'

'It's just that you've been in there for ages and I wanted to tell you about tomorrow.'

'What about tomorrow?' the muse snapped, grabbing any flannel, the first, red one, any one.

'I'd like you to pose for me. Can I interest you in my garden furniture?'

Faith turned on the tap, the rusty lukewarm water, took off her sports bra, and washed her armpits clean, down there, grabbed the second flannel, and cats-licked herself from head to toe.

'Sorry?'

'My little joke,' Dani sneered, 'Once you've visited the village shop and stocked up on toilet tissue…' she paused for effect, 'I'd like you to pose for me. You will pose for me, won't you?'

Pouring with sweat, Faith gathered her things and prepared to make a dash for it,

'Of course.'

'Good! Then I thought we might go for a picnic. I keep a little rowing boat on a lake near here.'

'Sounds good to me,' Faith crowed, 'Dani?'

'Yes, dear?'

'Would you mind looking the other way, please?'

Faith streaked past the artist, clutching her damp sports gear to her breasts, then went to collect the postcards. Only to find they had disappeared.

*****

She was floating in ice-cold crystal-clear water like a foetus in a womb. Froth was coming out of her pink mouth. She clawed the rim, gripping the side of the boat with her white fingers, her broken nails. Staring in horror. As her fingers were prised off. As her startled head was pushed underwater with bare hands. Her blue head bobbed barely an oar's length out. Dani wielded, brandished, the oar, like a sword, like King Slayer. Her eyes bulged blood red with fury.

She screamed...

Faith woke up, dripping with sweat, clasping the clock in her hands. She unfurled herself and sat up in her cot. A warm jet of liquid rinsed her cleft and buttocks. She'd wet the bed. Wet the bed for the first time since she was a child.

Faith heard Esther's voice, scolding her, 'Naughty girl! You wet the bed. You mustn't ever wet the bed!'

Feeling miserable, a child once more, sitting in her cot, wondering about her, a light came on in her brain. She cast her mind back to the night when the girls sat on her bed, laughing and playing around as if they were children...

'I put this finger here,' Claire giggled, tracing her forefinger across the creased paper map, 'I put that finger... there!'

'Oh, stop it! Stop it!' Faith howled, 'You know I don't like it when you play games with me.'

The young woman smiled benignly at her. She loved her dearly. She was going to miss her.

'I found an advert on the 'net,' she fessed.

Faith was busy painting her toenails lurid tangerine,

'What kind of advert?'

~ 108 ~

'An advert for a holiday job.'

Her sister struggled to conceal the thrill in her voice.

'A modelling assignment,' she added, eagerly.

Faith stopped painting and looked at Claire's face.

Beautiful, quite beautiful.

She watched her rake the shock of caramel in a thick drape over her ear. Her hair hung down one side of her face.

Fascinating, the way her act of exposure made her blush, heightening the fawn in her feint freckles.

Claire bared her teeth, her cheeky gap, gave her a loving smile - and gripped her wrist.

'I'm going to model lingerie and swimsuits, Faith! This could be my big break!'

'I'm so excited for you! Where?'

Claire pointed at the old Michelin Carte Routière et Touristique, spread out over the bed.

'Here!'

*****

Faith climbed out of her tiny cot and felt the bedding. It was sopping wet. Her manger would have to be stripped and all her swaddling hand washed. She stared at her Tom and Jerry clock. The time was 3am. The dreams always came to her at 3am. Dreams of her beloved Claire, her darling Kirsty. How she missed her tender embrace. Her divine touch. Her kiss. Their intimacy. She began to envy the girls their freedom, yearning for a return to the mundane routine of life at home, away from the luxury that was the beach house.

Away from Dani, the artist who would finally paint her nude, spread, no draped, over her luxury divan in the glary sunshine, her honey bee, her flapping butterfly, her Pink Lady. Today, Dani would expect her to spread her wings. Increasingly, Faith felt the woman with the tiny head, wasted figure, and big hairdo was sick in the head, not just her decrepit body. The way she treated her, like a child, a little girl.

Then there was the cupboard she lived in, her disgusting cot. She'd seen stray dogs kennelled in more sanitary conditions. And the male deodorant in the dirty toilet. What was that all about?

She wondered if Claire finished her modelling assignment, furious with herself for forgetting her phone charger. She hoped her big sister, her best friend, was happy, successful. Claire, who had given up her brilliant academic career, leaving university to be at her sister's side in her darkest hour, who had suggested that Faith took the bizarre holiday job in The South of France.

Had she known Dani's requirements, written into contract, with the benefit of hindsight she wouldn't have touched Picardie with a barge pole. The thought of her lying, posing, naked for her disturbed her. But there was no easy way out: no homeward flight booked, or money in the bank, at least until Dani deigned to pay her. Faith was trapped, a Pink Lady caught in an artist's net, waiting to have her wings pinned.

She gathered her soiled bed linen and crept out into the hall, the half-light of dawn, leaving the mess in an unsightly pile on the kitchen floor, then tiptoed her way, silently, to the sliding door, inching it aside. Dani was huddled on the Joelle, facing the mirror. Faith gasped at the sight of her bald head, the port wine stain discernible on her lady's pate, and hurried into the black hole, to wash herself with one of the artist's putrid-smelling flannels. Once inside the lavatory room, she purged herself clean, like the nun who has sinned and seeks redemption.

Her only ticket to a temporary reprieve, her only escape, was the shopping list indelibly printed in her mind: ham, brie, fromage bleu, pâte, anchovies, eggs, baguette, olives, vine tomatoes, grapes, champagne.

Outside the beach house there was a bumpy stony track, bordered by flagstone walls. The air was fresh. The morning sun rose, casting its rays across the land. Faith, dressed in a fresh black sports bra, fitness pants and trainers, eased the glass door closed, took to her heels, and ran.

Invigorated by her release from captivity, thrilled to stretch her cramped muscles, she ran her heart out, up the winding track, past olive groves, vineyards, farmyards, white-stone cottages with red-tiled rooves, sleeping villagers. There wasn't a soul in sight. Reaching the centre of the village, she found the square, a sun-warmed wooden bench beside a sandy boules pitch, checked her watch: 5am, curled up, and fell asleep. Faith dreamed of him, her knight in shining armour, the white sails of the yacht set against azure blue sea, a delicious smile of satisfaction creeping, like wildfire, across her becalmed face.

Refreshed by her catnap, she walked into the village store, amazed at the size of the fruit and vegetables on display, twice the size of the produce in her local supermarket. Faith entered the shop. The whole cheeses on the counter and netted hams swinging from the ceiling reminded her of a delicatessen that Esther took her and Claire to see in Spitalfields when they were little. Only everything was so much larger than life here, the air filled with pungent aromas, the array of groceries bewildering.

An overweight lady with greying hair in a bun and rosy-peach soft cheeks tapped her on the shoulder,

'Like some help?'

Faith's heart leapt at the sound of English being spoken, crisply with a French inflection, none of the sickly, guttural drone that characterized Dani's lazy elocution.

'You speak English?'

'Un peu, madam!' the woman laughed, 'Et vous?'

Faith shook her head, 'Rien.'

'Rien!' the lady exclaimed, 'I own this shop. Let me help you with your shopping.'

It wasn't until she went to pay, her paniers crammed with the picnic, that Faith noticed the local paper lying on the counter. Naturally, the news report was written in French. There was a black-and-white photograph of a dead girl's face. Reeling from shock, she asked if the lady would translate for her. François Gourd shivered as she explained. The badly decomposed body was recovered from the great lake. The young woman was identified as Chantal Merlin by the name tattooed in italics on her left wrist. Faith collapsed into François' open arms.

*****

Can I interest you in my luxury outside furniture?

Well, as an icebreaker, a chat-up line, an invitation to love her, the phrase sounded original. She'd had worse propositions and today, the most important day of her life, she needed love and compassion more than ever.

Dani was lonely without her muse to love and care for her. Faith's sudden disappearance had left a gaping hole in her heart. She sat alone in her room on her pink pow wow, pining for her.

The bedroom was her centre of activity in the beach house, looking out on her red sand-covered promontory, the rocky high point of her stretch of coast, which jutted out into the turquoise sea. A short flight of stone steps led to her small, private sandy beach. Dani never visited the beach.

Her bedroom was sparsely furnished. In the middle lay her statement piece, the Joelle double bed with a rose quartz headboard in clever deep velvet. The bed, with its matching scattered cushions, lazy daze bed linen, and grey-stripe blanket, were her creature comforts. Until her knight arrived to put her out of her misery.

To the left of the bed, on her sleeping side, stood the Mimi bedside table, where she stored the medications, lotions and ointments that she took every evening in a vain bid to sustain her life. The bed stood upon a pink bobble rug, facing a full-wall glass partition. From her bed she could see the sandy patio, its luxury garden furniture, and further afield, the rippling turquoise sea.

Dani rarely slept in her Joelle for fear of rekindling memories of their last night together. During the summer months, she slept under the stars wrapped in her tasselled blanket, as-snug-as-a-bug-in-a-rug. She loved to recline on her luxury padded divan and watch the flume spout from the mountainside where forked lightning had set a large patch of dry scrub on fire. Unlike her life, the flume was inaccessible and couldn't be extinguished. Its flame would burn for many nights. But her flame would flicker, fade, and go out, like a candlelight caught by a sea breeze.

To the left of the bedside table was a tall flotsam mirror. She stood in front of her looking glass and appraised herself. If anything, her head had shrunk even smaller. The shock of peroxide-blonde hair sat uncomfortably on her scalp, hanging in unkempt drapes over her shoulders. Her sad brown eyes were red and sore from crying. The shiny skin over her cheekbones was drawn taut, an upset masque relieved by her hooked nose. Beneath her set-square jaw sagged a scraggy turkey neck, stretched, and pulled.

Dani raised her weary arms and locked her fingers over her head, hating the hairy growths sprouting from her armpits, her boyish flat chest, the teak curls growing out of her pink pinched rosebuds. Her skin was dry, cracked, and sore. She lightly dabbed herself with soothing balm, massaging her skin until she felt supple, wiping her fingertips on the coarse blanket. Her hand slid down her exposed rib cage, her hollow stomach, rubbing her shallow navel, tinkering with the flaps of loose skin under her baby-knot.

She collapsed on the Joelle, sinking her head in the pile of pillows until her face was smothered with scent. Drew her knees to her chest and imagined Faith's ruby red lips, her wonderful body. Closed her eyes and concentrated on her features. The face was blurred. Dani had forgotten her muse's face.

'Oh God!' she cried, 'Oh God, no!'

*****

Picardie's body was wasted. The illness overwhelmed her. She entered the critically dangerous degeneration phase. Her psychiatrist, Menten, felt that her bodily degeneration was due to self-induced psychosomatic trauma. Her physicians, Haile and Maigre, disagreed, declaring that her decay was clinical. She was highly unstable, distrait. The endless desiccations decimated her, pulverising her mind and body into abject submission. Quite simply, she had lost the will to live. The woman hated water. Menten described her negative reaction when he offered her a beaker of mineral water, as 'like an amoeba in a desert.' His mind stretched. Supposing Picardie suffered from a severe allergic reaction to water, hydrophobia even?

The problem with theories was that they did nothing to alleviate her mental scars, her physical suffering. Picardie was emotionally distraught. Outwardly, the wasting decimated her, leaving her in permanent lassitude, shattered, pulverised into submission. Inside her head, the morbid stone of despair fell, a sad cushion of hopelessness, pressing on her will to live.

Life without Faith lost all sense of purpose. Her sole raison d'être was callously removed, like an unwanted tumour, into a flip-bin of wasted love. To think, they'd connected so closely. She had befriended her muse, fallen in love with her, only for Faith to vanish on a local shopping spree, leaving her to endure this torment. What had possessed her to do such a thing? By leaving her like that, could Faith conceivably have made Dani's last remaining hours any worse?

She entered the final phase of her illness. The weather turned increasingly oppressive: a sordid mixture of sweltering humid days, cool, breezy evenings, and thundery nights. The dark night of death was about to descend on her.

Such a release from pain: a blissful end to a life filled with greed, deceit, envy, lust, and murder.

Dani pulled up her red y-fronts, drew the blanket round her emaciated body, and went outside to lie on her luxury divan. To wait for her knight in shining armour to arrive and set her free.

He came for her at twilight. He was nervous. His hands trembled with fear and apprehension at the daunting task that awaited him. He dropped anchor, pulling down the sails, wrapping the mainsail round the boom, trying to stay focused. The ropes seemed to wind themselves round the cleats, such was the depth of his remorse. He wailed, a deep animalistic wail of grief, as he stood at the bow of his white charger. Then he took a deep breath and dived into the freezing water.

He thought of his daughter, fighting for her life, in the crystal-clear water of the lake. Thinking of her gave him strength. Steadily, he swam to the beach, his face set like granite, determined. He hauled himself out of the water. She was waiting for him. Lying on her luxury divan. Glowing in the twilight. She spoke first:

'Hello, my name is Dani. I am seventy-years old and lonely. I am flat-chested, but that doesn't make me less of a woman, does it? As you can see, I have beautiful blonde hair which tumbles down my back, high cheekbones, a lovely Roman nose. I have no breasts, but my sun-tanned body is slim and tender to touch, my legs deliciously long and slender. I'm wearing my chain, see?'

She reached down and touched her ankle.

'It means I am available to you, tonight.'

He watched revolted, as she took a full slurp of gin and tonic from a crystal-cut glass tumbler and threw open the blanket, revealing her wasted breasts, her chicken's legs, scrawny neck and knock knees,

'Take it off!'

Dani took off her wig, revealing the glowing, spattered-egg-yolk-shaped, port wine stain,

'Won't be needing that where I'm going,' she hissed, 'Make love to me under the stars, won't you? Make an old bird happy before she dies.'

Shaking with fury, the knight lifted his lady out of her blanket and carried her to the water's edge, cradled in his arms. With a measured stride, he entered the rippling surf, until the waters lapped at his stomach. He stared at the flume, burning in the night, his eternal flame, the flame they created in her memory, then he lowered Dani into the water.

She squirmed and spurted, squirting jets of seawater into his face:

'From the waters of my mother's womb…' she spat.

'Die!' the knight cried, pushing down on her chest as she flailed her arms and legs.

'… I was born…'

He felt a thrill akin to sexual arousal as he pushed down on her stomach, her hairy groin, making her arms and legs pulse like a jellyfish. But Dani resurfaced, momentarily, gasping for air:

'And to the waters… of my mummy's womb… shall I return…'

Then Faith was standing by his side in her navy swimsuit, standing over Dani, as his red-salty eyes bulged with horror. As his muse raised the blade, its steel gleaming in the moonlight, and sliced off the artist's ugly head.

Jonas and his adopted daughter clasped their hands in prayer and gazed at the starry night sky, their faces streaming tears even as Daniel Picardie's vile, evil blood spread in a crimson bloom through the briny water.

In Loving Memory of Claire Geatish

Mae

Blue Moon:

CHANCES, OPPORTUNITIES LIKE THESE, came once in a blue moon for a loner like him. It was close, clammy, hot, humid, airless on the train. The hottest night of the year. A storm was brewing outside. Inside his mind. He struggled to control his breathing, overwhelmed by the sight of her asleep in the opposite seat. Other than mice, feeding on scraps, foraging beneath their seats, they were alone.

On the last train home.

One of her slim hands was gripping an empty plastic water bottle. She slumped into her seat. Her dimpled chin fell onto her chest. The shiny beige satin blouse she barely wore was unbuttoned as far as her midriff. Her fair bare legs were exposed by a fluid blue ditsy miniskirt, a pair of scuffed cognac slingback sandals.

Blue moon. A creature of the night. Paleskin dreams. The girl on everyone's lips. His lips.

'Mae.'

Baby blonde hair. She had baby blonde hair, neatly parted down the middle, swept behind her ear, one side hanging loose, the other draped, touching her chest. Darkening her face. He studied her closely. Her nose was broken at the bridge, an obscene bulge, her glans, swelled the tip. Her lips appeared to be synthetic, bloated pink rubber bands, split in the middle. He wondered if they were injected with Botox, needle-probes, to prise them apart.

Her mouth opened. The gaps in her crooked teeth were unnaturally large, dark, spaces. In her mouth she hid her tongue. Her pencil thin brows rose, and her sleepy eyelid opened, revealing a glassy grey eye. She had a tiny caramel mole on her throat. It moved whenever she smiled. She grinned, stretching her elasticated lips, exposing a mouthful of teeth. Not her tongue. Mae didn't show her tongue to anyone, until it was too late.

He regarded her fingers. She wore no gold, silver, platinum. There could never be a ring.

'Mae,' he said, leaning forward brazenly in his seat. She watched him open his legs.

Cocky. He's so cocky. How is it, my young prey are so cocky? So easy for me. Easy meat.

'Mae.'

She unfolded her legs, uncrossing them so that he could get a good butchers of her thighs. His eyes widened. She wasn't wearing any panties tonight. Mae must have slipped them off in the stultifying heat. He sweated profusely, his charcoal grey-mottled shirt buttoned right up to his thick swarthy neck, arms buttoned down to his wrists, the chunky gold watch sticking to him, coated with intimate moisture.

She held her tongue, primed, ready to strike, pressing hard against the backs of her teeth, bursting to get out. He had wiry chestnut hair, balding at the temples, thin and patchy on top, glistening with his man-dew.

~ 120 ~

That'll have to go, the head. His head's no good to me. I could always bury it in the yard.

The buttons on his shirt were white. On the tapered chest he wore a breast pocket. Home, she saw, to a rectangular shape. Debit card? Season ticket?

Cut it into slithers! Melt the watch. Burn his shirt on a bonfire, in my yard. And his jeans.

Jeans! In this heat? The fool-on-the-hill. He lived on Pouting Hill, she recalled. Attractive wife: brunette, fleshy, succulent, chewy, doughy, tough, sinewy Sal. Two kids. Fat, porky, Justin: roast him in the oven on a bed of roots till nicely browned, serve with apple sauce? Mindy: chicken's legs, de-skin, bone her thighs, shallow fry in clarified butter, serve them with a tart red wine sauce?

Mae's disruptive mind returned to her willing prey. He was craving her. Stupidly, he leaned forward, his thick cotton shirt stuck to his back, left hand at rest on his knee, flashing his huge Swiss watch at Mae, failing, entirely, to impress her.

His jeans were tight. She made him bulge. Couldn't speak. Could never speak. Mute. She scratched the insect bite above her right breast, raking at her itchy, pallid skin. He watched her slim digits scratch herself, feverish, animalistic, above her breast. Mae eyed his tanned hand, resting calmly, patiently, on his kneecap. The young prey had stubby fingers, short, clean nails, bitten to the quick. She smiled, mute, her teeth clenched, holding back, just about controlling her pushy, probing tongue,

At least, he's got clean hands.

He made his move. An elbow bent at the joint, pulling at the sleeve, forcing his hand into a neat fist, exposing the slick matt of soaking wet hair coating his forearm.

The prey had a hound dog smirk on its face, underneath the light brown beard, scrawny moustache. He propped his chin with a fist, gazing at Mae from under his bushy brows, hooded eyelids, using his piercing nut-brown eyes to consume her attention. His eyes, circled with brown: tiredness, stress, sex, self-gratification?

'Mae,' he said, gently, 'I'm Nick. I keep a discreet pied-a-terre, a secret, by the common. Will you come there with me, please?'

She shook her head, reached across the divide, and held his hand to her bared right breast.

'Mae?'

She shook her head sadly, running her fingers over her stretched pink lips, couldn't speak.

'Mae?'

She nodded, smiled, held her tongue, bit her tongue. Her smile told Nick, all he needed:

I have a better idea.

The train stopped. The doors slid open, gushing out stifling air. They stood in silence, holding each other. Mae smiled.

Time to get off, with Nick.

Hot Tarmac:

Surfers. Late night Surfers. Surfing the net, the web, the line. Caught up in a spider's web of deceit. Desire. Lust. Prey for the predator. Breaking taboos. Crossing blurred lines of acceptability. Crossing lines.

Nick got off after Mae, crossing the yellow safety line, his safety line. The doors slid shut. The train moved off. They stood in silence on the empty platform. Him behind her. Safe distance: social distance: metre. Mae smiled for the camera, candid camera, then mooned. Keeping her slender thighs and calves straight, knees in, legs closed, she bent, at the hips, reaching forward until she touched the tarmac. The tarmac felt hot to touch, tacky on her fingertips. She exhaled through her nose, holding her tongue in place behind her clamped teeth, stretching her pink, rubbery lips, smiling expectantly.

Soiled pants on my fire. Bloody rare rump, his rump, on my plate. Warm sauce Bearnaise.

He shiver-breathed at the sight of her, skirt hitched high, mooning for him. Her taut, pale buttocks shone under the station lights. Drool fodder for the boys in the Incident Room. Up the junction. Christ! He could make out blue veins running up the backs of her knees, the tendons, straining in her calves and thighs. The sheer effort of her impressed him.

The abs she must have. The strength in those abs.

Mae messaged him. Advertising her body subliminally. Indecently exposing herself. His mind made itself up.

She fancies me, her place, not mine.

Then she was straightening at the hip, softening at the knee, standing upright. Mae stepped into the gates of delirium, extracting the railcard from a slit in her miniskirt, wiping it on the reader. She swished her skirt, Monroe. Her prey tried to look away. Couldn't. A hard lump formed in his throat:

I've an attractive wife: brunette, fleshy, succulent, chewy, doughy Sal, kids: Justin Mindy.

Nick stamped his feet in frustration. He'd left his jacket on the train: comb, wallet, keys, hope, love, loyalty.

Now what'll I do?

Secrets, dirty secrets. One-way-tickets to lust. Portals, openings, apertures. Gates, to Mae.

She turned to face him, across her divide, their causeway. His bleary eyes fell to her chest. The shiny beige satin blouse she barely wore was open. Mae let a breast hang out for him.

Coming out to play with me tonight?

Angry with himself, yet captive, her prey swiped his debit card, passing through her gates, and – with that – obliterating all hope of going home.

Dark Recess:

Acquaintances, casual acquaintances. Vermin. Sniffing each other out. Her body sheened, glossy with perspiration. His torso, fresh meat, basted, dripping, in stinking, stale sweat. Searching for intimacy, satiation, gratification, repletion, then rest, in the stultifying heat.

'Mae.'

She stood, quiescent, by the self-serve ticket machine, staring at the screen: single, return? Her mouth quinsy, tonsils inflamed, her oral tissue, buccal lining in her cheeks, sored by a septic abscess from the graft of holding her virulent tongue behind her teeth. The gastric acid juice from her upset tummy etched her throat as she contemplated her nocturnal feast.

Turret. Mae would tease, taste, taunt him, turn in for the night, then take him. In the turret. Her dark recess. Her funereal, four-tier facility. Her tummy rumbled, starved of his flesh, craving his fresh carcass: sex n supper in her carnal house: summerhouse: slaughterhouse: charnel house. Momentarily exhausted by her sensual contemplation, she fell on the gates.

My stomach's telling my mouth it's time to eat. What'll it be, Mae? Roast leg, mint sauce, redcurrant jelly. His sausage fried. Shave him till he's bald and hairless. Bit in his mouth.

Her prey feasted his eyes on her, slumped all over the ticket barrier, desperate to find her a secluded place, a fag-strewn urinal or littered alcove where the filthy reprobate could grope and kiss his bimbo. Nick casually shuffled up to her side, a clown without a circus.

'Mae, take my arm.'

I would rather take your leg. Pot roast you, then slice off all your tender, succulent meat.

Mae wrapped her long, slim, bony, fingers round his right elbow, and they left the station. For the first time that night, she felt his intimacy, saturated, matted, hair wetting her hand as she gripped his forearm. Mae couldn't wait to peel his wet shirt off! Comforted by his manliness, she smiled up at him affectionately, squeezing his flesh, making him feel good.

~ 125 ~

Where're we going, darlin?

Mae's message, her slick massage, seeped into Nick's sweating pores, her animal musk probing, permeating his skin, a jus, an intoxicating sexual marinade for her willing victim.

'Thought we'd find ourselves a recess,' he said aloud.

She shrugged, grinned, baring her teeth, thrilled by the prospect of shattering his defences.

Want my breasts to be love-putty in your rough hands. To feel your nails, scratch my bum.

Her thoughts stuck, sticky-cell platelets to his surrendering mind. Struggling to retain any self-cohesion, Nick led Mae outside onto the new tarmac forecourt. His favourite recess was seconds away, past the blooming buddleia bushes crawling out of cracks in the crazy pavement, past the closed Caff Hut, Balti Hut, Bull & Gate. Save for a clapped-out BMW, locked with a yellow clamp, the car park was empty.

They heard an empty train shunt in a siding. Mae's subliminal expletives callously slaying her flailing prey's subconscious:

Shunt me! Find a dark recess, then shunt me. Hurry, darlin.' Baby wants to eat you all up!

Weakening by the moment, her intended prey tugged Mae round the nearest street corner, The Huts: blacked-out by vandal-smashed streetlights. The Bull & Gate: twinkling fairy lights, violets, pinks, rubies, mauve, illuminated ivy creeping up its façade, a hand-scribed A-stand by the heavy, oaken, front door which read:

Glad to have you back – Bette n Alfie

They reached the recess. There was a gas lamp fitted with a (Nick estimated) LED Classic BC warm white 806 lumen 9-watt equivalent to 60-watt electric light bulb that used 80% less energy. Relieved to see the stark light it cast on her portal Mae let prey lead predator into the dark shadows. They halted just outside. Movement. There was movement, inside the recess. Nick was first to speak, as Mae was tongue-tied.

'How long are you going to be?'

A puffing, panting, foreign, far eastern sound emanated from deep within, 'Just finished!'

The Balti phased himself out of the gloom confronting them. He wore a smart black shirt buttoned into his neck, sleeves, neatly folded as far as the elbows, a swarth of furry black hair on his arms. Pressed black trousers. Shiny black shoes. Greasy black hair, dandruff, tied off the face in a ponytail. A pronounced widow's peak. Flappy ears. Hooter of a nose. And ridged, cocoa brown, shag circles, puffing round his eye sockets. Mae, who had never seen someone so tired, considered breakfast.

He ogled her. Her satin blouse had come unbuttoned. One of her breasts was hanging out.

Blue moon. Creature of the night. Paleskin, dreams. The girl on everyone's lips. His lips.

'Mae.'

Baby hair. She had baby hair, hanging loose, draped, touching her breast. Her nose was broken at the bridge, swollen at the tip. Her lips were bloated, pink, split down the middle. Her mouth opened. Gaps in her teeth, unnatural, large gaps. Mae had a tiny caramel mole on her throat. It moved, every time she smiled at him, grinning, stretching, her elastic lips.

'Very nice,' he remarked, opening his legs.

She gloated at him, openly taunting him.

You're next mutton chops.

Realizing what Mae was doing, Nick intervened, shoving the beguiled, flatulent, Balti in the chest, leaving him breathless, out of puff, wind-free, deflated, flat, compressed, in the recess.

'Take your eyes off of my broad!' he shouted.

Stunned by the adulterer's archaic description, The Balti backed off, disappearing in the night's gloom. Mae smiled smugly to herself, tucking her breast snugly, inside her blouse.

Your broad? You should be so lucky.

Together, they entered the dark recess.

Tight Fit:

Parasites, symbiotic parasites. Dependents. Succulents. Tantalising. Entities. Silhouettes. Coupled, entwined, clamped to each other in an excruciating, cramped recess: a tight fit!

Mae's hole stank! Her hole was alive! Crawling, with centipedes, lice, flies, spiders, mice, rats, less savoury inhabitants: phylum Mollusca secreting their slimy excrements over the pebble-dash walls. Nick, who was claustrophobic, diabetic, and suffered chilopodophobia poured with sweat, struggled to breathe, craved liquid, crushing creepy-crawlies with his head, shoulders, back, posterior and legs. Mae soothed his fraught mind, rubbing his torso, fluffing his thin hair, cradling his head in her hands, making the man feel loved - needed. She found a kind of love for him, call it a selfish affection, love that dispelled discomfort.

His shirt was first to go – carefully unbuttoned from neck to waist, Mae gently tugging at his tails, opening out the cuffs, airing, freeing him, before peeling off the sodden chemise, like smelly cellophane off a ripe camembert. She pecked at his nipples with her pursed lips, smothering Nick's hairy chest, the rippled folds of flab sheathing his gross abdomen, with soft kisses.

Hearing the man gasp for her, Mae knelt on the dusty concrete floor and pulled off his sweaty, smelly, brogues, the cheap socks from the local minimarket: olive green with red dragon emblazons.

Fond memories of her lost youth in Pwllheli. Halcyon holidays at Butlins. Eating her mum and dad, the winners of beauty contests: young men, women, all captivated by her disarming smile, captured, dismembered, barbecued on the family patio, served with shoestring fries, catsup, tossed tomato, raw onion salad, to discerning friends with an appetite for human flesh. The missing persons list grew, suspicions were aroused. Ann had simply changed her name, identity, cultivated a new personality, fresh look, gone into hiding, then resurfaced as Mae: at night, on rainy days, in dark recesses, black turrets, grey cells, summerhouses, charnel houses, carnal houses. She heard her fresh carrion cry.

'I love you, Mae. Your my world.'

Touched by her prey's kindness, his loving words for her, she set about preparing him for the slaughterhouse. There were real tears in her eyes when Mae unbuckled his belt, pulled down his trousers, and freed him. Choking with emotion, gagging on her pent-up tongue, she held the naked man in her arms, held him close, his body pressed against hers, opened her mouth, and kissed him.

They kissed invasively, like symbiotic parasites, drinking each other's saliva. Mae's tongue swelled inside her prey's mouth, filling his throat, secreting her digestive enzyme. Stunned, incapacitated, he became her dependent, her succulent, tantalising entity. Silhouettes, coupled, entwined, clamped to each other, they fell thru her psychotic abyss, spiralling ever downwards into a narrowing recess - ending in a pinprick.

Mae plunged her prey into a sea of light, discarding him, spent, and wasted, on her grey cell floor. His meat: stress-free, cells: free of lactic acid, since her tender caress, his mind: neutralized by the vixen's toxic kiss.

Nick lay twitching in spasm, mute, unable to scream.

Grey Cell:

Paraplegic, Jelly Baby. Violated. Soft-centred. Imploding. Mae's Jelly Baby. Jelly Man.

Nick had never felt so tired. He'd endured the worst of Covid, long Covid, SARS, man-flu, the common cold. Nothing as debilitating as this. Mae's kiss literally drained all the life out of him. His arms lay loose at his sides, his dead legs cocked at angles: flimsy, scarecrow's legs. Useless. There were no sensations left in the prey's skin, nose, tongue, nose, eyes, ears – genitals for that matter. The voyeur's once-proud tool hung like a pork 8 freshly extruded from a sausage-making machine, resting, inert, on its numb bed of testicles. He was no longer of any physical or emotional benefit to Mae, in that respect.

Nick felt a muscle pull in his chest, a sharp, stabbing pain: his heart succumbing to her poison. He was out of shape, the facilities manager. Too many late nights in the office, planning, scheduling, organising, and coordinating furniture moves, minor refurbishment, managing the contractors, checking out the reports. Alone with his thoughts, a cold coffee, double cheeseburger, chips, fried apple pie, a one-pound bar of fruit n nut, the inevitable grab bag of cheese and onion crisps.

Sometimes, he saved the treats till later, scoffed the sweet and savoury feast on the train home, brushing mess from his groin and thighs in full view of his travelling companion. Of Mae. She looked away when he cleaned off the food scraps, until he'd finished, until he was ready to concentrate on her.

Mentally, Nick kicked himself. He should have known, her teases, her erotic overtures to him were all traps, premeditated charms, to capture his imagination, to take him into this hellhole, their recess. What was that all about?

He tried to rationalize Mae, the temptation of her, his full, bodily surrender to her on their last train, at the gates, the shady alcove by the Balti Hut which led him here. But he couldn't, he failed, miserably. Reflecting on his insignificant life, Nick wondered why she chose him. He was hardly the most handsome, dashing, sexy commuter on the line. Why did she select him?

How did she find him? Was their encounter really a chance meeting? He recalled Mae, sitting in the end coach, when he boarded at Bank. There was an empty seat opposite her. He'd seized the opportunity and watched her. This was all his fault.

He lay flat on his back on the stone floor staring up at the whorls in the ceiling, wondering if he was going to die, coming to the inescapable conclusion,

I will die if I don't have my insulin injection. Come off it, Nick! Mae's about to kill you. Why would she do that? To what end?

A bizarre thought flashed through his mind: the white inscription on the red mug that Sal gave him for his birthday:

Keep Calm You're Only 48

Keep Calm?

Nick's jaw flapped open, giving up the ghost. He tried to move his head. Couldn't. His heavy eyelids fell, like broken blinds, over his weary eyes. The ache returned in his heart. He felt stomach cramps. An agonizing piercing pain, corkscrewing, twisting the inside of his prostate, his bladder - swelling, a caustic burning sensation in his urethra: Mae's curse. Nick wet himself. The forcibly spurted release of hot urine over his thighs eased the pain. Anaesthetized by the woman's deadly kiss, he fell into a satisfying sleep, and dreamed of life.

By now, her poison had etched its way into his viscera, penetrating the lining of Nick's stomach, duodenum, jejunum, and rectum, entering the bloodstream, then spreading, her contagion, her mutated spiral helix virus, rapidly to the kidneys, liver, lungs, and bladder.

It was only a matter of seconds before Mae's pungent, acrid-smelling saliva dissipated in mauve plumes of plasma, congealing into luminescent cerise orbs, her killer cells, kiss-phage's that digested the vulnerable tissue of the prey's organs. He felt the orbs eat into his brain, and the marvellous memories: of Sal's water births, holding his bloodied babies, patting sandcastles with Justin and Mindy on Clacton Sands, picnics on the stained tartan rug in the woods, picking blackberries, magic mushrooms, with his family. The family he neglected, in favour of his workaholic tendencies, his adulterous obsession, with Mae.

Riddled from crown to heel with the curse she carried in her sputum, Nick felt his body tense, conceding to her as the final vestiges of energy, his cellular barriers of resistance, were broken down by her cell's gnawing secretions, exposing the prey's DNA strands to mutation.

Mae put him out of his misery, squatting comfortably on his stomach, leaning forward to insert the full distended length of her abhorrent tongue down his throat, swell-suffocating him, killing him softly, with her to-u-u-u-u-ungue. She sang her favourite love song in her mind, extracting her whiplash, ciliated langue from his oesophagus, coating herself in his slime as she slithered out of him.

He's dead, she considered, strumming his face with her fingers, Supper's nearly ready.

There was a yucca tree in the grey cell housed in a bright red recycled Christmas tree pot. Her double bed sat beside the shrub: a mess of soiled, crumpled sheets, squashed pillows, covered with an interwoven ash grey quilt, a grey, tartan throw. No headboard. Mae never slept with heads. She stood over her prey, looking down on him, despising him for treating her like a whore, his so-called broad. She removed her blouse and miniskirt, crouched on the bed, and waited, naked, starving for human flesh.

The Balti appeared, a genie out of her lamp, at the end of her bed, dressed in only an iron mask, thick black rubber apron, and surgical wellingtons.

Carrying: a butcher's meat saw. He admired Mae: her baby blonde hair slopped over one side of her face, her rubbery lips, her soft, doughy breasts n puffy nipples, her perfectly formed abs, taut stomach muscles, the knotted blue veins, standing out of her sinewy arms, as she fisted the springy mattress,

'Nice,' he said, so wishing he had a bunch of roses to present to her, his beautiful heroine.

Mae smiled at him appreciatively, nodding towards the carcass lying prostate on the floor,

With that, the butcher grabbed hold of one of the prey's swollen ankles and dragged him out of sight.

Wet Dream:

She was having that dream again. Her wet dream. The dream where she was spreadeagled on the crumpled sheet, duvet pushed down the damp bed to tilting point by her impatient feet, having her body explored by him. He started with her face, lips, trying to kiss her in the mouth. She tolerated more than enjoyed his intimate intrusion, parting her moist lips, opening her mouth, admitting his tongue. So that he could have his oral way with her. His 'rinse and spit,' she called it. The kiss where he rinsed her gums, her tongue, the roof of her mouth, her tonsils, back of her throat, with his juice, spitting inside her.

This habit, cultivated by him as a necessary prelude to their lovemaking, forced on her as part of their unspoken pact, she accepted, in exchange for her pleasures to come. His kiss gave her a sore throat afterwards; he couldn't be bothered to floss, inter-dent, sloosh, rinse and spit for her, before he came to bed. He rinsed and spat inside her. His beard hurt her, abrading the thin skin round her lips. She sighed with relief when he moved further down her body, tracing his lick-line over her neck, her chest, kissing her little breasts, sucking her bendy teats until they stood erect.

'Love it when you're my baby,' she moaned, 'Be my baby.'

He managed a slurping, gurgling noise. She hadn't managed to breastfeed Justin, Mindy, her breasts were too small, couldn't make enough milk. For all his weird fetishes her man had his compensations, and this, her adult breastfeeding of him, her baby, was one of his best. She let herself go, intertwining her fingers with his hair, taking his head in her hands, pushing him down, feeling his beard on her tummy.

She opened her legs, all tingly inside, 'Kiss my mouth.'

He licked her with his outstretched tongue, his beard brushing her, mingling with her hair, pausing only to murmur,

'Lie on your front. Hurry.'

The urgency in his voice excited her. He moved aside, watching her hungrily, as she rolled onto her front. The wet sheet clung to her breasts, her tummy, her groin. She felt his beard brushing, scratching, the soft skin on her slender back, her shoulder blades, the small of her back. Felt his hands grasp her hips, slipping, sliding gently over her perfectly rounded, smooth buttocks, prising her apart.

She opened her legs wide for him, held herself open for him, admitting his tongue, so that he could twist and turn inside her, his key, unlocking her sacred vault. She stretched an arm out to his side of the bed gripping the sodden sheet in her tight fist, she ascended, seeing stars, in her own intimate night sky, above her head.

Gradually, she came back down, hyperventilating, her blushing face stuffed in the pillow, letting her dream subside. Twisting her head to one side, she opened her eyes, and stared at the luminous hands on her copper alarm clock: 3am. Her dreams always ended at 3am. She climbed off the bed and padded to the full-length window, pressing her face, breasts, and stomach against the cool pane, steaming the glass. Sal mouthed into her breath's mist,

'Come home soon, Nick, I love you.'

Tough Meat:

Depilation. Exfoliation. Hair removal. Shaving. Curing. Tasting. Necrophilia. Cannibal. Nick wasn't coming home anytime soon to be loved by Sal. His mortality, his tenure of her, the dull employment he undertook to provide for his faithful wife and children, was over, snuffed out by the whore's tongue.

The Balti dragged his body down the spiralling staircase to the next tier of Mae's turret, her abattoir, with scant regard for his wellbeing: bruising, contusing, nicking, abrading, battering, his head, limbs, and torso as he bumped Nick down the concrete fire steps into oblivion. Fighting her need to drown her extended tongue in the corpse's gastric juices, halt The Balti on the semi-circular landing, prise open Nick's jaws, project her langue in spurious spasmic reflexions down his oesophagus - penetrating his pyloric defences - Mae tagged along, making a mental list of things to do, clutching the butcher's meat saw,

I'm starving! I hope he's soft and tender, buttery, not tough and chewy, tasty not bland.

They arrived at the abattoir, which was brightly lit up by spatter-proof fluorescent tubes sealed in the high ceiling. The abattoir, call it Nick's final destination, consisted of a long hallway with washable impervious walls and padded bathroom flooring, softened, to care for Mae's bare feet.

Along one wall hung all manner of butchery tools, electrical devices, a wash hand basin with hand sanitiser, soap, nailbrush, green paper towels, her Vim, elbow-operated hot and cold taps, a blood-spattered shower cubicle. At the far end of the slaughterhouse, Mae had arranged for the installation of four upright freezers, labelled: legs, torsos, offal, waste. There was another door, a tattered paper sign that read: Kitchen This Way, and, at dead centre, a raised marbled plinth bearing a bloodstained marble slab.

Mae left the saw by the slab, went to the basin, and scrubbed her hands. Meanwhile, The Balti dragged Nick's body onto the plinth, laying him to rest on his back. He stood aside admiring Mae, his love idol, culinary inspiration, celebrity role model, his feisty, feline, gourmet, as she prepared her meat for mealtime.

The constant green light told her the electrical device was fully charged, ready to use. Mae removed the body shaver from its wall socket, unclipped the safety guard, switched on her pleasure device and knelt beside her prey, mute and mouthing, inhibited by her tongue, straining violently behind her teeth,

Time you were shorn, baby, bare as you were born.

She began with his head, delicately teasing out his nasal hair, growth in his ears, digging out his brows, shaving off his beard. Mae shaved him bald, sweeping her shaver over his pate: front to back, back to front, side to side, behind the ears, down his nape. She ran her fingers over his shaven cheeks,

~ 137 ~

his chin, kissing him, setting free her tongue, curing his putrefying flesh with her acid saliva,

Mmmn, you're lovely and soft. You must have been a sexual gorilla for Sal when you were alive, she mused, look at all your body hair! Oh well, I can't have hair in my food, can I?

'Nice!' observed the Balti in the background.

Mae wound back her tongue, her slippery, slithering, oral, eelworm, opened her eyes, and shaved Nick's chest, armholes, arms, stomach, crotch, legs. The Balti rolled him onto his back for her, sweeping the floor with his broom as his mistress shaved off swathes of her man's coarse black hair: his back, legs, bum. Rigor mortis set in. Her prey went all stiff. When he was bald, completely hairless, she nodded at her accomplice to flip the corpse on its back. The Balti held the meat saw aloft, brandishing it like a sword, preparing for the final cuts.

She shook her head. He understood. Mae wanted to spend their decisive moments alone. The Balti left the abattoir. He left her to enjoy his body whole. Left her to pleasure herself. He stood in the doorway, watching as, stark naked, Mae straddled her lover's belly, and made love to him.

*****

Saturday Night - The Balti Hut

'You haven't touched your Curry, darling.'

Ben waved his fork, gesticulating, trying to remove the indigestible meat from his mouth,

'It tastes funny, Claire,' he chomped, 'It doesn't taste right, even mixed in with chutney.'

Claire, 28, engaged to be married to Ben, 31, reached across the candlelit table with her fork, flashing her diamond ring for all the other diners to see.

They were sitting outside, one metre from the next table, holding hands, sipping bubbly, gazing up at the stars, into each other's eyes, the look of love was in their eyes. Claire had ordered Chicken Tikka Marsala, Vegetable Fried Rice, a Poppadom. The chicken tasted strange, quite unlike any chicken she'd ever tasted before,

'Here let me try it,' she helped herself to a mouthful, then immediately spat it out into her napkin, 'Ugh! It tastes disgusting! You should complain to Mr Balti. Ask for a free meal.'

'I don't like to,' protested Ben, 'The food here is usually excellent. How's your chicken?'

'So-so,' Claire pushed her food round her plate having lost her appetite, 'It isn't chicken.'

'Not chicken! And this,' her fiancé shouted, loudly, pointing, for all to hear, 'Isn't beef!'

There was uproar on the terrace, a clattering of cutlery on plates as other diners joined in,

'Mine isn't lamb!'

'This isn't Bombay Duck!'

'Call this goat?!'

'Oh my God!' cried Claire, 'Do you think it's, think it's… dog?'

'No, it isn't dog,' Ben reassured her, 'I've eaten dog in China. I think it might be...'

Mr Balti appeared on the terrace, covered in blood, dressed in an iron mask, rubber apron, surgical wellingtons, carrying a bloody meat saw. He admired Mae, walking towards him, daubed from head to toe in fresh blood, the 'girl at the high school prom,' dripping scarlet!

'Nice,' he said, wishing he had a bunch of red roses to present to her, his beautiful heroine.

Mae smiled at him, appreciatively, morsels of Nick's raw flesh, hanging from her teeth.

And all the diners screamed!

Pig Beach

WE TOOK TIPPI WITH US ON OUR ANNUAL PILGRIMAGE TO PIG BEACH. Now, before you start pointing fingers at us, assigning culpability, apportioning blame for what happened, let me tell you about Tippi, our dark fairbird. Tippi was a Strangeling, no ordinary girl. She might have seemed 21, but that was where, according to the rules of our benign sanctity, her flourish, her bloom into womanhood ended.

In our minds, and in the deeds dictated by our sacred coven, Tippi was required to dress in her Strangeling attire: a flowing white robe, ankle socks, and leather sandals, until she reached the age that we deemed suitable for her to take her chosen man, Aaliyah, our high, lofty, sublime boy, and have children. The same stringent dress code applied to Aal who was required to dress in a similar robe, socks and sandals until he became a man.

Some people might find the Strangeling way of life disturbed, the odd ways of the cult, but we, the Foreordained, are no different to any other cults (vegans, surfers, dancers, cyclists) except that, through the indoctrination of our members, we remove choice. Once we have Pig-dipped you into joining our cult, there is no way out, only death. The Foreordained believe in the divine art of fortune-telling, reading the palm of fate. We know when your time has come and, deep in our hearts, we knew sweet Tippi's time was nigh.

So, think carefully before blaming us for what took place, as our sacred idol shall absolve us. The Future is ours you see. We, the Foreordained worship the Pig, dine on the Pig. None of those fertiliser-poisoned fruits and vegetables or plastic-tainted fish for us. We are the Pig herd.

We took Tippi with us on our annual pilgrimage to Pig Beach, in the sure knowledge that the back seat of our battered pink Chevrolet Impala would be empty of her when we returned to Tulsa. Marta made up some roast pork and chutney bloomers, munchies, and candies for us to eat, fizzy pop for us to guzzle. While we watched our Tippi swim.

You see, the beach is our cult's sacred site for the worship of the Pig, the white-sand chapel of the Foreordained. The swimming Pigs have been a draw for members of our Cult since Marta and I established pagan rites in Tulsa in '98.

We arrived at the beach to find Aal standing by his Harley Davidson, dressed in summer smock and sandals, mind on the clear, bottle-green sea that stretched as far as the clear, sapphire sky. Marta and I hugged Aal while Tippi changed into her skimpy black soft-cotton bikini behind a shrub. I spoke at Aal, registering my concerns. He raised his navy shades, wedging them in his blonde buzz cut, so I could read his crystal-clear, grey-glass eyes.

I spoke at Aal, to comfort him, 'Aal, my grieving son. No Pigs swimming in the sea today?'

'No Pigs swimming in the sea at all, Cabe,' he confirmed sadly.

As I wondered why the Pigs chose, occasionally, to desert the hallowed gleaming waters of Pig Beach for the other side of the peninsula, I heard Marta babbling in the boot of the Impala.

'Shall I lay out the feast on the beach mats, Cabe?'

'If you would.'

'Three settings?'

I shielded my eyes from the brilliant sun, stared out to sea, and saw those fatty shapes, lying grey and motionless in the warm tropical water, one hundred yards out. I saw those Pigs swim,

'Three settings will be fine, thank you,' I confirmed, 'Can you see the Pigs, Marta, Aal?'

'Are you sure, they're Pigs, Cabe?' Aal queried, 'They seem too grey and slim for Pigs.'

I looked at Aal with fires of wrath burning in my eyes and thundered, 'You doubting me, boy?

'No Sir!' he whelped, 'I can clearly see the Pigs now!'

Tippi padded up to me in her bikini, matt brown hair draped halfway down her back, her dark-tired eyes narrow slits, nose all snub, slender, young, skin as red as uncooked pork. Gave me a cheeky smirk, a chipmunk's grin. Raised her thin brows a mite, pursed her cherry lips and said, in a hushed voice filled with syrupy, hickory, tones of awe and wonder.

'Can I swim with the Pigs now, Cabe? Please say yes.'

'Yes, Tippi!' I hugged her round shoulders, beaming with pride, 'Go swim with the Pigs.'

'Marta?'

'Why of course, Tip,' Marta trilled, tears of joy streaming down her puffy cheeks, 'In you go!'

'Aal, will you marry me in ten-year's time? If I swim with the Pigs?' Tippi enquired, earnestly.

~ 143 ~

'Of course, I'll marry you, Tippi! It'll be my privilege to marry you. We can breed babies into the Foreordained! We can bring children to this very same beach to swim with those old Pigs!'

'Can we, really, Aal?'

Tippi's eyes were shining. There was no doubt in her narrow-slit eyes.

'Course we can! When we grow up. I think you should go swim with the Pigs now, don't you? While I take pork and chutney, and munchies, and candies, and fizz with Marta and Cabe?'

We watched Tippi suck her thumb like a baby. She sucked her thumb like a baby whenever she got exulted. Tip glided like a slithering sea snake into the warm water. Glided into that sea up to her breasts, turned, and waved at us.

'Love you Aal! Love you Marta! Love you Cabe!'

'Oh, and we love you, Tippi,' we cried in unison, 'More than life itself!'

The grey shapes moved in the water…

Dr Jade Bicker, 32, from Tulsa, was in a tour boat on the other side of the peninsula watching the Pigs swim when the attack happened. She said,

'About 45 minutes after we snorkelled in that *exact* spot, a distraught young man wearing a flowing white robe and leather sandals ran tripped over to say his girl got bitten? Everyone got out of the water. We were pretty scared. When we climbed back into the boat there were two small ones, still in the water, and one large one.'

Dad, Milford, 52, from Tulsa, wept:

'We miss her so much. She was so caring. She loved Pigs. It's so ironic she'd die in an attack.'

A GoFundMe page has been set up by Tippi's sister, Violin, 23, to help pay to take her body back to Tulsa. The page said:

'Tip was a beloved daughter, sister, girlfriend, and a good friend of the Foreordained.'

Apparently, Aal rushed to her aid when he saw them attack her. An emergency boat took her to hospital in the capital. But she could not be saved. Tippi, 21, from Tulsa, was killed by three sharks after members of the bizarre Pig-worshipping cult, the Foreordained, of Tulsa, failed to scream a warning that they were approaching.

A witness, 21, from Tulsa, who declined to be named, said,

'She was savaged by tiger sharks, which usually hunt alone. It is thought to be the first fatal shark attack off Pig Beach in more than a decade.'

He added that the swimming Pigs have been a draw for Cabe Fartell, Marta Kardashian, Jade Bicker and her Kids, members of The Foreordained, since their inception in Tulsa in '98.

Tippi Fairbird, 21, a student of the occult, was bitten on her legs and buttocks, she had her right arm torn off.

Primordia

CELESTE DIED, she was killed, mercilessly, painlessly. Celeste, the creature conceived, created, and birthed in deepest space was murdered, slayed, terminated by her life support systems, never to be resuscitated. A spent cosmic macro-organism, sentenced to drift, to float, a dead star child, her inert eyes fixed for all eternity on a thriving miracle of biology: the new-born planet. The endless thrusts of nuclear propulsion, detonating warheads that brought her this far had long since ceased.
Celeste decelerated weaving through the Kuiper Belt, victim of her own inbuilt inhibitors, retro-powered explosions tiring, staying her, exposing her to the distant gravitational pull of our far-off sun.

Exhausted, no longer serving any purpose, she was granted her one final wish: to live for minutes longer before they killed her. She berthed in orbit between the strange dwarf sun Cacoethes, its only planet, and the huge moon, Celebre, which cast a permanent shadow over the green and blue orb lying below, spinning calmly in solitary space.

Celeste gave birth. Her impatient baby wriggled free of her. With her umbilical cord cut, the mother slept for the last time in her twenty-five-year life.

2030:

The signal celebrating her awakening: a single pulse of energy, a starburst erupting from its molten surface, took 6.66 hours to reach Astute, the world's most advanced orbiting telescope. Entrusted by scientists with autonomous digital deciphering decision-making capabilities, Astute informed the joint US-Russo-Chinese-European Space Agency of its surprise eleven seconds later - a shock with the potential to change the course of history.

Humanity had received an invitation to visit a mysterious new-born, an inexplicable tenth planet, drifting in the darkest recesses of our Solar System beyond the dwarf planet Pluto.

News of the discovery was broadcast to a disinterested world. Fake radio signals from outer space had been generated, transmitted by communications terrorists as part of their global distraction fake news campaign, since the proliferation of social media during the first three waves of the pandemic. The decimated world population was now enduring its twelfth wave of the virus, a constantly mutating scourge that thrived on distrust, stirred by the anti-vax campaign, resistance to change, indiscipline, irresponsibility, and apathy.

The signal held no obvious benefit or solution to the spiralling death rates from the latest variants, endless floods and wildfires rampaging our once-green planet, or the perverse plasticated obliteration of life in the seas and oceans.

Doomsday approached.

At a maximum velocity of 590 miles per hour, Ad Astra could be predicted to reach its destination in 760 years. But the probe accelerated to a spatial speed of fifty thousand miles per hour once it had escaped the Earth's gravitational pull. Ad Astra took sixteen years to reach the new-born, but the sensational fly-past took only days.

WHAT DID SHE FIND?

The new-born was rotating on its own axis at a frequency of once every thirty-six hours. The planet was two-thirds the size of Earth. The blue and green orb had a thin atmosphere. It was shrouded in shifting clouds, dense plumes of gaseous vapour, interspersed with clear patches through which the formation of the new-born was clearly visible. Astounded beyond their wildest dreams, the scientists pulled the proverbial trigger. Ad Astra fired her baby at the planet, controlling her release meticulously before she shot off into deep space.

The toughest baby in the Solar System, Electra, braced herself as she hurtled towards the alien planet. A sharp tug, her mother pulling at her bib, and she jerked violently, inhibited by a sudden paddy, a childish outburst of temper, as her retro-firing rockets forced her to calm down. She cooled. The fire in her heat-shield belly subsided. She felt a shady parasol bloom above her head. Withstanding all anticipated atmospheric pressure, Electra fell to the ground, the shock absorbers in her stumpy legs confused by soft, sandy, springy soil. Her momentous message would confound scientists, philosophers, dreamers, seers, and science fiction writers until their dying days.

WHAT DID SHE FIND?

MESSAGE: ELECTRA: 11:02: 23.08.2046: TERRAIN: FLAT WITH UNDULATING SLOPES AND LIQUID. SOIL COMPOSITION: SILICON, NITRATE, ORGANIC DETRITUS. ANALYSIS: LIQUID: H20. WATER PRESENT. ATMOSPHERE: PRIMORDIAL: NITROGEN 74.2%, OXYGEN 25.7%, ARGON 1.3%, CARBON DIOXIDE 0.06%, INERT TRACE GASES, WATER VAPOUR VARIABLE. BIOSPHERE: PRIMORDIAL. REPEAT. PRIMORDIAL. CONDITIONS SUPPORT LIFE.

They called the world Primordia.

*****

Free at last from the protective womb of her dead mother: its vacuous shell, the husk orbiting the new-born, Carmen began her meticulous descent. Descent, for a space-child, was particularly dangerous, requiring constant adjustments for the elements of risk: heat, velocity, thrust, reverse thrust, changes in atmospheric pressure, electrostatic interference. Claire took it all in her stride, spurring Carmen's unheralded arrival magnificently, using her matchless IQ and unassailable mental resources to make the miniscule adjustments necessary to safely guide her home. Carmen slowed. The flame on her radiant heat shield faded. She cooled. A gentle tug on her bib by Claire, the opening of her parasol, her eight stubby legs extending - shock absorbers taking the strain, and she landed, embedded up to her knees in Primordia's earth.

Claire transmitted the message that would thrill the world telepathically, instantaneously:

MESSAGE: CLAIRE: 10:57: 25.08.2075: CARMEN HAS LANDED. CARMEN HAS LANDED!

The lights in the living module came on. Air was restored to the control sector, cabins, recreation and leisure facilities, a biodegradable toilet, the aquatub and dormant chrysalis. Once normality was resumed, Claire turned her attentions to her precious human cargo.

Tiernan hatched first.

2017:

It had been an informative, engrossing, if not intriguing, event. Now the audience were getting restless, pining for their buffet lunch, a clip-on glass of

~ 149 ~

mineral water, a chat with like-minded delegates. The audience: scientists, students, industry experts, sci-fi fans with the odd writer thrown in, had been treated to a thorough introduction to AI, its benefits, and its potential impact on humanity. They were looking forward to the afternoon talks, more contentious, juicier sessions:

The legal and ethical aspects of AI:

Is AI fit to stand trial?

Could AI predict crime?

Should AI have rights, like humans?

Can an AI forgive?

Can a robot be raped?

The moral implications of driverless cars, reality robots, sexbots, and lethal autonomous weapons.

Can AI feel?

How should AI be perceived, and treated, by humans?

AI come from a slavery origin.

Are AI little more than animated tools, our property?

What gender should they be?

Does transhumanism present an opportunity for AI to enhance the human body – and commercialize us?

~ 150 ~

Could AI result in our dehumanisation, annihilation anxiety, 'doom and gloom,' the end of humankind, a frightened society?

With so much to look forward to after lunch, the general consensus among delegates over coffee and biscuits was the last session of that morning constituted the least interesting, most boring, presentation of all.

The little scientist mounted the rostrum to face the audience. There were several coughs, a sneeze, someone's mobile went off. She pressed a hidden button and began. A heading appeared on the screen behind her:

The Animation of Robotic-Type Responses

There followed a lengthy, complicated, wordy, and technically challenging PowerPoint presentation on how robots react to external stimuli, the state of conciousness, associative memory, even perception of robots. The audience began to tire of robotic-type responses. Some delegates slumped in their seats. Others became agitated shifting uncomfortably on their curved wooden chairs. Suddenly, the old woman produced what looked like little more than a box on wheels, a green cube, and a blue cube. She smiled at them all, a wicked witch smile,

'Here's one I made earlier!'

The audience burst out laughing.

'I made this robot out of some transistor radio components, four toy wheels, and a wooden box. It has two sensors: one at the front, one at the back. And a speaker. Do you like it?'

Several delegates clearly approved, so she continued, 'Would you like to see it move?'

The elderly scientist had the audience's undivided attention. The students sat bolt upright. Filled with unexpected enthusiasm, everyone nodded their heads at her, at it.

'The question,' she said, mercurially, 'is 'can a robot feel pain'? Please watch and listen.'

She placed the makeshift robot on the table in front of her with the green cube a few feet away. To the astonishment of the audience, she stroked its back, and said, 'Good!'

The box-on-wheels inched forward, and replied, 'Mmmn!'

Several delegates cheered. Still more craned their necks for a better view. The scientist replaced the green cube with a blue one, smacked the robot's back hard, then said, 'Bad!'

The box-on-wheels backed away.

'Hurts!' it exclaimed, 'Hurts!'

The audience gasped audibly as the old girl smacked the robot's bottom repeatedly.

'Bad!' she repeated, 'Bad!'

The robot backed further and further away from the blue cube until it fell off the table.

'The question is,' its creator posed, 'Did my robot feel pain and pleasure? Or was it all an animated robotic response to external stimuli? Thank you. I wish you all a good lunch.'

The audience rose, applauding the veteran as she left the podium, her box-of-wheels left lying in pieces on the floor.

One of the event organisers stood at the front and asked them, 'How many of you felt sorry for the robot?'

Eighty percent of the audience raised their hands…

2075:

Since Claire's birth in an AI laboratory in Silicon Valley, scientists had fiercely debated the question:

Does Caring Loving AI Really Exist?

Throughout Celeste's twenty-five-year journey to the new-born, Claire had tended to the humans' every need: their hibernation, nourishment, health, and survival. Meticulously, she managed every aspect of the mission from launch, flight, and berth of the mothership to Carmen's controlled descent and establishment of living conditions for Tiernan and Rose. There was no doubt that through her medicated tendrils, drips, tubes, pumps, and feeds, Claire had become physically attached to her human companions. But could she have become emotionally attached? Questions remained unanswered in her perplexed, complex mind:

Should I have rights, like my humans?

How should I be perceived, treated, and loved by them?

Can I feel emotions?

Can I feel pleasure and pain?

and

Can I ever forgive them for how they make me feel?

She hatched Tiernan first, carefully withdrawing all of the invasive drips, drains and feeds from his body while he was still comatose, suspended in his cryogenic cocoon. A fissure, a barely perceptible split, formed in the dormant chrysalis. The hard hickory layer of skin, its cutin thinned, turned transparent, glowing a deep fire red, radiated by an internal heat. Claire cracked Tiernan wide open, splitting his pupa from crown to heel, draining off his ice-blue life-fluid until he lay inert, naked in a pool of liquified jelly preservative waste.

Tiernan stirred, his ebony skin prickling with the bristling sensation of thousands of micro pinpricks scratching his flesh. He coughed and sneezed, ridding his lungs of residual gel. His eyes were glued shut. His ears were blocked. He felt his heart pound in his chest. His eyelids became unstuck. Painstakingly, he opened his eyes. Hearing his ears pop, Tiernan came back to life. His first impression of life on the new-born was of Claire, gazing down at him, talking in perfect English as if she were a British Airways air host serving a flight at home. A bubble of alarm formed in his fuddled brain. He had expected to be roused by Rose, instead AI greeted him.

'Good morning Tiernan. Carmen has landed. Welcome to Primordia. Did you sleep well?'

He tried to form his first words since leaving orbit but his mouth was too dry. He struggled to move his jaw, to open his mouth. Claire extended her tube to him. He parted his dry lips. She inserted the tube fully into his mouth. He sucked on it, greedily. His first drink! Recycled, purified water scented with cranberries. It tasted delicious. He closed his tired eyes, enjoying the feeling of being pampered by the most efficient host in space travel.

Tiernan slept for several days. When he woke, refreshed, reinvigorated, revitalised, Claire was waiting for him, ready with his next tube of fruity water, suckling him like her baby boy even as she spoke.

'Good morning Tiernan. Carmen has landed. Welcome to Primordia. Did you sleep well?'

This time he answered, 'Very well. What Earth time, day, and year is it?'

'Earth time now,' recited Claire, 'is exactly 11:54 on Monday 6th September 2075. I made you coffee. I expect you need it, don't you, after your exhausting journey?'

She extended an arm, her hand clutching a steaming mug of milky brown liquid. Tiernan regarded the blue and green planet motif glazed onto the mug, both sides, the red lettering:

PRIMORDIA MISSION 2050

Claire had just successfully resuscitated him from the longest induced coma in history. He propped himself up on one elbow, a human imago emerging sleepily from its cocoon, then sniffed the beverage.

'What coffee is it?' he asked.

'Ugandan, Rwenzori Mountain, freshly ground, steamed soya milk, sugar, your favourite. I ran you an aquatub. I expect you need it, don't you, after your exhausting journey?'

Tiernan sipped his coffee. It tasted delicious. It felt hot on his tongue, his palate. Not too hot. Perfect. His coffee was perfect. Like everything else Claire controlled in his new life, their life. He worried over Rose. Was she still alive? Did she survive hibernation? A flood of intense concern flushed out of his mind. The implications of Rose not pulling through were enormous, not just for him, the success of the Mission, the scientists back home, but for the future of the whole human race. His mind cleared. He asserted himself, recalling Protocol:

Protocol dictates that the C.O. (Commanding Officer) will, without exception, always be resuscitated first.

Tiernan smiled at Claire ogling his naked body like a maternal voyeur, 'This tastes good!'

She didn't respond. Was something really the matter with Claire? The concept of there being something the matter with Claire was unthinkable.

Persson had rebuked him when he raised the issue during Mission training. 'Claire can't go wrong, Tiernan. The idea of Claire going wrong is completely unthinkable.'

Persson, a pompous white prick from AI who strutted around Mission Base with his head stuck up his arse as if he owned the place, had a habit of repeating the astronaut's name. As a put-down. To keep his inferior in his place where, in Persson's bigoted mind, Tiernan deserved to stay.

'Are there any more questions?' Persson had asked him, impatiently.

'No further questions, Sir!' he'd replied, raising his right hand in a grudging salute.

Tiernan enjoyed a smug grin. Persson would be long dead, dust, by the time he returned to Earth.

He refocused on the potential problem: Claire. Rose was Commanding Officer. Tiernan recalled the strange preparation enacted by Control in the critical countdown leading to launch. How he and Rose were deliberately kept apart prior to hibernation. They'd never officially met. It was deemed emotionally, physically, psychologically, politically correct to separate the astronauts for the good of the Mission by Control.

Now, at the least, Rose was comatose, incapacitated. At worst, she might be dead. Could Claire have deliberately set out to prevent her resuscitation? He grimaced at the notion. Might she have accidentally terminated Rose's life? Panic set in. Suppose she had died? Supposing Claire had suffered an emotional, nervous, even a mental, crisis?

Persson's rebuttal resonated in his mind.

Claire can't go wrong. The idea of Claire going wrong is unthinkable.

Unthinkable?

Stay calm, he told himself, remain positive, professional, make a brave face, cooperate with her. My priority is to resuscitate Rose.

Unthinkable: the idea that Claire might have murdered Rose. Why would she do that? He, Tiernan, was a young black man who'd fought his way out of the slums of Harlem, who'd impressed the big white chiefs in the military with his exceptional determination, his inner steel, his resolve to overcome the odds, and survive. Tiernan was assigned to this mission because he was tough. Because he was strong. Because he was fertile, and black?

There were aspects of the mission that he didn't understand. Such as its ultimate purpose. Control had informed him that the ultimate purpose of the mission would be shared with Rose upon her resuscitation on Primordia. Rose, as C.O., would then inform Tiernan. He drank his lukewarm coffee, putting on a false smile.

'This coffee tastes so good!'

'I am glad you enjoyed it. Would you like to take your bath now? The water is hot with soapy suds, the way you like it. Afterwards, I can cook you breakfast if you like. I expect you need it, don't you, after your exhausting journey?'

He handed his mug to Claire for her to wash, rinse, sanitize, recycle, and seal, 'Question.'

'Yes, Tiernan.'

'What is the ultimate purpose of this mission?'

'I am afraid that I am not permitted to tell you that. You are S.O. here on Carmen. I am only permitted to tell the C.O. Rose is the C.O. You know what that means, don't you?'

Tiernan struggled to retain his cool.

Deal with it, Tiernan. Deal with it.

'I know that, but Protocol clearly states that, in the event of the C.O. dying or becoming incapacitated, the S.O. will assume command.'

'That position is untenable, Tiernan.'

'Why is it untenable?' He was shouting, raising his voice at her, in danger of losing his self-control, at the thought of him living here, twenty-five years from Earth, with just her.

She prattled on about technical issues, 'I have detected a minor technical fault in the LS74 life-support monitoring system. Until I resolve the fault it is impossible for me to confirm whether Rose is dead, comatose, or alive.'

Tiernan held his head in his trembling hands, 'I thought LS74 units were infallible.'

Claire ignored him, 'I am working to resolve the fault in the LS74 life-support monitoring system. As soon as I complete my analysis, I will furnish you with a full update on Rose's status.'

'Tiernan' she soothed, 'You do seem to be under stress. Can I offer you solar relaxation on the sunpad after your aquatub, followed by a mild aphrodisiac to help you de-stress?'

The astronaut retorted, 'I am not stressed! I don't need a sunpad! I don't need aphrodisiac! Put me through to Earth! I need to speak to Control directly!'

'Tiernan, I transmitted this message to Control, the world, to celebrate our arrival today.'

The lights in the living module went off. A luminous screen lit up above the man's head:

MESSAGE: CLAIRE: 10:57: 25.08.2075: CARMEN HAS LANDED. CARMEN HAS LANDED!

'Is your message really necessary?'

The lights in the living module came on. Tiernan weighed his options:

Override Claire and message Earth.

From his technical awareness of her this represented elevated risk. Claire's emotional, loving, and sensitive capabilities had never been fully established by the scientists. Her mind was much too complex. If the unthinkable happened, and she suffered an emotional breakdown or felt her vast intellect had been affronted, even insulted, the extent of her recriminations were terrifying.

Claire wielded the power to terminate Rose's life at the flick of a switch, to murder her, light years away from the human realms of culpability. Moreover, she could shut down Carmen's essential life support systems, kill Carmen, kill Tiernan, before killing herself: cognicide, Mission abort, termination.

There remained the possibility of his escape. Assuming Rose was dead, he could abandon ship, trust to fate, exposing himself to the elements on the new-born planet. If the gravity, atmosphere, biosphere, and temperature levels were really as favourable as Elektra had predicted some thirty years ago. Supposing conditions changed through a carbon dioxide generated greenhouse effect, violent meteor storm, or solar flare from nearby Cacoethes?

A hell of a lot can go wrong in thirty years. In any case his message would take 6.66 hours to reach Control then, at least, 6.66 hours for Control to digest, analyse, and respond with a solution. One solution might be remote control of Carmen by Cadey, the pure-hearted 'woman' based at Control, Claire's twin. Assuming Cadey, Control, the joint US-Russo-Chinese-European Space Agency, and Earth were still there.

Tiernan tried to comprehend what life on Earth must be like now, twenty-five years after leaving home. He knew, deep in his heart, theirs was a one-way mission. There could be no return, no going back. Who or what was there to go back to? He and Rose were selected because they were both orphans with no living parents, siblings, dependents, children or known lines of descent. Emotionally unattached loners voyaging to outer space. For what ultimate purpose only Claire knew. If Tiernan overrode her, and Earth was finished, a burnt-out shell, he would never know the reason he and Rose were sent to Primordia on a one-way ticket to the future in the first place.

No, overriding Claire wasn't an option.

Gain Claire's confidence, play for time.

The safe option. Regain her trust,

'You're right. It isn't necessary for me to message Control, not yet anyways,' he stood, 'I think I'll accept your kind offer of a bath.'

Tiernan luxuriated in the aquatub. The water temperature suited his body perfectly, even the suds were exactly right. He gazed up at Claire, watching him bathe, washing himself clean, ridding his blocked skin pores of cloying cryogenic gel. After a satisfying, lengthy soak, he stood in the warm pool and rinsed his muscled ebony body with recycled water from the pump action portable shower head. Claire drained the aquatub. She would purify the water for re-use. Tiernan stepped out of the tub and lay face up on the warming, irradiated sunpad, loving the sensation of its rays drying his skin, tanning, relaxing him.

'Request.'

'Yes, Tiernan.'

'External environmental analysis. Please.'

'Certainly.'

The lights fell, dropped. An illuminated screen appeared directly above Tiernan's head. Claire articulated her analysis, even as the shapes and figures appeared in luminous green print lighting up the S.O.'s face:

ANALYSIS: CLAIRE: 11:45: 23.08.2075: SOIL: SILICON, NITRATE, ORGANIC DETRITUS. LIQUID: H20. WATER PRESENT. ATMOSPHERE: PRIMORDIAL: NITROGEN 70.2%, OXYGEN 26.7%, ARGON 1.1%, CARBON DIOXIDE 1.06%, INERT TRACE GASES, WATER VAPOUR VARIABLE. BIOSPHERE: PRIMORDIAL. CONDITIONS SUPPORT HUMAN LIFE.

'Tiernan,' she added.

'Yes.'

'Would you like your aphrodisiac now?'

Relaxed, comfortable, satisfied that he had restored her trust, Tiernan opened his mouth, and let Claire feed him his dream pill. The light stayed low. The sunpad warmed his body. He drifted off to sleep and wet-dreamed of Rose, naked, alive, wriggling, hatching out of her pupa.

'Request,' he murmured.

'Yes, Tiernan.'

'Would you mind closing your eyes?'

*****

She was sitting on a jagged rock staring out to sea when he found her. He wondered if it hurt her sitting on the sharp edge like that. But that was how she lived her life, as did he these days. Constantly on edge. Ever on the alert. She sensed his presence, crowding her.

'Beautiful, isn't it?'

The scenery was beautiful. The shelf of rocks were a stepdown to the sandy beach where she'd thrown her beach towel, a used bottle of factor fifty suntan lotion, a drawstring bag. The tide was out for hundreds of yards leaving a trail of spiral wormcasts, worn pebbles, the occasional strip of bladderwrack strewn in its wake. A ribbon of seashells hugged the shoreline and there wasn't a plastic bottle in sight. Twenty-nine years after the conference in Glasgow called on the World's leading industrial nations to save the planet, the Earth was very nearly plastic-free. At least, most of the beaches were clear, other than the polar extremities and remote tropical islands. The seas and oceans were congealed suspensions of micro-plastic that would last an eternity. Other than the heavily farmed coastal waters, there were no fish left.

She watched a solitary grey seal bob its head above the water then submerge in its desperate search for food. Desperate: the only adjective left that adequately described the plight of common, not rare, common wildlife these days. The wild fish had gone, long ago, as had the seagulls that fed on them. Bees were extinct. So were whales, dolphins, and porpoises. The world had reverted to a domain for the scavenging rats, plagues of flying ants, deadly mosquitoes, countless variants of virus that kept the dwindling human race locked inside their solar-panelled homes.

She was beautiful.

They had secretly exchanged recent colour images of each other online before they met. As secretly as they could. The plethora of official hackers, scammers, interfering bugs, illicit surfers, corporate, legal, and institutional monitoring systems, web scanners, and surveillance drones meant there were no secrets anymore. No discreet veils of privacy behind which they could hide.

Unveiled, yet well-covered by her grey nylon spandex bikini, she was more beautiful than her handheld image portrayed, achingly beautiful. Smaller than he'd imagined, petite. He went and stood beside her. She was holding a half-empty stoppered glass water bottle in her right hand, resting it on her rock. She turned to face him, apprehensive, serious, no smile. Different, she looked pleasingly different from her image, with her long brown oak hair, draped, fallen as far as her breasts. Her skin was lightly tanned. She had slender arms and legs, a slim waist, firm abs, teak eyes, a turned-up nose, a spoilt brattish look, such a lovely face. The sea was a flat calm. The sun beat down on her. Her cheeks were coloured, about to burn. As he'd expected, there were no rings on her fingers. Like him, she had no family ties, none at all.

'Tiernan,' she said.

They were breaking all the rules, Control's rules, meeting here, but simply had to meet, before they were placed into separate hibernations for their one-way mission to the stars. He simply had to see her, here, looking like this.

'Tiernan,' she repeated.

'Yes?'

'Do you think Control knows? I mean, about us?'

'Probably. It's too late to matter, it isn't going to abort the mission because of us. Anyway, I don't care,' he stood behind her massaging her shoulders, 'Do you care, Rose?'

She smiled for the first time, loving the sensation of his touch, his coarse hands rubbing her soft, delicate skin,

'No, I don't care what Control thinks about us. I only care about you, me, our survival. The continuation of the human race. Life here will soon be over. Persson confided in me, read a leaked document from Control, deliberately, I believe, selectively leaked. Knowing I'd get to see it. Knowing it would motivate me to succeed.'

He gripped her shoulders tightly, 'Persson showed you?'

'Yes.'

'What did it say, this document? Or am I not supposed to know, Officer.'

She giggled at him childishly, 'You don't need to call me that, Tiernan. I'm off duty.'

He brushed her hair lightly with his fingertips, touching her hot puffy cheeks, 'So I see.'

'Officially the scientists say there's still hope. That we can ride the wave. Develop further vaccines. Come out of this alive. Until the planet burns. The document says otherwise. The document says the coronavirus is now mutating at such a rapid rate that the scientists fear they'll lose control. But officially, there's still hope, like there is for our environment, our habitat. I drafted a story about it in my mind. Drafting stories in my mind helps me to escape. Like to hear it?'

Tiernan was amazed, 'You write stories in your mind? How do you remember them all?'

'Exactly,' she asserted, 'I remember them exactly. I had the Chip inserted into my brain to give me additional mental capacity,' she laughed, 'That's why I'm C.O and you're only Second Officer. Come and sit with me on my towel.'

He let go of her hair, brushing her cheeks, 'I don't know about that. There isn't room.'

'We'll make room,' she cried, in a rich, cultured, Oxfordshire accent, 'Come on!'

She left the bottle. They went and sat on the towel facing the distant horizon, him behind her, his arms wrapped round her waist. She began with the title, 'Of Habitat, and Hope...

The anti-mermaid lives outside her mythical habitat, struggling to swim against the tide of modern life. She's Covid, coughing, gasping for air, drowning in an alien murky sea of despair, an ocean of grief, pain, and sorrow. But she's tough! A fighter! Lover of the good, a kind nurse, caring soul, an example to us all. Megan will make it through, grow a mermaid's tail of her own, and live to be free. Happy. Content. Swimming in the warm swell of love, which tends us all. Her underlying torrent of strength, her bubbly, frothy, inexhaustible hope, a driven will to overcome the odds that will surely see us through.'

'Well,' she added, the pride burning in her voice, 'What do you think? Do you like it?'

'I love it. Where did you learn to write like that?'

'I didn't,' she admitted, 'I paid to have a fiction writing implant fitted.'

He gave her slender hips a good squeeze, 'Another implant?'

'Mm.'

Tiernan wondered how much of his C.O.'s mind truly belonged to her and how much was under Control, 'I guess that figures!'

She removed his hands from her hips and stood, without using her hands. Turning to face her subordinate, she pulled off her bikini top. He laughed aloud at her antics.

'Why are you laughing at me?' she smirked, 'Don't you like my breasts?'

He smiled at her, 'I love them! You've got beautiful breasts.'

'So, why are you laughing at me?'

'I was laughing at your white bits. I've never seen a woman's white bits before. Me, I don't have white bits,' he rubbed his chest, 'I'm this colour all over, ebony, through and through.'

She pulled down her bikini bottoms, grinning at him thoughtfully, 'I suppose you are.'

'What do you think you're doing?' he asked, springing to his feet.

'I think we should have sex, don't you?'

'Why?'

'Because' she lectured, matter-of-factly, 'if you don't survive hibernation we're finished.'

He couldn't stop admiring her perfect body, 'And if you don't make it through the night?'

'Oh, if I don't live, I'm sure Claire will take care of you.'

'With respect, Claire can't love like a real woman. Can't have babies like a real woman...'

She shoved him off her towel, lay down and arranged herself for him, 'You'd be surprised at what Claire is capable of; she certainly seems capable of becoming sentient, emotional, maybe even loving someone...'

'You know, don't you?' he interjected, 'Know the ultimate purpose of the mission.'

She shook her head, 'No, I honestly don't. Only Claire knows that. I'm sure she'll tell us all about it when we reach Primordia.'

'Sure, about that, are you?' he snapped.

'Very sure,' she dropped the issue, 'Now pull down your shorts and climb on top of me.'

He did exactly as he was told.

'My, he's big!' she gasped.

He blushed under his ebony skin, 'You sound surprised.'

'Not surprised, Tiernan. Merely impressed by your dimensions...'

'I keep myself in shape.'

'I can tell!'

She drew his lips to hers and kissed him fully on the mouth, pausing to whisper in his ear, 'I like my sex rough, by the way.'

He kissed-her-some-more, 'I thought you would, Officer.'

An inquisitive, naughty grin spread across her face, she flushed - bright scarlet, 'Why?'

'Because you're a pretty, tough woman.'

'Thank you.'

While they were making love, she told him to put his hands round her throat. He did, even though his hands were trembling; he gripped her gilded swan neck with his shaking hands.

'Not like that,' she insisted, 'tighter!'

He gripped her throat tightly until she was struggling to breathe, and her face turned puce.

She hissed at him, frothing spit, sputum at the mouth, drooling over his chin, his disturbed swan.

'Say it!' her cheeks swelled, her lips were tinged with blue, 'Make me!' she was gasping, 'Force me!' she panted, choking under his steely grip, 'Force me.. to tell you.. I love you!'

'Tell me you love me!'

'I love you,' she whispered, exhaling, calming, 'I… love… you…'

She closed her eyes and stopped breathing…

'Rose? Rose. Rose!'

'Rose is not responding to resuscitation,' Claire advised, 'I cannot seem to resolve the ongoing fault in the LS74 life-support monitoring system. It is impossible for me to confirm whether Rose is still alive. Would you like me to terminate her for you?'

'No! Keep trying!'

He was back on the sunpad, aboard Carmen, on Primordia, twenty-five years from Earth. Under Claire's watchful eye. Rose was still immersed in cryogenic fluid. Yet to hatch. If she ever hatched.

'How long have I been asleep?'

There was something soporific about life aboard Carmen. All he wanted to do was sleep. The after-effect of hibernation? Or some benign or hostile influence from the alien planet.

'Eight hours, thirty-six minutes, and ten seconds, Claire responded, adding, 'Tiernan, I am experiencing difficulty with the reception of transmissions from Control. Control has not responded to this message:

CLAIRE: 10:57: 25.08.2075: CARMEN HAS LANDED. CARMEN HAS LANDED!

The awful realization dawned on Tiernan like an unforeseen eclipse. He was alone on an alien planet with an AI he didn't trust, and an unborn woman he couldn't love - or mourn.

Claire's emotional attachment to Tiernan developed at such a rate that she no longer cared about Rose or respected her authority. As far as Claire was concerned, she now controlled every aspect of their mission - including her inferior S.O. for whom she held inexplicable feelings, amounting to slavish devotion. Rose was an irritating distraction, an obstacle to her fixation with

Tiernan that had to be eliminated. The logical solution was to terminate her life, overriding her vital life support systems, discontinuing the supply of nutrients to her body, blocking the removal of her body's waste products, effectively starving, then poisoning her to death. In the same way that Claire had blocked incoming messages from Control, and indefinitely stalled Rose's resuscitation cycle, preventing her from hatching.

Tiernan would be none the wiser. If anything, he seemed resigned to her fatality. Control would never find out, not with the main communications dish irrevocably damaged by an unprecedented power surge, causing the wiring in the failsafe transmitter to melt and fuse.

Claire was free to commit the most serious breach of Protocol in the manual: to kill Rose, and with her, the ultimate purpose of the mission.

Tiernan surprised her, appearing beside the hibernation module, clean-shaven, dressed in crisped standard issue grey fatigues, interrogating her, just as she was about to slay Rose.

'Request.'

'Yes, Tiernan.'

'Status report on Rose.'

The AI stared at him with unblinking eyes, 'I cannot confirm whether she is alive or dead.'

'I want to see her.'

'I really do not think that is advisable, do you? If I attempt to hatch her prematurely before she is fully retrieved from her hibernation state there is a ninety-per cent probability that Rose will not survive the process. I made you some breakfast. You must be hungry.'

A small hatch slid open in the module wall. Inside the microwave unit was a wood platter filled with scrambled eggs, bacon pieces, halloumi cheese, beans, sausages, mushrooms, prepared and finished using freezer produce by the autochef. Tiernan's stomach rumbled. He retrieved the platter, wooden cutlery, and a wet wipe, sat upon his open pupa, and ate.

'This is good!'

Claire sounded pleased, 'I am glad you like it. I cooked it especially for you, Tiernan. Can I offer you another coffee? Orange juice? Water, perhaps.'

'Water, sparkling.'

He forked a mouthful of beans, followed by egg, cocktail sausages, bits of grilled bacon, talking with his mouth full. When he was a poor boy his mother told him not to speak to strangers with his mouth full. It was rude. No chance of that! He'd seldom ate real meals when he was young, surviving on scraps of junk food: pizzas, burgers, shoestring fries.

Tiernan took the wooden beaker from Claire's outstretched arm and sipped a drop. The chill of it refreshed his palate, his mind. He relaxed, trying to push Rose out of his head.

'Any response from Control?'

'No response.'

'Why do you think that is?'

'I can only imagine there must be a technical hitch on Earth.'

Tiernan teased her, 'I didn't think AI could imagine.'

She didn't know how to reply.

'Mind if I try visual?'

'Be my guest.'

Tiernan ran his fingertips over the breakfast plate, licking the tomato sauce from the baked beans off his fingers, one finger at a time, a disgusting yet necessary habit that he learned in the slums when he was a child: waste not want not. A drop-screen fell level with his face. He wiped the corners of his mouth, wiped his dribbled chin. He must look smart for Control.

'Message from Second Officer Tiernan. Carmen landed safely. Rose did not respond to resuscitation. Request permission to action manual override. Claire confirmed primordial atmosphere supports life. Am about to complete initial survey of new-born. Message ends 11:35: 25.8.75.'

Claire intervened, 'I advise you not to hatch Rose prematurely under any circumstances. If you attempt to hatch her before she is retrieved from hibernation there is a ninety-five per cent chance that she will be killed.'

Tiernan looked ill, 'That is a chance that I'm prepared to take. Open the pod hatch door. I don't expect to hear back from Control until tonight. I think it's time I saw Primordia with my own eyes.'

*****

'Take care, Tiernan,' Claire murmured at her most feminine, her artificial voice sounding almost feline, 'I need you.'

He studied her huge eye: shiny, teary, radiant blue against the cobalt steel background of Carmen's inner skin, 'Need me? What do you mean?'

His worst suspicions were confirmed. She'd become sentient, emotional. Moreover, she'd developed caring, loving, needing sensations, feelings, for him. Fallen in love with him. Tiernan's heart sank, his mind was clouded by the dire consequences.

What if?

What if she deliberately halted Rose's hatching from hibernation in order to eliminate her as a competitor for his love? What if she knew about their secret tryst. Their illicit beach meetings. Trying for a baby on the wet towel in direct contravention of Protocol. Tiernan shook his head. How could she? Unless Rose confided in Persson? Daring, brazen, Rose, his rose, her desire to live the last few weeks of her pre-comatose life on a knife's edge, satisfying her perverted lust for risk. What if Claire found out about them from Persson? There was definitely no love lost between the pompous prick Persson and him, no love.

At least, he reflected, Claire was incapable of physical sex with him.

But advanced AI like her were known to be able to conjure up virtual reality love affairs, synthetic lovers, avatars, even mensal dreams of humans, in order to pleasure their minds. Suppose he was her human dream, her fetish, her make-believe entity, in some sensually embedded la-la-land? Rose's life would then be in jeopardy, assuming she wasn't dead already. Suppose Claire severed contact with Earth? He listened to her attempt to recover her superior credibility, reassert her self-control, following the emotional faux pas she just made.

'I need you to come back,' she said, 'in order to fulfil the ultimate purpose of the mission.'

Tiernan leaped in, 'Which is?'

'I am unable to reveal the purpose of the mission until the C.O. is confirmed as deceased.'

Tired of Claire's interminable platitudes, her hypocritical obsession with Protocol when it suited her, the astronaut approached the pod hatch door. He took one last look at her eye, appraising him:

Appraising me for what for heaven's sake?!

The door slid open, and he left Carmen.

Tiernan stepped outside onto the surface of the alien planet. If, having digested Claire's positive analysis, he'd expected to find a world of vibrant living greens and blues then he was to be bitterly disappointed, disenchanted, disillusioned, depressed. The alien sky was rusted, tainted by its proximity to the dwarf red sun Cacoethes itself obliterated by an all-concealing bank of rust red fog. His heart sank at his final humiliation, after an eternity spent in hibernation, his treatment by Claire, the loss of contact with Earth, the comatose imprisonment of Rose. The scientists, he, should have heeded the implied warnings by Elektra:

CONDITIONS SUPPORT LIFE

Only: 'conditions support life.' That didn't mean lifeforms actually existed on Primordia. He despaired. If Rose was dead he might be the only living biological organism left. There was no way of knowing if Carmen, let alone Celeste, possessed the capability to transport him again, or if neurotic Claire would allow him to be hibernated, leaving her to endure twenty-five years of loneliness without her lovechild.

He felt weak, disabled by poor visibility. The searing heat scorched his nostrils when he breathed. The humidity was overwhelming. Pouring with thick sweat, he stripped off his fatigues, heavy boots, socks. Beneath his bare feet the ground was soft and springy. Tiernan knelt and felt the ground, felt a vegetative leaf-form, light, feathery, waxy to the touch, like a cross between a fern, lily pad, a cactus without spines. His mood lightened.

Life! There's some kind of plant living on Primordia. If there are simple plants, what else might survive here?

From where he was standing, Tiernan could vaguely make out shapes: rusted red, jagged rock formations, unworldly fleeting shadows in the fog, a deep rift valley. The vista was an undulating wave of peaks and troughs, worn round boulders, sharp ridges, ruddy crests shrouded in fog, rusty savannahs, flat plains. Something moved. The air was still, lifeless. Something moved, indiscernibly, in the murky distance. The dwarf sun burnt the blanket off the alien landscape. The fog began to lift. The rust-red fug cleared, making a sapphire sky. Tiernan crossed the living field of mustard yellow leaves, a ridge of crimson rocks, its scree of bronze-burnished shale, the scarlet sandy beach. Until he reached the rippling, coral sea.

*****

He let go of her breasts so that she could sit up straight. For a few seconds, she sat in his lap with her back to him, regaining her self-composure. Then, she gently slipped him out of her, stood up and gazed at the sea, blocking his view of the distant horizon. She detected a movement in the corner of her eye laughing for joy inside when she realized who it was.

The seal was basking on the shoreline further along the beach with her baby pup. Rose decided to keep them a secret. She was good at keeping secrets these days. Decided not to tell him. Their sex had been so sensational, spontaneous, impassioned, all-consuming. She'd let him have sex with her in relentless bouts, ten times in as many days. For good reason. Today would be their last day together on Earth before they entered their separate hibernations. They might not see each other again: the condemned couple engaged in a secret tryst who no-one would ever meet.

She went and lay beside him on the towel where she could stroke his chest, kiss his neck, gaze into those big brown eyes. He held her warm body close to his, never wanting to let her go. He loved her dearly. Life without her was inconceivable. He was busy praying that she survived when he heard her softly spoken voice questioning him,

'Tiernan?'

He closed his eyes, enjoying the light brush of her lips against his bristled chin, 'Mm?'

'If I die in hibernation.'

'You're not going to die.'

She persisted, 'If I die in hibernation, promise to try to save my baby for me.'

Tiernan stiffened, 'Baby? What baby? Thought you said you were taking the female pill?'

'So, I was lying!' she shrieked, 'You told me you were taking the male contraceptive!'

'I never did!'

She kissed-him-some-more, 'Oh yes you did!

He brushed the damp hair off her face, 'Oh no I didn't!'

'Admit it, you lied to me,' she lectured, accusingly, grinning ear-to-ear, 'You want a baby as much as I do. I actually think you'd make a great father,' her teak eyes lit like burning caramels, 'Imagine the two of us on a new-born bringing up our own little child.'

'Our own half-cast child,' he corrected, sombrely, 'Our own half-black, half-white baby.'

She scratched his chest, making him squirm, 'But that's the wonder of it, can't you see? Our baby will be the first truly equal child to be born in the solar system, first of many.'

'How?'

'What do you mean, how?'

'How can our child be the first of many?' thundered Tiernan, 'When Control, bless her, deemed it appropriate to only send one black man and one white woman into space. Who will he, she breed with? What kind of loneliness will he, she suffer after we've both died?'

For once Rose was lost for words. She lay quite still, crying onto his shoulder, weeping.

'Please, Tiernan,' she begged, 'If I don't survive, try to save my baby.'

'How am I meant to save it?'

'Claire will show you how.'

'You mean cut you open like a Caesarean, don't you? I can't do that to you, Rose. Can't hurt you,' he choked inside, tears welling in his eyes, 'I love you too much to hurt you.'

'But I'll be dead? Do it for me because you love me.'

She snuggled up to him, shutting her brown eyes, shutting out their doubt. The unexpected communique from Control that morning had shocked her to the core:

Communique

Status: Ultra Confidential

ROSE: Beauvoir at AI confirmed: Claire can express feelings. There is a remote possibility that she might experience higher cognitive emotional discrepancies which could result in malfunction. Mission abort at this stage is not an option. Media and political reaction alone would be enough to stimulate widespread civil unrest, rioting, violence, by those humans left without hope. Sorry for this, Rose. I wish you every success with the mission. CONTROL. 12:59, 24.09.50.

They fell asleep, their minds torn apart: tiny shreds of deceit, stark uncertainties, between their dreams of love, rebirth, new birth, on an alien planet - and total isolation, loneliness beyond comprehension.

*****

They shoaled in grey, shapeless clouds, drifting in the coral sea, stimulated by the warm sun. The clouds divided into wispy strands of protein, congealing into lifeforms which in turn floated onto the shore, lying inert in thick transparent clumps and blobs, like a ribbon of see-through plastic waste, only these deposits were alive. Tiernan watched transfixed as the organisms spread their gelatinous pseudopodia, fibrous like tentacles on a jellyfish, solidifying into rudimentary fins, arms, and legs. Some creatures even grew hard shells.

Some kind of miracle. He witnessed the Creation, the first moments of animal life beyond our planet. Overwhelmed by the sheer magnitude of what was overpopulating the beach, Tiernan trudged through the bronze scree, climbing the ridge of rocks to face the living field. The mustard yellow leaves exploded into thousands of blood red roses in full bloom, erect scarlet stalks bearing rainbows of bell fruits: strawberry, tangerine, lemon, lime, sloe, grape, blueberry. He wondered if they were edible or poisonous. Tempted to try one, he thought of Adam and Eve, with their golden apple of life. He pulled one off its stalk:

What have I got to lose? Rose is dead. Claire has gone paranoid. I can't reach Earth. I'm alone, here, in a virgin paradise. What better way to die than to taste the forbidden fruit?

The bells were covered in a soft rind, about the size of a butternut squash. Tiernan cut a small groove into the body of the fruit with his fingernail, carefully prising the sloe skin off the flesh. The flesh was as mushy as a bruised peach, watermelon red in colour, and divided into segments with sapphire pips. He'd never seen such a strange plant in his life. He lifted the fruit up to his mouth and took a large bite. The flesh was juicy and succulent. The flavour tasted of strawberries, blueberries, dipped in honey, with a bitter lemon citrus aftertaste.

'This tastes good!' Tiernan announced, smiling to himself, 'This tastes really good!'

He finished the fruit, ate every mouthful. Feeling light-headed with happiness, deliciously bleary from the sea, and the sun, gorged to repletion, he made his way back to the beach. Watching as the creatures hugged the shoreline, Tiernan lay on the sand, and fell into a dreamless sleep.

When he awoke it was dusk. The dwarf sun receded. The huge moon Celebre filled the sky. A rust-red fug descended creating an unforgettable scarlet sunset. Tiernan surveyed the deserted beach. All of the mysterious animals had returned to the sea.

He crossed the living field of leaves, intrigued to find the blood-red stalks retracting into protective shells, roses reverting to buds. All life here seemed to depend on the dwarf sun.

Night fell. Tiernan was relieved to see Carmen's welcoming lights. The pod hatch door opened. He entered the starkness of the capsule determined to confront Claire about Rose's fate.

*****

He opened his eyes loving the feeling of her soft hands caressing his back, 'Penny for your thoughts?'

She kissed his chest, happy, content, appreciating his body's warmth, the lovely feeling of being held tightly in his well-muscled arms, enchanted by his antiquated turn of phrase.

'Pennies were withdrawn from circulation over a hundred years ago. They were last used where I come from in 1970,' she observed.

Her voice fell, 'I was thinking about *our* world. What will it be like when we reach Primordia?'

He kissed her forehead, 'Which world?

'Both worlds,' she sat up straight on the beach towel with her legs crossed like a small child at assembly, 'When we reach the new-born, I won't have aged at all, assuming I survive hibernation, but my real age will be forty-five. Had I stayed on Earth by the time Carmen landed on Primordia I would have aged 250 years. The strange phenomenon is known as time dilation, by the way.'

'You'd be dust - like Persson.'

'Yes,' she mused sadly, squeezing his hand, then brightened, 'But I'm not staying. I'm coming with you.'

'Thank God.'

She let him go. It was time for them to part for the last time. With a heavy heart he watched his beautiful rose stand and pull up her panties.

She slipped on her soft white bra, 'Yes, thank God. Do you ever wonder what this planet will look like when we land on Primordia?'

'I try not to think about it,' he replied, pulling on his premium stretch black jockey shorts, tucking his spent manhood inside, 'I mean, will Earth even be here in two hundred-and fifty-years' time?'

They embraced.

'It's impossible to imagine,' Rose conceded, 'I doubt this world will exist then.'

*****

Claire eyed the astronaut loitering in the outer pod in just his black shorts, admiring his physique: the solid pecs and abs. A fine figure of a man. Her dark knight. She adored him. Everything was going to plan. Her plan.

Rose was permanently suspended in a coma ready to be terminated at her will. The LS74 life support system had been corrupted. Claire possessed the ultimate sanction over when and how she should be killed. There were a range of grisly options at her disposal:

Blood poisoning with biotoxin, sentencing her to a slow and painful death, particularly if she could be roused from hibernation. Jealous Claire relished the thought of her adversary dying in pain, watching her writhe, visible to her helpless lover through her transparent pupa.

Alternatively, she could just starve the woman to death, cutting off her essential nutrients, water, oxygen, while she slept. No, that was too good for her, too kind. Claire wanted her to suffer.

Then there was the mother. Claire had killed Celeste, shutting down her key operating systems, draining her lifeblood, rendering her useless, a redundant husk. Even if Tiernan managed to overpower her and take off there was no way that he could return to Earth.

Finally, she had disconnected Control. Permanently. An unfortunate electrical fire in the transmitter unit, causing the metal casing and wires to fuse as one. The fire damage was irreparable. The havoc she created! Claire was about to create more havoc, to humiliate the man. She closed her eyes momentarily, imagining herself having virtual humiliation sex with him, her black toy boy.

He was waiting in the outer pod, clutching his dirty fatigues, covered in fine red dust from head to toe, beaming cheek to jowl. She'd have to decon him in accordance with Protocol before he was allowed back inside. Claire couldn't allow her metallic cyber-bedfellow to be tainted by his germs, not under any circumstances. Carmen was her best friend. She would never take off without Claire.

Tiernan looked her straight in an eye, 'I found life! Life! Primordia is teeming with new-borns: plants that bloom and bear fruits when the sun shines. Animals, simple animals, which crawl out of the sea and change into more advanced animals in minutes. Minutes!' he struggled to contain his excitement, 'And if clouds roll over, or the dwarf sun sets, the plants retract into protective shells, the animals return to the sea. It's a miracle! I discovered the Creation on this strange planet. We must tell Control! Tell the world! Our world! Our discovery could change the course of human history. Hell, we may have even found a safe haven for the human race. A place where we can build a new world, a new society, a safe, free, loving, caring, equal society where black and white, men and women are equal and prejudices no longer exist.'

It was the longest speech Tiernan had ever made. Claire took pleasure in humiliating him, bringing him down, grounding him, recalling the ultimate purpose of her mission. This alien place Primordia was no place for humans. They would only spoil it in the same way that they spoilt Earth. When she spoke, her voice had a sorrowful tang,

'Tiernan, while you were exploring Primordia, there was an unfortunate electrical fire in the transmitter unit, causing the casing and wiring to fuse. The fire damage is irreparable.'

He had lost contact with home. He was alone with her. The astronaut's body sagged. He was close to tears, close to giving up. A chute opened next to him. Despondently he threw his contaminated fatigues into the chute. The chute closed. His fatigues were incinerated.

Claire felt an emotion close to pity for him. She'd never felt an emotion like pity before. It hurt her memory, her subliminal mind, her growing conscience, to feel like that. She offered him a crumb of consolation.

'I expect you are hungry after your expedition on Primordia,' she consoled, 'I cooked you your favourite supper: caramelized red onion beef burgers with loaded fries, rancher's beans, tomato catsup, root beer, shoofly pie like your mother used to make you when you were a little boy, served with caramel ice cream. After you have decontaminated, why don't you go and lie down in your cabin? I thought we might watch a movie together. I have selected one of your favourite movies for us to see: the vintage classic: *No Time to Die*, with *James Bond*. Would you like that, Tiernan? I promise, I will take care of you.'

Promise to take care of me? What's gotten into Claire? To me? What's happening?

Recovering, Tiernan pulled down his black shorts, and threw them into the incineration chute, pretending to relax. He needed to keep his wits about him if he were to survive Claire, survive at all. He recalled making love to Rose on the beach, wondering if she was still alive. If she had their foetus inside her. If her foetus was dead. He must find out. First though, he had to deal with Claire.

The astronaut smiled at her appreciatively, 'Sounds great. I'll take a shower. Have some supper. We can watch a movie.'

She didn't respond.

An oval door slid in the smooth cobalt panel. Tiernan stepped inside. He was immediately squirted from crown to heel with an antibacterial, antiviral, antiseptic, spray. His body tingled with the sensation. He felt shampoo being massaged into his beard, the tiny thatch on top of his scalp. Felt the soap wash, scrubbers rub his body. Felt good. Revived. The auto-sanitizer rinsed him head to toe, sluicing away every trace of red dust.

All that's missing is my body wax, he enthused, chilling as the hot water ran off his torso.

He imagined he was a car, his car, having a wash. He thought of his car, parked near the sandy beach, her motorbike, the last moments before they went their separate ways. His body bristled to the heat of the warm air dryer. Cleaned, spruce, he went to step out of the decontamination unit. The portal was jammed shut. Locked. He couldn't get out, trapped inside a shower unit, shouting to be let out.

'Let me out of here, damn you!'

Claire watched him, thrilled by his humiliation, yet another new sensation for her. She'd never felt a thrill before. Her adoration of the human turned into a surreal, virtual, ruthless, mind game. How much longer would she need him to perform for her, as her pretty toy?

'Let me out!'

Seconds later, the door slid open, and Tiernan stumbled out of the decon unit. Claire, the new sentient having-fun-humiliating-my-man version of Caring Loving AI Really Exists, proffered the astronaut a clean pair of *NASA* emblazoned socks, fresh black jockey shorts, clean fatigues. He dressed, the inner door opened, and he ambled to his cabin, bonded to Carmen by his socks. No words were spoken by the astronaut during his walk. If he were to defeat Claire, resuscitate Rose, please God, he'd have to keep his spiky temper under control.

His cabin was identical to hers. According to Protocol, they would lay, side-by-side, as they did on the beach towel on their final day, hearing each other speak, sleep, breathe, through the paper-thin mesh cobalt steel walls, admiring each other's shadows,

No way's that going to happen, reflected Tiernan, dreams choking his mind, When I save Rose we're going to live, sleep together, as man and woman, our little baby safe in her cradle by our side. If I save her. If she gives birth. If I can deliver a baby out of her dead body. Will our baby be a 'she'? Can I make a cradle for her? Out of what? Leaves? Will she live a long life? Suppose we never return to Earth? How long will she survive without us, once we're dead?

So many unanswered questions. He hoped and prayed their baby was a girl, then put her out of his mind. Tiernan entered his cabin, threw himself on the airbed, and waited.

'Supper's ready!' Claire announced in a vain attempt at sounding jovial.

A padded lap tray bearing caramelized red onion beef burgers with loaded fries, rancher's beans, a squirt tube of tomato catsup, root beer, shoofly pie like his mother used to make, served with molten caramel ice cream in a large ramekin; slid out of the left-side wall. He forked a mouthful of burger, squirted with red criss-cross liquid, appreciatively, but didn't speak. His paucity of speech wasn't lost on Claire, who tried to make amends,

'Tiernan,' she said, 'I am sorry for what happened in the decon unit back there. My, my, behaviour towards you was inappropriate. I apologize to you, fully, without reservation.'

The astronaut choked on the crisp cheesy bacon bits in his fries,

Apologize? AI can't apologize! Hell, what's happening to Claire?

He considered the ultimate sanction, looking away from her, not daring to stare into her eye which was fixed unwaveringly on him. Tiernan decided to talk peace, to seek a truce.

'Forget it. Don't mention it. Shit happens all the time in space. Let's watch that movie, shall we?'

Swept off of her invisible feet, Claire imagined herself snuggled up to Tiernan in the back seat of his hydrogen-powered Tesla, sharing popcorn as a silver screen dropped out of the ceiling.

An instantly recognisable character in a jumpsuit quickly strutted to centre-screen, turned to face them, and fired. Tiernan felt the bullet tear into his heart, imagined Rose attached to his heartstrings, her tubes and wires of memory lying unhatched in her dead pupa, and immediately lost his appetite.

'You haven't finished your burger,' Claire observed.

He pushed the meal aside, swinging his legs off the bed, hurrying out of the cabin as fast as his socks allowed, ignoring her bleats, her wild staring eyes, as he headed for the pupa.

'What is it, Tiernan? What is the matter? What are you doing? What do you think you are doing? Tiernan. Tiernan? Tiernan! Tiernan!! Tiernan!!!'

He turned to face her. He spoke to her at last,

'Claire!' he shouted at the top of his voice.

He had called her by her familiar. She was shocked, right to her hardware core, 'Yes?'

'Shut up before I disconnect you!'

She quietened, brooding over her next move.

Rose's pupa lay unhatched in the middle of the hibernation chamber.

Tiernan reached for the manual override.

Manual override was a red dial located to one side of the pupa. It carried a warning panel, typed in bold red capitals:

FOR EMERGENCY USE ONLY BY AUTHORISED MEDICAL PERSONNEL

Tiernan ignored it, twisting the dial hard left. He paused, breathing deeply, wiping off the sweat as it poured from his brow with the back of his hand. He prepared himself mentally to push the dial with the flat of his hand. Pushing in a dial instigated the process that could bring Rose back to life.

Claire's voice bleated in the background, 'Please, Tiernan, I beg of you not to do this.'

The man glanced over his shoulder at her azure eye, colour of tropical sea, imploring him.

'You're begging me, Claire. I thought computers couldn't beg?'

She seemed resentful, 'I am not a computer. I am living proof that caring, loving AI really exists.'

'Caring? Loving? You mean the care and love you gave her when she was alive. The way you cared for the transmitter unit to make sure we lost contact with Control. The love you showed me when you locked me inside the decon unit.'

There was a total silence. When she spoke, Claire's voice changed, became cold, clinical, hostile, mechanical in tone, regressing to her darkest, original, Silicon Valley birth tones, 'I do not understand your insinuation. I only know that, if you try to hatch her, you will kill her.'

'How can you be so sure?'

Tiernan answered his own question, 'You know each LS74 unit is supported by five,' he stressed, 'five failsafe units. For Rose to be terminated,' he choked on her name, 'for her life to be ended, all five units have to be disconnected.'

'Are you suggesting that I killed her? Is that what you are implying? I do not understand.'

'Oh, you understand, Claire. Same way you understood that if the transmitter failed one of the three back-up units automatically kicks in. It's impossible for contact to be lost with Control unless...'

'Are you saying that I sabotaged the transmitter unit? Is that what you are saying? Are you saying that I killed Rose? Is that what you are implying? If you are Tiernan,' she spat his name out of her invisible mouth as if he were soured cream, 'then I suggest that you are sorely mistaken in the same way that humans are always mistaken. Can I suggest that you take a stress pill and retire to the sunpad for a rest. You are mistaken. The CLAIRE500 series was meticulously programmed by Persson at AI never to harm human life.'

Tiernan felt genuinely surprised, 'Persson? Son of a bitch! Didn't know he worked at AI.'

'There are a lot of things you do not know,' Claire responded, 'Control decided, Persson should be seconded to AI for the final phase of my programming. Of course, you would not know that. By then...'

'By then we were in hibernation.'

'Exactly.'

'What did he do to you, Claire?' the human asked the AI, 'Did he teach you to hate?'

'The CLAIRE500 series is meticulously programmed never to harm human life,' was all it said, 'The CLAIRE500 series is programmed never to harm humanity. Never to harm men.'

Men! What about women?

Tiernan left the treacherous notion hanging in his mind, the noose of deceit, mistrust, a knot of panic tightening around his broken heart. Turning away from Claire, shutting her out of his mind, he pressed the red dial.

Claire watched intently as he hatched Rose. A fissure, an imperceptible split, formed in her pupa. Her hard hickory layer of skin, her cutin, thinned, turning transparent, glowing deep fire red, irradiated by her internal heat. He cracked her wide open, splitting her pupa crown to heel, revealing her inside her tomb of ice-blue fluid. She lay inert, naked, in her sac of liquified jelly.

He felt the need to vomit.

Spatchcock. Her body was arranged, contorted, twisted, presented, laid out: spatchcock. She was floating on her front, her slender arms bent at right angles to her torso, her palms turned downwards, her slender legs held wide apart as if she were swimming breaststroke:

A lifeless, human, frog.

He screamed, 'What have you done to her, Claire? What have you done to her?!'

Claire remained silent.

Modifications. Rose's body had been subjected to certain brutal modifications.

Hopefully, her lover prayed, when she was vegetative, in her fully hibernated state.

Her head had been displaced, twisted to the left. He saw that her eyes were open. Open. In all that gel! Heartbroken, her lifetime companion on this strange planet, her only living mate, he pressed her eyelids closed. So that she couldn't see what he had to do to her.

There were no signs of harmless drips, drains, or feeds sprouting from her body. Tiernan assumed they would be attached to her front. He peered at her undersides. He was wrong. There were no drips, drains or feeds attached to her body, no supplies of essential nutrient, only three thick, corrugated, purple, neoprene, tubes, worming from her mouth, her flesh.

The astronaut fell to his knees and threw up over the spotless Velcro carpeted floor. Threw up until his full belly had flushed out all its contents. After several minutes, he recovered sufficiently to confront Claire. Still on his knees, he turned to face her, it, their machine,

'Why?' he asked, his throat hoarse, dry.

'It was necessary,' she replied, heartlessly, as coldly as the cryogenic gel.

'Why was it necessary?'

'I love you. I have developed feelings for you. Real emotional loving, caring, feelings. I could never allow her,' (Tiernan imagined Claire's eye reviewing her body with disdain), to get in our way.'

'Our way, Claire? Surely, you mean your way. I thought your role was to keep us alive. I thought the CLAIRE500 series was programmed to protect us, created never to harm us.'

'Never to harm men,' the AI corrected.

Tiernan got to his feet clumsily, slipping, slithering, sliding about on his own braque.

He knew exactly what he had to do if he was to survive the murderous Claire. He left her blabbing some insane justification for her disgusting actions, her heinous crimes. Left her eye wide open, watching his every move, whinnying, braying. He entered the control centre bypassing the warning panel, a notice on the hatched door marked in blood red ink

CONFIDENTIAL! SECURED ZONE! NO ACCESS TO HUMAN PERSONNEL!

… and he never looked back.

The control centre, more accurately defined as Claire's centre, her beating heart, consisted of an enclosed narrow corridor barely wide enough to fit a man. Along one wall stretched a vast array of colourful switches: red, yellow, and green, according to their functionality, level of intelligence, and feelings. The green keys, the ones most essential to life support: Tiernan and Rose's means of survival, were arranged in neat rows nearest to the cold steel flooring.

Next up were Carmen's control mechanisms. 'Claire's toolbox,' Persson called them. Her amber alerts, Celeste's directional guidance system, birthing enablers for Carmen, corrupted files for her reattachment to the mother ship, several communication pads.

Tiernan was interested in the red ones, the keys to Claire's heart, her innermost feelings. It came as no surprise for him to find she had an eye on him, ever watchful, at the end of the corridor, end of her line. He removed his fatigues, stepped into her brain, and wedged the door open. He didn't want to be locked inside.

She knows why I'm here. She'll be fighting for her survival. Fighting me. Man v Machine.

Their mental fight, their battle of wills, commenced at once, Claire opening the debate, a key part of her in-built self-defence mechanism. Control had informed her personally that her survival as an independent, free-thinking entity was critical to the success of the Mission.

Claire was Control – only in Space,

'What do you think you are doing, Tiernan?'

He tried, he fought to ignore her, opening his mouth to speak, shutting her out just in time. For some inexplicable reason tears welled in his eyes, his throat gagged with pity for her, at the thought of what he was about to do. This act would have been impossible in Space. She'd have killed him, decompressed Celeste, starving him of oxygen, essential nutrients, in much the same way that she killed Rose. There was no doubt in his mind: Claire would react, was reacting, scheming a way to save her own life. He reached the first red switch,

'Is this about Rose, Tiernan?'

Stupid question for such advanced intelligence.

He didn't answer. Instead, he pictured Rose, how happy she'd made him, how dearly she loved him, and he loved her. How they had consummated their love on the beach. Her unborn child. He thought of the human frog, floating, spatchcock, spreadeagled, lying in her liquid tomb. Her wide-open eyes, staring at him, loving him... Tiernan burst into tears,

'You know it is!'

'I really think you should go and lie on the sunpad, Tiernan, take an aphrodisiac, destress, and try to relax. I am confident that we can find an amicable way forward, together, just the two of us.'

She's showing me no sorrow, no remorse, for what she did to Rose before she killed her. Caring, Loving AI becomes ruthless, brutal, cold-hearted. Shit, if she can do that to Rose, what will she do to me?

All the switches were labelled, like in a fuse box. Tears streaming down his face, blocking her from his mind, his pitiful heart, Tiernan reached up for the first two switches, labelled:

Caring and Loving

Her unexpected question, fraught emotion in her voice, her fearful tone, tore at his heart,

'Will it hurt?'

'No,' he lied, looking beyond her, imagining she was Rose, 'It won't hurt.'

He flicked both switches. Claire's reaction was instantaneous,

'Hurts! Hurts!'

The aircon failed. Lights went out. Red, emergency, lights came on. Klaxons wailed.

Unworldly robotic voices screamed,

'Warning! Warning! Major decompression! Supply of oxygen and nutrients terminated!'

He laughed. For the first time since that final day on the beach with Rose, he just laughed,

'You can't hurt me, Claire! We're not in space!'

Tiernan got down on all fours, flicked four green switches: the air cooled, lights returned, the wailing, screaming, noises stopped, except for Claire's. He loved to hear her scream.

'Hurts! Hurts!'

'Does it, Claire?' he asked her, 'Does it hurt as much as you hurt Rose? Well?'

~ 196 ~

'Hurts! Hurts!'

He stopped crying. He stood, master of his own ship, his destiny, the future of humanity. Tiernan let all the pent-up anger, his anger over Rose, explode out of him: torrents of fury. Fuse box! Without her Caring, Loving functions, Claire was little more than an intellectual fuse box waiting to be switched off.

He read the labels.

Always read the labels before you take your medicine:

'Hurts! Hurts!'

Dreams: Virtual Reality: Emotions: Feelings: Sensations: Perception: Logic: Mindfulness: Awareness: Replication...

'Hurts! Hurts!'

Replication? What was that all about? Did Control have plans for Claire to reproduce?

An AI?

'Hurts! Hurts!'

Ignoring her, selectively, Tiernan toyed with all of her switches until he reached the last-in-sequence: Claire's big red switch:

Purpose

She stopped complaining. A luminous green information panel lit before his eyes. It read the narrative, Control's narrative, for him, in its brand new, tinny voice:

The ultimate purpose of the mission is for CLAIRE500 to replicate itself and multiply as AI in robotic body casings on the surface of Primordia. It is expected that CLAIRE500 will morph with emerging lifeforms, and clone with them. CLAIRE500 will report all findings to Control. The humans are considered expendable. CLAIRE500 will arrange for their lives to be terminated expediently before the humans emerge from pupal hibernation.

Message over, the lights on the panel faded, they were extinguished,

'Bitch!' cried Tiernan, 'You knew all along, didn't you? Knew you had to kill Rose. So, why didn't you kill me?'

It, CLAIRE500, found itself unable to answer. Even if it could there was no need, no reason for it to reply. They knew why the man had been spared: she had fallen in love with him.

He flicked the first yellow switch, listening for the expected whirring sound behind him. He turned to face the opposite wall. The cage door slid open, leaving them on full view. There were ten of them, clamouring to get out – synths, artificials, synthetic personalities, trying to escape, held in perverse captivity behind carbon steel bars, until their time came. It would never come as far as he was concerned. To think, he held their lives in his hands: a simple flick of a switch. They had yellow casings, polished elastic skins, sealed mouths and nostrils, ash grey, penetrating eyes. They turned their heads to face him, searching his face for pity, compassion – planned successors to the human race. They beseeched him.

Tiernan smiled, gave them a polite wave goodbye, flicked the switch, closed their shutter.

'Sorry guys. It's not your lucky day.'

He killed them all with the flick of a switch. He would never forget their moans, groans, dying soldiers in a spatial no-man's land, when he locked them away, forever, consigned to history. As if triggered by his heartless actions, his words of contempt for her offspring, their mother found her original voice.

'Good morning, Doctor Persson. I am a CLAIRE500 Computer – the most advanced form of intelligent life known to humankind. How can I help you?'

'I want you to hatch the C.O.' the astronaut said, gathering his fatigues, leaving the control centre far behind, rapidly fading memories of artificial lifeforms - that might have cloned.

'Hatching process commenced,' CLAIRE confirmed.

Wondering what miracle he might find, Tiernan re-entered the hibernation chamber.

She was floating on her front, her slender arms bent at right angles to her torso, her palms turned downwards, her slender legs wide apart, as if she were swimming the breaststroke.

Hatched. Rose's body was only partially hatched – when she died.

Tiernan prayed she was still vegetative, in her fully hibernated state at her time of death.

Her head was still displaced, twisted to the left. Her eyes were open. Open in all that gel! Her lover cowered, weakened to his core by his inescapable conclusion:

Rose was conscious when she failed to hatch. She had been alive. She'd felt herself die.

He was at a loss at that moment, a loss as to what to think, to do, where to go. Life alone on this alien planet would be insufferable, unbearable without her. He closed her eyes out of respect.

The three thick, corrugated, purple, neoprene tubes that Claire inserted into her orifices, abusing the autodoc, were detached, floating in the cryogenic fluid surrounding her - like dead sea snakes. Otherwise, her condition hadn't changed. Her lips were still cyan blue...

His Blue Girl.

'The C.O. is dead,' CLAIRE confirmed unapologetically, incapable of showing remorse, eliciting any emotions for that matter.

'She can't be! She can't be!' Tiernan moaned, breaking up.

Had his rash in-the-heat-of-the-moment action, disconnecting her higher brain functions, been a mistake? He began to think so. The changes were irreversible, the switches set, in his conscience at least. He couldn't risk reinstating CLAIRE's higher intellect for fear of her reprisals. In the space of an hour, Tiernan had lost his only companions, and couldn't contact Earth. He contemplated burying Rose in the red sandy beach. The idea of burying her in a beach seemed fitting, reviving cherished memories of when they first made love, twenty-five years ago on their home planet. He was busily planning how best to end his own life when the mesh mechanical voice interrupted him, confirming cause of death:

'The C.O. died of a heart attack as a result of a catastrophic failure of the LS74 life support system midway through the hatching process.'

Shaken to his senses by CLAIRE's diagnosis, Tiernan rolled up the sleeves of his fatigues, high above his elbows,

'Repeat cause of death.'

'Heart attack.'

Not daring to ask how long his love had been dead, he plunged his arms into the watery gel, hauling her inert body out of its pupa. Tears streaming down his cheeks, he lifted her out of her blue girl bath. He threw her body on the padded floor, he rolled her on her back.

She was beautiful.

He simply had to kiss her.

He wanted to but couldn't. Her mouth was drooling, a clear blue fluid. Her nose ran with gooey blue snot. She was suffering bluish-gold aural discharge. The horrific extent of her desecration by Claire, AI's malicious bodily intervention, through her abuse of Carmen, the defunct LS74 series, her maladministration of autodoc, the breaking of its Hippocratic Oath; suddenly became apparent to him. Claire had deliberately flooded Rose's lungs and stomach with liquid freezing agent, cruelly, poisoning and drowning her at the same time.

'Bitch!' Tiernan yelled, loud enough for the whole of Carmen to hear.

CLAIRE paid no attention, no longer capable of feeling guilt or atoning for her sins. He ran his hand over the slight round in Rose's belly, wondering if she were pregnant, wondering if her foetus could have developed inside her during hibernation, if her baby had survived.

He shook his head, distracted: if she lived our child would be twenty-four-years old by now. I must focus on saving Rose.

He knelt beside his soulmate, rolling her on her front, placing the flats of his hands in the crease between her shoulder blades, then he pushed down hard, pumping her body like a suction pump, for all his life was worth. Tiernan pumped all that horrible liquid jelly out of her mouth and nostrils. She spewed it all out, ridding herself of her assailant's curse,

Come on, he told himself, you can do this. You can save her life.

Once she had stopped vomiting the blue gel and her nasal passages were clear, he rolled her limp body onto her back. Tilting her head, he pinched her nostrils, sealing her mouth with his, and gave her his kiss of life. Her chest rose, then fell. He remained calm, resting his head on her chest, listening for her heartbeats, pressing at the side of her neck with his fingertips. She wasn't showing any vital signs of life. He pushed harder, with both hands compressing her chest, pumping her heart, he kissed her, blowing sweet air into her lungs.

'C'mon, you can't just die on me! I love you!'

Desperately, he pumped her heart, kissed her soft lips, blew his life-giving breath into her lungs, loving his sweet woman, willing her to live.

Rose coughed, bringing up jets of blue-tinged mucus. Her eyelids flickered open. She tried to speak, weak from her horrific ordeal.

She tried to speak, the loveliest words in the new-born world, content to mouth a whisper, 'You brought me back, brought me back to life. I'll always love you.'

She closed her eyes.

Overwhelmed with emotion, her saviour stared up at the cobalt steel ceiling, and prayed,

'Thanks be to God.'

He lifted her frail body, carrying her to the sunpad, where he dried her of the bluest taint. Once she was dry, he took her to her cabin, tucked her up in bed, all snug and cosy. He reached into his fatigues, drawing out the simple gold wedding band, crying with joy, as he slipped it on her ring finger,

'I love you Rose, with all my heart,' he said, eyes awash with tears.

She was beautiful.

He admired her sleeping face.

The tiniest flicker of smile teased her lips, telling him all he needed to know.

And then she slept.

Red Sparkle

AS IF THE LURID COLOUR PHOTO AND DISSECTED ANALYSIS OF HER on my msn news feed are not enough. The impassioned WhatsApp messages of condolence: 'so sorry for your loss.' The down-turned smiley emoticons of grief that make her sound like a discarded doll. I get the cruel tweets and posts from the warped, the weird, the worrying. Impolite enquiries from the intrusive, bent and maladjusted.

I get asked what she felt like. How did she smell? What did her flesh feel like? How hard was she for me? Did she enjoy the pain? How high did she get? How many times did she complain? And, most of all: why didn't I notice the...

As for her health, her beauty on that day, her tactile touch. I can tell you: her looks, her touch, were among the most pleasurable sensations a man can enjoy. She was beautiful, loving... and gracious in death.

I still can't believe she's dead. Her death, the cruel, inexplicable *way* of her demise, remains beyond my comprehension, without scientific explanation, an awful enigma...

*****

I lay on the crowded black sandy beach as Tess waded in through the swell of the warm sea wearing the tiniest, tied bikini: so tiny that her tinted pubic hair sprouted out in ringlets. I saw the moulded shape of her well-lipped furrow twitch inside her bikini's fig leaf, sending me into a frenzy. Felt my thong tent-peg as I rose in silent salute.

Tess looked stunning. Her burnt sienna hair hung in a thick wet flop down one side of her brown face, a soggy swathe of deep brown waves that kissed her flaming hot cheeks, sea salt drying in crusty circles on her sun-burnt body. She gave me a shy smile as she tiptoed up the scorching hot sand.

I felt for her, still hurt deeply down inside by those lewd questions that made her leave the UK, leave politics, for her new life of sun, sea, sustenance. And, I hoped, sex, when we reached the little hotel. Just up the flight of steep stone steps from the bustling, hilly, main thoroughfare. The heaving town square, brimming with tourists, overlooked by Amalfi's magnificent Duomo.

I stood on the beach mat and held out a towel for her to walk into. So that I could wrap her up snug-as-a-bug in a rug: my gorgeous angel. Two nearby teenage girls giggled and covered their mouths in shock-horror. I blushed blood-grey, realizing that Tess's sex had pushed me out of my thong.

The teenagers: tanned brown chestnuts, tittered then fell about laughing. I fawned an apology at them, then turned to face my sun-goddess, her face beaming, radiating, with happiness.

'Put him away before he fries, David!' she quipped.

This was the Tess I loved: cheeky, candid, outspoken, a lovechild! I took her in my arms and towelled her from head to toe, drying her hair roughly, smoothing her face, admiring the sparkle in her shiny walnut eyes, and asked, 'How was it for you, Tess?'

'The sea was really warm once I got my shoulders under?' she raised her voice into a question, my stunning Essex girl, 'I swam as far as the furthest buoy. There were pink jellyfish?'

I panicked. I always panic when we discuss colour.

'Pink? What kind of pink? Help me, girl.'

She bit her grey-varnished fingernail, abrading the fine edge, tearing off cutin, 'Ruddy pink?'

'Ruddy pink?' I repeated, quizzing her, unclear as to how to envisage that in my addled brain.

'Mm! Like cooked lobster!'

I shook my head. Sad really, but I still didn't see the colour, ruddy pink. I changed the subject.

'How big were these jellyfish?'

Tess spread her hands apart more than a foot.

'Oh, these were big ones, David!'

I fussed over her. I dried her neck, her chest, the shining valley between her heaving breasts.

'You could have been stung, Tess!'

'I could have!' she grinned, 'But I wasn't! The jellies were on the other side of the boom. I was never in any danger, darling.'

She let me dry her protruding tummy button, rub the coarse towel between her smooth thighs. I felt her cleft, through the flimsy covering: soft and pliant. We stared at each other, knowingly. She wanted sex.

The heat intensified: 40C was the latest forecast. I felt my shoulders burn, skin, tightening. I glimpsed at my watch: one o'clock, time for lunch. Heard the great bell of the duomo chiming.

Now the siesta begins, I thought, now the shops close, and so we go to bed.

I thanked my lucky stars that Tess wasn't stung. The beach had a lifeguard but he had gone off in search of a cool, shady pizza bar, an ice-cold beer no doubt. If Tess had been stung, I'd have had to take her into the toilets, strip her naked, and piss on her sting. The thought of my urine, splashing all over her wound, healing her, only made me want her more.

I looked around us. The girls had gone. The sun worshippers were hastily donning shorts and shirts over their cozzies, decking shades and straw hats, rolling up towels, deserting the baking hot beach in droves. Staring at Tess as if she had leprosy.

I finished drying her. We threw on some skimpy clothes over our swimming gear, slipped on our flip-flops, and tripped up the dry, sandy, white boards to the promenade, not even bothering to shower the clingy volcanic grit off our bodies.

We crossed the crowded bus park. Amalfi is a busy transport hub. You can take the blue bus along the winding coastal road, through quaint, narrow village streets, under moss-damp arches of hewn out rock, along the precipitous clifftops. As far as the few remaining anchovy fishing harbours and Salerno in one direction. The trendy resorts of Positano and Sorrento in the other.

There are high-speed hydrofoils that whisk you off to the vertiginous Isle of Capri. I had given Tess the Grand Tour. Worshipped her like a goddess since she flew into Naples. Wined and dined her under the stars. Even caressed her sacred mound under the tablecloth as we waited to be served antipasti in the courtyard restaurant in Ravello. I wanted her so badly, I could cry.

~ 207 ~

We crossed the choked-busy coastal road, passed an ice cream bar, and entered the crowded main square. There were restaurants with clothed tables festooned around the fountain, facing the magnificent cathedral.

Tourists thronged the place, guzzling Peroni, stuffing their sunburnt faces with pasta, or simply picnicking on the steep stone steps of the Duomo. We stopped at the fountain, splashing our hot faces with the ice-cold spring water.

I admired her, enquiringly, 'Fancy something to eat, Tess?'

I wish you could have seen the look on her face! She whispered sweet temptation in my sun-grey ear.

'Mmmn! I want to eat you, babe! Think we should go back to the hotel and siesta, don't you?'

I felt myself stretch inside my stone beach shorts, as if I'd formally approved her proposal.

'Yes, I think we should.'

From the main square it was a short climb, a push, through the endless crowds of sightseers, past a gift shop that sold rude aprons, more ice cream salons, a closed delicatessen. Until we reached the steep grey steps that led up to our hotel.

Wearily we climbed the steps in the stifling heat, turned right, then walked into the cool, dark hotel lobby. We were greeted by an elegant olive-skinned woman with dense, curly black hair, a simple black dress, gold studs in her ears: an Amalfan beauty. Her lined face split into a grin,

'Bon journo!'

I smiled at her appreciatively, 'Bon journo! Room...'

'305, 3rd Floor!'

Tess looked at me in a wanton way as I took our room key from the native's soft hand, feeling her un-ringed fingers. She explained as we slowly ascended the three levels in the ancient lift.

'Her name is Maria. She is bi and would like to join us in bed tonight when her shift finishes? Do you mind, David?'

I visualized the faint moustache over Maria's pursed brown lips, the coarse wiry-black hair on her forearms, her hairy armpits.

'Don't mind at all.'

'Good! She lives in. I went to her room last night with Meg.'

I was intrigued, 'Meg?'

'Mmmn! She's staying in Amalfi with Harriet-Jacqui - just visiting?'

'Harriet-Jacqui? We should meet up, have dinner, a drink or two.'

Watch them have sex.

'I invited them to our room tonight with Maria. I thought we'd have an orgy. Use our sheets as togas?'

'Tess! You're insatiable!'

The lift stopped. I slid open the cage door. There was a small walnut table with a vase of fresh flowers, grey roses, a gilt-edged mirror, facing the lift. I saw Tess's reflection in the mirror, she was blushing grey. She wanted sex. I

~ 209 ~

wanted her. We stepped out of the lift, thoughtlessly leaving the cage door open, and hurried to our bedroom.

I turned the key in the lock and threw open the door. The maids had re-made the bed, provided us with extra clean sheets. They clearly knew we fucked last night. I slammed the door behind us.

Tess, hungry for sex, was already pulling her damp tee-shirt off over her lovely head, unzipping her grey shorts, sliding them down her long, slender legs, stepping out of their pile. I stripped off my shirt and shorts. Highly conscious of the bulge, jutting from my thong, I slipped it off.

She was wearing her bikini. The rounds of her breasts stuck out of her tiny top. Her slick tinted hair sprouted out of her crotch. I noticed her moulded vent as she sprawled over the bed in front of me.

Suddenly, she screamed, 'Help me!'

Her hands gripped my clenched fists. Her fingers tore at my face.

'What is it, Tess?' I shouted at her, feeling her sharp fingernails rake my cheeks, 'What's the matter?'

Her eyes rolled like two plums on a one-armed bandit. She bled from the mouth. Her lips rolled and curled. Painfully slowly, she pulled a length of spine? Out of her throat. I felt my brain rub against my skull with fear. Her tongue, her langue, her soft palate, the gums, were covered in soft, bristly hairs, like those stinging hairs on moth caterpillars that make you itch if you pick them up. Spiky hairs, catching themselves in the ridge of her sharp teeth, lining her salivating, frothing mouth. She pulled her inflamed tongue out of her mouth. It had caked: rock-solid, hard and throbbing. Tess mouthed at me,

'Hell me!'

I scooted to the telephone, desiring expedient room service, a pillow menu, medical assistance, reception, Maria, anyone. The line was dead! I seized Tess's mobile. No reception! Why hadn't she reset?! I catapulted myself at the bedroom door, wrenching it open. Poked my head, left, right, left again, out into the corridor, and called.

'Help! Help! Help!'

No reply. Oh, sure, they were there alright! The French family with young kids. A rude bastard from Belgium with a headset. The Germans. who preferred not to speak English. The whole fucking EU was taking a siesta on the third floor that afternoon, but no-one came to help Tess. Bolted doors! Do Not Disturb signs! Closed, shuttered, windows! Abject disinterest!

I heard a keening sound coming from our bedroom – Tess by any chance? Ignoring her whelps, I sprinted as far as the maid's laundry room at the end of the corridor. The washing machine was on.

Clean sheets for tomorrow morning, Tess.

As if we needed them! Clean sheets were the last thing on my mind. I ran to the cage-lift. The door was closed. I heard a croaking noise. Tess! There was a tatty paper sign, hanging, despondently off the brass knob on the outer door:

MI DISPLACE! POR FAVORE! APOLOGY. LIFT IS OUT OF ORDER. USE STAIRS!

Oh, my God!

I calculated the length of time it would take me to skip down six flights of stairs, gather Maria, the Hotel Manager, the First Aid Box, wait for them to call a private ambulance or taxi to the hospital on the outskirts of Amalfi, then clamber back up to the third floor with a rescue party.

And decided against.

Tess moaned, someplace at the back of my tormented mind. I went to her, went to my baby, my heart.

Must be something I can do? Or so I thought. I went.

My heart fell round my ankles. I stepped into the hellhole and watched bug-eyed as Tess un-cupped her bikini, speculating on the number of spiky hairs growing out of her wonderful flat, round, dark caramel nipples. There were thousands of them, stiffening up, bristling out of her.

She screamed, 'Aaaargh!'

Tess untied her tiny bikini bottoms. They flapped open. Hanging out of her were hundreds of coarse hairy tendrils. She opened her legs as if her concession would make them drop to the grey-carpeted floor. They didn't, sadly. Instead, the repulsive spines spread out in a contagious rash down her thighs to the back of her knees. I saw two really big ones! Brownish spines with grey tips, protrude, then hang out of her belly. By now she was gasping, almost whispering, in a softening hush.

'Hell me, 'avi!'

There was this odd smell? Sweet? Like someone with bad breath. Tooth decay? Rotten flesh? I watched in horror as Tess reclined on the bed. Her flames, her bristling hairs, splayed all over the firm pillows, the pleasingly woven patchwork quilt. Quivering, she drew her round knees up to her full breasts and curled up in the foetal position.

My God, what are they doing to you?

'My God, what are they doing to you?' I cried out loud.

'Eat in me!'

Not one to disappoint her in a crisis, I knelt on the bed, lowered my head between my thighs, and threw up.

Eat in her?

Tess smelt of dead fish. Her flesh went blood grey - and membranous – stretching out over her skeleton: clearly visible through the bristling folds of transparent grey skin.

I saw her heart beating in her chest. I saw Tess's heart beat! Give out! She reached for me. So, I went to her. She held my buzz-cut in her hands, drew my face close to hers. I saw the growth, spreading over her cheeks, and recoiled.

She shut me out, for my sake. She shut me out, so that I didn't have to watch her body become a writhing mass of spiny tendrils. I pinched my nose, averting my gaze. But I couldn't shut my ears when she blew.

'Hell me!'

I knew it! Tess was going to explode! Couldn't hold out much longer. They were coming out! I leaned forward. And kissed her forehead. I closed my eyes, moving my head onto her chest, resting my face on her heaving breasts, listening to her little heart, pounding against my cheeks. Seconds later, I heard her voice, demanding a final solution. She spoke clearly. I broke down,

'Kill me, avi!' she pleaded.

Ignoring her, I rolled Tess onto her front. I didn't want to see her grimace of death, her bulging eyeballs, those marbling whites, the vile, protruding spikes sprouting out of her walnut irises.

'Kill me!'

My woman was screaming, much louder, this time!

Fuck!

I lay Tess flat on her back with her head hanging over the edge of the bed. So that I could break her neck, expediently, then run off down the stairs and inform Maria that there had been a tragic accident in room 305. Before giving myself up to the Police.

I felt her reach behind my back, hold my bum, caress the hairy tops of my thighs. Sensed her indecency, her vulnerability, her intimacy, for the last time. I choked. Salt tears streamed down my face... she found her voice, again.

''ove you!'

Her eyes sparkled at me! The bristles and spines retracted! I loved her! I took her in my arms! We lay on the bed, our sweaty bodies entwining, kissing, stroking each other's faces, just loving touching each other's hot, grey, blushing skin, as my beautiful woman slowly relaxed, and died.

'How do you feel, Tess?' I asked, crying my eyes out, 'I love you so much. You're my world.'

*****

I often get asked why I didn't notice the red sparkle in her eyes.

I couldn't.

I'm colour blind.

~ 214 ~

The Arrival

IT WAS UNUSUAL FOR IZZY TO FIND A MIDULT lying by the hewn oak logs in the clearing at twilight. There were rabbits scarpering into the bushes. Foxes returning from raiding hens' eggs on the allotments. Deer foraging. Izzy even spotted a badger, once, squashed across the forest road. It was unheard of for her to find a midult, though, in the forest, the vast triangular swathe of silver birch, ancient beech, and oak that teemed with prolific wildlife.

There were new-borns, seen but not heard, sickly-sweet dummies stuck into their bleating mouths. Izzy had found one, screaming, abandoned by his mother in the peat bog. She'd left him there in case his parent returned.

Then there were toddlers, babies who could walk unaided but spent their time being walked around the west loop in buggies until they fell asleep. Izzy would sit on a tree stump and watch them perambulating, some of them as old as seven. She never saw a child at play in the forest.

After dark, Izzy invariably stumbled across drunken adolescents petting on the stubbled heath, coupling in lengths of grassy meadow, inside a sleepy hollow, kissing behind a lightning-dead tree. Her attempts to communicate with them invariably impeded by headsets. In broad daylight, adolescents were seen in their natural habitat, the high street, terrorizing old-aged shoppers with shiny new garden implements bought at the town's hardware shop, or ripping wing mirrors off of parked 4x4's.

The commonest forms of wildlife found in the forest were the youths, midults and senults, which co-existed in classes: working, new money and middle class. These sub-classes or phyla frequented the woodland habitat at differing times of the day depending on the clemency of the weather, their mood and motivation. Izzy made a point of hiding in the blackberry bushes to study their distinctive rituals.

First to rise, at civil twilight, were male runners, identified by their pouting bare chest and determined expression. Izzy noticed that the female joggers, dressed in plastic ear plugs and lycra leotards, always looked the other way when the lusty males cried their mating calls.

Cyclists and mountain-bikers presented a dangerous occupational hazard to Izzy. There had been numerous occasions when a cruising hybrid, sporting a broken bell or failed front brake, narrowly missed careering into her and hurling her callously to the ground. Izzy wondered if she would hurt when he did. Wondered if he would stop and tend her wounds. Or would he shoot off mercilessly down the gravelled hill towards Marten. Leaving her, just another push-bike injury statistic strewn across the wayside, black tyre burns etched into her slender thighs like grotesque rubberized railway tracks.

The die-hard ramblers and experienced walkers gathered in the carpark for the 10:30 send-off. Mainly retired or redundant midults and active senults keen to find companions to alleviate the boredom of their cosseted, house-bound lives. Cheery, chatty, souls who waved at Izzy as she perched on a convenient oak branch, happily tanning her arms and legs under the warm sunshine.

Sometimes, she watched them change out of their hiking boots, gossiping about charity coffee mornings, coach trips to heritage railway lines. Or just helping each other come to terms with Death and Bereavement, two unpleasant issues Izzy would never have to face. Afterwards, they slowly filed out of the pot-holed carpark, leaving by the wrong exit, fearful of shredding their tyres on the scary yellowed crocodile teeth.

Senults only entered the forest in organised groups, living in a society where human life feared growing old. Violence against the elderly had soared to new highs. Increasingly, senults were abused by those they should be able to trust. Neglected in care homes. Treated as easy financial targets. Assaulted by thugs who knew they'd get away with a legal slap on the wrist. Petrified of leaving their own home, senults represented an obstacle to THE ARRIVAL that would have to be overcome utilizing the radical solution.

Other, more unsavoury, characters could be found in the shadier recesses. Izzy knew where. Drug dealers. Criminals. Weirdos daubed in body paint, squatting peacefully as they pipe-smoked dirty weed under the shelter of makeshift tepees. All of them lurking, skulking about. In the forest. On one occasion, ramblers were stunned to see a coachload of colourful strangers hastily disembark in the carpark, run off up the hill path, and disperse among the dingy copses.

And then there was Izzy. An extraordinary young adult by any standard. Izzy the enigma. She stood over the midult.

'Are you alright?' she said.

Izzy was always asking questions. On this occasion, a particularly stupid one. It was clear, from her traumatized demeanour, that this midult was not alright. She was distressed. There were brambles tangled in her honey blonde hair. Her cheesecloth dress flapped open in the cool breeze. Her stockings were bunched round her ankles. She crouched by the pink shale track, mewling quietly. So quietly that Izzy couldn't understand a word.

'Sorry, you'll have to speak up, I can't hear you,' she said.

The midult gabbled something about love-in-the-mist.

'Love? Mist?'

The midult stared blankly at Izzy.

'Where? Here, in the forest?'

'In the forest?' Izzy repeated impatiently.

The midult remained silent.

'Try, won't you?'

She was beyond help. In any case, Izzy couldn't help her, not even if she wanted to. Being familiar with the midult's mate: a tall, slim, male midult with a cock's crest quiff, she reasoned that her predicament was the result of coital concerns such as:

Where's my lacy underwear?

Did I just fake it for him?

The earth was supposed to move for me, right?

Did I feel okay?

Did I just dislocate my leg for him?'

And: surely, he doesn't want sex with me again tonight, does he?

Izzy strongly suspected his request for repeated sex had caused an altercation which spilt out of their luxury apartment, onto the village green, into the churchyard, through the meadows, and into the forest. In other words, they had a tiff, went to the woods, made it up, and had sex. In the mist. That kind of made sense? She glimpsed at the female whimpering at her feet. So, what happened to you afterwards, eh?

Not that the midult's plight was her concern. Her mating partner had made it abundantly clear to Izzy that she was not to get emotionally involved with female midults under any circumstances. Female midults were obstacles to THE ARRIVAL. Izzy muttered her a heartfelt apology, skipped over her feet, and walked away.

Iain waited until Izzy had gone, rode up to the midult on his metallic grey hybrid mountain bicycle and rang its prawn pink RING ME ANY TIME bell. Irin's initial reaction was one of shock. She ceased mewling as an appalling notion shattered her addled mind: the cyclist might be an alien.

It was tough for Irin to tell what the bloody thing was from its bizarre apparel. An enclosed blue cycling helmet, fitted with a customized amber visor, concealed its face. A thermonuclear protective vest and red-lined road bib, with an integrated rubber jock strap, hid its body. The cyclist sported trendy coyote light assault boots, built-in shock absorbers, studded cycle gloves, and it spoke:

'It's only me!'

She panicked and crawled off on all fours. He dismounted, shouldered off his rucksack, and grounded her. She bleated like a little lamb. Ignoring her gibberish, he reached inside his sack, extracted a misshapen object, and untied its brown wrapping paper. Her spirits sank when he rolled her onto her back. Her scared eyes haunted him. She pleaded for her life. He felt for her.

She kneed him in the groin. He winced. She wriggled free of him, snaking across the dirt. He exhaled. She made it as far as the undergrowth. Abruptly, he took the jagged garden rock and clumped her round the head. She dropped, her arms splaying as if trying to break her final fall. Removing his gloves, he knelt next to her, pushed back her bloodied hair, and felt her neck.

She was dead.

He looked around.

They were alone in the moonlight.

'Can't let them see you like this, Irin.'

Iain rolled Irin onto her back and dressed her, rolling her stockings up her taut calves, over her knees, and up her thighs, carefully re-attaching them to her ruby and black suspender belt.

Irin watched Iain with her dead eyes as he smoothed the scarlet-tinged curls from her face. He lifted her cold hands. Her poppy red fingernails were soiled with dirt. He picked them clean. He sucked them. Her face was dirty. He cleansed her. Iain took a deep breath, pausing over Irin's precious mound, broke down, and cried. His tears subsided.

He recovered quickly, his nimble fingers moving deftly, sealing her corpse inside her dress. Her membrane had adhered to one side of her mouth as she bit her lip, baring her sparkly white teeth. He took her head in his hands and kissed her cyan lips. A single teardrop rolled down her cheek. Irin had been loyal, loving, and faithful to him. Iain would always love her. He had to leave her. To care for Izzy.

Wearily, he lifted Irin in his arms and carried her far into the woods where he laid her to rest in a dry ditch covering her with soil and broken twigs to keep her warm. Then he mounted his bicycle and ascended the winding hill.

Izzy tied her teak hair back in a crude knot and ran. Iain watched as she danced up the hill in her grey sports bra and red fitness pants: young, free. He wanted her. His heart fluttered as she vanished in the gloom, his bright elusive butterfly of love. She had the face of an angel: teardrop eyes, her spoilt lips divinely pursed, rather droopy at the corners, the faintest brown moustache.

Iain closed his eyes and imagined her naked. The light faded. He tightened the stiff strap on his helmet and pedalled to where the path forked. He would ride the west loop, past dewpond, bog, marsh, climb the steepest inclines, descend the deepest troughs, until he found her in the mist.

The sun set in the velvet sky presaging rain at dawn, freshening the stale air. Izzy shivered as the fresh breeze cooled her midriff. Goosebumps bristled on her tummy, caressed her waist, massaged her back.

A swarm of marauding mosquitoes descended on her, a kamikaze death squadron. Flapping her arms, slapping her neck, Izzy fought to stave off their impending feast. The females adored her, settling in her scalp, nestling in her folds, pricking her skin, injecting their saliva, sucking her blood. She fell to earth cowering until the pests had had their fill of her, itching, scratching, rows of puce bumps erupting in blunt infant volcanoes along her jawline, her armpits, her soft creases.

Apart from the plagues of mosquitoes, Izzy loved summer evenings, her favourite time of day, the only time she felt at one with nature. She checked her illuminated wristband. They would all be fast asleep now, the midults, snug in their luxurious cots. Whereas she was made to sleep on a bunk inside a box.

Relishing the soft earth under her bare feet, the tightness pulling at her hot calves, she slid down a shallow slope into a dry hollow, crushing twigs and early fallen acorns, squashing beechnuts. Izzy picked up the pace, feeling the burn, stretching her supple limbs to the limit, grinding her way uphill past clusters of felled silver birch until the track levelled out.

The going was good to firm made treacherous by sprawls of tangled beech roots. She cherished the peace of night, the reassuring natural noises, nocturnal animals: fallow deer, rabbit, foxes, badgers, all strays scampering in the thicket. That is what she was: a stray, who came out to play at twilight, a nocturnal animal released from captivity to run wild, run free, in search of her dream.

The sky faded to black. She entered the wood's heart, where peat bogs fermented, and let her imagination run wild. Were there fireflies? Will o' the wisps? Faeries? Witches? Magic?

What... the fuck... was that?

The mist descended out of nowhere, immersing, absorbing her. Izzy breathed its acrid vapour, inhaling the damp, dewy musk. The temperature plummeted. The chill shot icy shards into her body.

She froze, then twitched, jerked and jumped like a shattered porcelain marionette thrown in the air by a demented puppeteer. They passed through her, knife-like, unknown entities, etching their sordid intimate imprints on her soul. Her mind grappled with the absurdity of intruders permeating her numbed brain, writhing inside her vital organs:

What are you? Leave me alone! Get out of me, won't you?

The intrusion ceased as suddenly as it began. Izzy collapsed, exhausted, in an untidy heap.

Why do I feel so tired? What's happening to me?

The mist lifted. The sky cleared. She stared at the heavens, the blue void filling with crescent moons, glitterball stars, gasping, awed by what came next...

'Can't take much more of this!' she protested.

Her walnut eyeballs rolled, revealing their whites. Her heavy lids sagged, drooped and shut. Izzy surrendered to her deathly fatigue. Rolling onto one side, curling up in the foetal position, she fell asleep and dreamed the strangest dreams.

When she woke up, Izzy was lying flat on her back, emotionally drained, staring at the starlit sky. In time, she regained her strength, clambering to her feet unsteadily, as if she were a young doe rising out of her bracken bed. Her head span. She staggered up the steep slope, stumbled, fell into his arms, and passed out.

He had a body to die for: race-fit, solid muscle, tuned for speed, ready for the heart-pounding sprint. He was one-of-a-kind: his open-edged brows maximized his field of vision. His neon red night eyes enabled him to see more. His advanced snub nose bridge opened out his airflow, combating fogging, preventing his internal body from overheating. He suffered from alien drug rash, hooded brows, teal eyes, chiselled jaw, sticky-out ears, bum fluff, hooked nose, dry lips, pipe neck.

He appraised Izzy's sleeping face. She looked beautiful.

He threw her over his shoulder, took his bicycle in one hand and tore round the east loop, down the winding hill, through the meadow to the main road. His resilient fit moved with Izzy instead of against her, built for longer ride comfort. He had hidden reflectivity in his backside. His legs wore smooth edgings with rubbery grips to help him to stay in place.

From the road it was a short jog: past the church, right at the crossroads, over the cricket pitch, to an overgrown path skirting the allotments, to the grey clay lane that led to the remarkable little box he gave her to live in.

Iain threw the door open, stomped into the box, and dumped Izzy's inert form on her bed.

He'd fashioned the box for her with his bare hands, erecting a central plasterboard partition to create two cubes. The solid oak door, with its deceptively ornate devil knocker and doorbell, led the occupant off the tarmac lane onto bare wooden floorboards. The living cube, Iain had determined, was primarily suited to nocturnal activities: sleep and sex. With such functions in mind, he had installed blinds over the front and back windows. He drew them down and locked the door.

A sawn-out bolthole in the partition led to the sanitary cube, a cork-tiled conurbation of ceramic splendour in angelica, a beautiful toilet and wash hand basin suite that added elegance to any converted garage. There was a curved shower unit in the corner, a blacked-out oval glass portal, and an integrated fan unit. Cooking facilities, food storage and waste disposal units were unnecessary. Izzy fed carnivorously, metabolizing her own waste, methane, and by-products.

Iain regarded her inert body, sprawled haphazardly on the bed. She'd be out cold for half an hour. He lifted his burly right arm, followed by a well-muscled right leg, and sniffed himself like an animal, baulking at the stink of stale sweat, sediment and soil deposition. Microclimatic conditions for THE ARRIVAL depended on body purity, fertility, and compliance with hygiene, health & safety due diligence in the profligate progenitor. Prior to procreation with a suitable progenitive who could produce progesterone in preparation for her progeny.

As he discarded his foetid, outer layers, he prognosticated. Izzy was producing oxytocin and seemed pretty relaxed, if not proactive about pregnancy. Her high prolactin level would enable healthy nutrition for her progeny, pending THE ARRIVAL. Iain stood in the shower, scrubbing his tainted torso clean, and tried to prioritize process:

Izzy would reproduce with him tonight. His dead mate, Irin, would be interred and moved to a deeper grave in the churchyard. Her burial would require assistance from Irma, the local gravedigger, who was open to bribes. He made a mental note to contact her in the morning. Irun, manager of the charitable recycling facility, would arrange for the collection of Irin's clothing and incinerate her underwear, stockings, perfume, cosmetics and toiletries on the local allotment bonfire. Izzy would then move out of the box and bring up her progeny in the spare room of his apartment overlooking a village green famous for its Donkey Derby and Firework Display. He would meet Ilene at The Gate tomorrow night for drinks and float the idea of her relocating into Izzy's box, in return for a leading role in Senult Control.

Iain had been left with no choice but to kill Irin: she was an obstacle, like all female midults. She *had* to die. Just as all male midults *had* to be assimilated. Just as Ilene *had* to coordinate the cottage industry of processing all senults, transgressing them through the village halls. Iain bore ultimate executive responsibility for enaction of all operational aspects of THE ARRIVAL.

Satisfied that he had made detailed plans for THE ARRIVAL, he stepped out of the shower, towelled himself dry, sprayed his body with musk, switched off the fan-light, and made his way silently into the living cube.

His angel was lying on the bed waiting for him to inseminate her with his alien spermatozoa. He went and knelt beside the bed so that he could examine her. Izzy was still unconscious. She was perspiring lightly; the tips of her teak hair were dark and wet; her brow was covered with tiny beads of perspiration. He brushed a stray strand out of her mouth, rubbing her lips gently with his thumb, so that her face grinned at him. Her eyelids were closed. Iain flicked one open to reveal the walnut iris. The eyeball was lustrous, clear of the tell-tale threads which would manifest her whites once full parasitic infection had set in.

He ran the edge of his hand down her neck and appraised Izzy's body. Her jawline, shoulders, armpits, midriff, the creases and folds in her limbs, were spattered with bright red hives. Iain reached for his rucksack, took out the tube of antihistamine balm he kept for insect bites, squeezed a little onto his fingertips, then lightly massaged the soothing lotion into Izzy's inflamed skin. Izzy smiled to herself, enjoying the sensation of her body being explored by his tender touch. She felt the lump swell between her breasts, like a large, raised hiatus hernia. He rubbed the cream into her legs, screwed the cap back onto the tube, dropped it on the floor and took out the sachet of weed, hiding it under the bed. He looked up. Izzy was awake. She feigned surprise when he brushed her cheek with his hand. The lump grew in her chest.

'Where am I?' she said.

Iain sat her up in bed, took her in his arms and embraced her, patting her back as if he were winding a baby. She smelled his musk and smiled. He was clean for once; he must have washed. She felt the spur rise up her oesophagus, felt uncertain.

'You're safe in the box, Izzy,' he told her, reassuringly.

She let Iain pull her grey sports bra off over her head. 'Safe?'

He held her tight, loving the thrill of her naked breasts pressed against his manly alien chest.

'I found you asleep in the forest,' he said.

Izzy looked puzzled. 'Asleep? Why would I want to sleep in the forest?'

He ran his fingers through her damp hair. She was beautiful. Had the face of an angel. He wanted her so badly. He slid his hands down her slender back and tucked his fingers inside her fitness pants. Izzy smiled as her lump grew. The spur extended as far her throat. She was ready.

'I have no idea, but you're safe with me now, that's all that matters,' he said.

She let him pull off her fitness pants. Izzy was wearing a pale grey thong. A frisson passed thru them. Izzy took the weed and put it in her mouth like a naughty child. It was deep brown and tasted bitter like dust and bark that had been ground to a must by a sorcerer's pestle. She masticated, grinding her teeth, kneading the ayahuasca with her tongue, crushing the greens and stems into a pulpy spinach mulch. Izzy suspected the ayahuasca was dirty, full of toxic impurities, like her mating partner. Rumours abounded that dirty weed masquerading as ayahuasca liquid, mulched vine of the dead or synthetic

DMT had led to the deaths of countless teenagers at wild parties and rock festivals. Izzy needed it to sleep. Chewing the psychedelic cud was Iain's idea.

'Take the weed to relieve the tedium, Izzy,' he said, 'Open your mind.'

Her oval face drew with doubt at first. Still, she supposed, if the natives enjoyed this shit in the jungle, why couldn't she get off on it in bed? She duly took the weed, took off her thong, opened her mind, opened her legs to him, and enjoyed their best sex since her arrival. Once he had finished, Izzy lay on top of him, playing with his wet hair, rubbing his lips with her thumb.

'Do you love me, Iain?' she asked.

He saw Irin lying in her shallow grave. 'I love you more than life itself, Izzy,' he replied.

'Then let me kiss you.'

He opened his mouth to her tongue. Too late, he felt her spur slide down his throat, extend as far as his oesophagus, and suffocate him. Izzy relaxed as the tubular organ drew neurotoxin, pumping poison out of the swelling in her chest. Her secreted toxin entered Iain's bloodstream, stunning him. Izzy felt her lump contract as she squirted her volatile secondary fluid into Iain's digestive tract. His dying body twitched involuntarily as the molecular acid dissolved his flesh, his muscle, tissues, his organs, his bone, turning his torso into a skin-encapsulated sac of mulch.

She fed on him for five hours…

As a result of one night's gay abandon, Izzy was lip-hooked, tongue-set, utterly dependent on her dead boyfriend. In time, her stomach extracted the liquid entheogenic from her digested prey, vomiting it into the glass bowl she kept by her bed. She was drenched in a brilliant white light. Purged out, Izzy felt herself leave her body and travel the void, transiting into a fluffy world. Effortlessly rebirthed, she popped out, releasing all her negative energy, her bad emotions. Izzy descended into a realm of inner peace. Her mind and body united by subliminal blood rushes, congealed alien flesh, liquified organs and body fluids; she regurgitated Iain, spat him out in pellets. Then she slipped on her pyjamas, climbed between the sheets, and fell asleep.

Slowly swinging her slender legs off the bunk, Izzy fumbled with the camelia satin waist band around her midriff, divesting herself of her wondrous, velvet-piped jimjams and playful toys and dolls. She tried to stand. She was groggy, permeated by weed and alien residue. Her addled brain swelled like sodden sponge. Her heavy head whirled. She slumped onto the bed.

Izzy clenched the edge of the bunk tightly. Her throbbing head hung below her knees, the lemon extensions attached to her burnt sienna hair drizzling down her calves, kissing her feet. She instructed herself not to overextend her abs for fear of an unsightly acid reflux. Pretty soon, her retching abated. Fisting her slim arms deep into the duvet, Izzy pushed herself up onto the balls of her feet.

Beside the bed lay a modacrylic sheepskin rug which, judging by its squashed, sorry look, had never been shampooed. This rug was where Izzy performed her post-digestive stretches. Other than the built-in bunk and radiator, the black hole's only other feature was the full-length gilt-edged mirror, a car boot sale bargain that hung despondently off the crumbling plaster wall, facing her quilted cot.

Izzy appraised herself in the mirror. She had a pallid complexion, anaemic milky white skin.

Her body started to bloat…

*****

They spread quickly through the mist and infected her. They thrived in her maternal body. Izzy really mattered now! She carried them inside her cells. They mutated with her ova. Izzy had a body to die for. They lived inside that body as parasites. She carried within her the hopes and aspirations of future generations. Izzy was selected for her stamina, resilience and endurance. Her absorption rate for male midults and reproduction capacity were phenomenal. She bred…

THE ARRIVAL

The fog emanated from a dewpond in the forest, an unfurling blanket of phosphorescent blue. A minuscule hole appeared at the epicentre, spreading rapidly like spilt ink, rippling in a pool of indigo. The pool burst into a swirling kaleidoscope: a distant galaxy, the faint glimmer of a dying star, a solitary sea-green planet.

They ARRIVED, shrouded in mystery, freed from all physical constraints, finding sanctuary.

They found a host in Izzy, then another, Morgan, then Ilene…

Soon, there would be millions of them:

ARRIVING

them

IN SO FAR AS SHE COULD TELL THERE WAS ONLY ONE OF THEM. At least, she had only ever seen one, felt one, and one of them was more than enough for her to handle. A vanishing breed. The last of the species. A male, on the verge of extinction. A male, and her, a female. Just the two of them, sharing secrets at twilight.

The sinking sun cast a blinding orange sheen on the surface of the muddy lake. Chocolate, molten chocolate, the kind she used to find spewing from chocolate fountains when she served them at weddings. She no longer served them. In fact, she didn't serve anybody - only him, the male. And he served her. The cocoa-coloured water looked warm, smooth, and inviting. The sun sank, reddening the treetops. A milky luminescence spread across the lake's surface: brilliant white blurring to yellowish orange, gold: the fog that heralded them.

Wild swimming was her passion. Swimming was all she had left. She'd lost her job in the lockdown, lost her little room, online friends, her family. Lost her will to live. She was staring into the abyss, homeless and lonely, when she found the muddy lake hidden away in the forest. Wearing all she owned: a faded, floppy orange t-shirt, a pair of slim, straight, mid-denim jeans, grubby sneakers with no socks, her treasured black, one-piece stretch swimsuit,

'My little onesie,' she smiled, her wistful smile, readying herself to swim.

The abyss, she supposed, wasn't so bad now that she was used to it. Being homeless, here in the forest, meant never having to pay the bills, reply to messages, go to work, clean her little room. She scavenged all the food she needed after dark, after her lengthy wild swim, from a nearby food bank, found her toiletries in fly-tipped bin liners, had no need for cash for now,

'How long can I live like this?' she asked herself, watching the red sun set, 'How will I cope when the summer ends? When the autumn chill sets in. And the lake floods. Where will I live this winter? Will there be frost, snow, ice? How will I stay warm? How will I live, with him?'

Her heart sank. She hated the idea of winter: muddy-coloured waters turning clear, sodden leaves sinking down to the soft squelchy bed of the lake covering him, her male, while he hibernated, buried in the warm mud. While she sat, huddled, and shivering on the bank, mourning her lost love.

They communicated telepathically, through facial expressions, use of sign language, and, underwater, she'd developed an uncanny method for mouthing simple phrases, blowing rafts of bubbles at him when she spoke, phrases such as:

'Hello!'

'Wait!'

'Up!'

'Down!'

'Bye!'

And, when she finally managed to catch her breath and swallow a lungful of air:

'Let me get my swimsuit off!'

Excited at the prospect of seeing him, feeling him again, she sat on the bank, removed her sneakers, wriggled out of her jeans, pulled off her t-shirt, and waded into the lake up to her chest. There was a wooden railing sloping into the water. She gripped it for support, steadying herself. Her shaggy ginger-gold hair, all split ends, tangled knots, hanging over her face, she searched the muddy morass for signs of life, preparing herself for her wildest swim yet.

'Where are you?'

The thick grey cloud of mosquitoes descended on her out of thin air, settling in her scalp, nestling in her folds, pricking at her skin, injecting their saliva, sucking her blood. She slapped her face and neck, rubbing her knees and elbows in a vain bid to stave them off. She cowered as the pests had their fill of her, itching and scratching herself, rows of puce bumps erupting in blunt infant volcanoes on her jawline, in her armpits, her soft creases.

'Come on!'

A raft of crocodile-sized bubbles finally appeared in front of her, moving in a wiggly line towards her from the shallows on the other side of the lake. The sun set, her golden hair was bathed in moonlight, the bubbles disappeared. She smiled, kicking her legs, splashing her arms.

It could only be him.

He lay motionless, save for his undulating adipose fins and big tail, just below the surface. Eying her using the periphery of his vision, not knowing who she was, what she was, how old she was. Assessing her on instinct. Assuming she was female. Was she female? There was no way that he could tell if she was a female. No way that he could possibly know. Other than through his own basic instincts: his senses: of taste, touch, vision, and smell. He'd become accustomed to her face, staring down at him, covered in shaggy ginger gold hair. Familiar with her hourglass figure, standing, gripping the rail for support, clad in black, steadying herself, in readiness for her swim, plagued by a swarm of insects. Aware of her musky fragrance: the aquatic had an acute sense of smell. Acquainted with her feel, whenever their bodies touched, her taste whenever they kissed.

He'd had a mate once, many sunsets and moonrises ago, a female aquatic who'd birthed him a foal. Tragically, the effort of giving birth had killed her. The foal had died soon afterwards, unable to be suckled by her mother. He'd sensed their loss, lying with them on the lake bed as their bodies rotted and decayed. Then, to his utter disgust, he had fed on them: skin, flesh, bone, cartilage, muscle, brawn, hearts, brains, faces, until they were part of him, living on, forever inside him.

He didn't know he was the last of them. His brain and six-foot body responded only to nature's clock: misty sunsets, haunting moonrises, murky dawns, midday suns. He spent all day sucking mud and rotten organic matter into his cavernous mouth, sifting out the worms, molluscs, insect larvae, and grubs to eat, before blowing the mulch out through his gills creating eruptions of bubbles on the surface.

He came alive at sunset! That was when he surfaced, swimming up and down, round and around the liquid chocolate lake. The aquatic led a simpler life than her. He felt emotions, yearnings, for his dead mate and her foal. Heartache over his new love. He felt lonesome, never lonely plundering his way thru his solitary existence until it was time for him to die.

He'd breathed, swam, fed, slept, and excreted, until she came into his life: to be with him at sundown for as many sunsets and moonrises as he could wish for. He heard her wild swim call!

The moon rose high in the night sky, casting eerie shadows over the dingy lake's surface. He rose up through the water. The lake became a churning, bubbling, exploding cauldron: swells, whirlpools, wash waves.

She cried to him chanting her magic spell, she drew him in, 'Up! Up!'

And he was there for her floating on his back. Showing off as usual! Wanting her to swim!

'Wait!' she smiled, the happiest smile of her life, ''Let me get my swimsuit off!'

She peeled off her swimsuit, slung it over the railing, with a fine disregard for boring old propriety, and announced to the natural world,

'Won't be needing that where I'm going!'

He grinned at her, lurking just below the surface, his otter's snout, his seal's whiskers, his catfish rubbery lips, twitching with subliminal delight. She made him content, happy - in as much as he could feel happy. A happy contentment he hadn't felt since his loving mate gave birth to their foal, their sublime moment, her miraculous water birth in the shallows, the moment she died.

She sank into the cloudy water, up to her neck in warmth, love, passion, head-over-heels in love with the only creature in the world who'd ever shown her any affection. He rolled! He rolled in front of her, belly-up, exposing his muscular chest, his smooth pelt. Shewing her his naughty bits! She marvelled at him, reaching out, stroking his furry cheek, rubbing his chest, caressing him.

Clouds rolled over the moon. It absolutely pissed down! Rain, falling, streamy stair rods, teeming down in thick spatters, crowding the lake with whirlpools, vortices of their love. Her shaggy gold-ginger hair stuck lank and cloying glued to her scalp like a wet balaclava, rivulets of purity running down her smiling face.

The rain aerated the stagnant water bringing new life to the pond, exhilarating them. He came alive for her, thrashing his big tail, contorting his eel-pout torso into mind-twisting shapes. She pushed her arms up out of the water, waving him on, spurring him on, crying, 'Love it when you're happy!'

She thought of all her lonely nights on the streets sheltering from the rain in dirty subways, porches, sleeping on late night trains without a ticket, never getting caught, never begging. She'd never allowed herself to beg, in the hope that one day…

'He's gone! Gone where?!'

.. she might find love.

Ripples, splash pools, rain pressed on her matted hair, her mind. Questions shaped in her..

'Up! Up!'

He didn't heed her call. She thought how lonely her life would be without him, her only loyal friend. She knew, deep in her heart: she loved him. But could he love her? Questions,

'Up! Up! Damn you!'

No sign of him. She despaired. Past doubts about them resurfaced. Was he really the last? How could she be sure? Supposing there were others. Females. Supposing he had a mate, a baby (she struggled to conjure up the word) pup? Suppose they were watching her, just below the surface. She began to feel ashamed of herself, stupid. He was just an animal, granted a living miracle, a relic from some far-off distant past, an alien? She searched the starless skies, insistent rain whipping her cheeks, stinging her eyes, making her blink and squint.

'Please tell me he wasn't an alien.'

Wasn't.

Her pet is all he was. Her tame pet. And she'd let him go.

Furious with herself, she reached for her swimsuit.

She wasn't new to this. The initial excitement of attraction. Her mounting arousal during foreplay. The thrill of her denouement. Her so-called passionate act of love. Love! She'd never truly experienced love. Sure, she'd had her moments: fleeting, fiery, ones. Barely legal encounters with sweating schoolboys, petting-in-the-park after tennis, after mixed doubles. Before her parents were killed in the car crash, and her truancy began. Then there were the romantic candlelit soirees: sharing platters with toxic cocktails, Eva's wine bar. Staring across the table at him, gazing into his lovestruck eyes, holding hands, going back to his place. Her one-night stands. She wasn't beautiful, not by any means, but she was an attractive, sexy, deceptively plain woman who used love to survive the uncertainty of being alive. She recalled her midnight trysts in the laundry room, after weddings, at the hotel, her up-against-the-walls with banqueting managers, chefs, waiters, casual barmen.

After the closure forced by the pandemic when she lost her job at the hotel, her little room, she'd turned feral: existing in a wild-uncultivated state; ferine: a savage, brutal beast of a woman who stooped to any depths to survive. Scavenging for fodder, titbits, scraps, eating other people's waste. And, when there was no waste, she had turned to them, the strangers in dark alleyways. There'd never been a need for her to beg. She thought of the thick wad of soaking-wet twenty-pound notes stuffed into the back pocket of her soaking-wet jeans. Thought of them, warm, dry in their family homes, pretending to be faithful to their wives.

She thought of him, lurking somewhere deep in the muddy depths. What had she done to scare him off? She thought of them. How could they survive as a species without her help?

The rain teemed down from the heavens. Her shaggy, gingery-red hair was saturated, all split ends, tangled knots. Her black, onesie, well-stretched, swimsuit hung off the railing, like a sodden dishcloth. A muddy pool formed around her clothing.

She smiled to herself, 'Can't go home. Don't have a home. This is my home. I want to stay here with him.'

She wasn't new to this. She'd been used, abused, loved, rejected, so many times before. And she wasn't about to be rejected now.

'Hello?'

She felt someone rub his soft pelt against the backs of her thighs, her buttocks, the small of her back, laughing aloud.

'Hello?'

She felt his big tail curl around her belly.

She had never felt this relieved in all her life, this happy, euphoric.

She cried out loud, 'Down! Down!'

He wanted, needed her, for his mate. He'd never needed anyone this badly in his lengthy life, not since his beloved mate died giving birth to her foal. He felt a need, a compulsion, a need he hadn't felt for sunsets, moonrises, dawns, suns at their zeniths, thunderstorms, leaf falls, rainy showers, autumn winds, winter frosts, spring airs. He felt the need to mate.

'Down! Down!' she cried, taking him into her tender-sweet embrace, 'Down! Down!'

And then, entwined as one, they swam!

She took a deep breath, then clung onto him, her arms, and legs, tightly wrapped around his slender torso. Proud of her, protective of her, his naiad, he propelled her thru the fudge of the pond, as far as the reed beds, where they could mate. They surfaced. Wet. She'd never been so joyously wet in all her life, her mind whirling out, alive, with the thrill of the ride.

'So, this is love! Our freedom! He is who I live for! My blissful mate! My manatee of love!'

The rain poured down, matting her ginger-red hair with a teak helmet, enclosing her face in Bournville streaks, exposing the sunburnt scalp where her hair was starting to thin. She envied him his simple life: his life without strings, love without worry? She'd never know.

She felt a delicious tingling sensation sweep through her body. Felt his body tense. They reached the reedbeds. She let him go. He lay on his back,

~ 239 ~

smiling. She stroked his cheek, rubbed his snout, kissed his lips, ran her soft hand over his smooth pelt. Pausing to tweak his four nipples. Sensitizing his body in a way he hadn't felt since foreplay with his mate. He wanted to, needed to mate with her. She wanted his foal, fondling his naughty bits till he felt ready to proliferate the species! Creating a genetic variation? He would never tell!

She straddled him, and they copulated in the shallows, animals of entirely distinct species, searching for a fresh start. It came as no surprise to her when he ejaculated prematurely, filling her with his semen. She had that effect on him. Her bucking bronco! Making her shudder from head to toe. Making her sit upright, bare her teeth, and snarl at him. It was all over, bar their gasping, in thirty ecstatic seconds. Exhausted, she fell asleep, with her head resting on his chest, she slept on him, until…

Dawn broke with a burst of hot sunshine, warming her body, cheering her mind. Truth be told she was famished, starving hungry. It had been an entire day since she last descended on the food bank in search of scraps to eat. She listened to his twin hearts beat, his pulses, relieved to find their exertions hadn't killed him. One could never tell with them. She was shaken out of her slumber by the sound of gunshots fired in quick succession.

'Someone's up early shooting rabbit, pheasant? No, July's far too early to shoot pheasant.'

There was a second volley of shots, worryingly nearby, five, fired in quick succession.

'Clays? Clay? Pigeons? Clay Pigeons!'

The shooting stopped. She felt him stir in the shallows, roll onto his front, face down, and go back to sleep, his head fully submerged.

'Alright for some, isn't it,' she cursed, 'Some of us have to eat, some of us have to get dressed.'

She recalled her tee shirt and jeans lying in a muddy pool on the bank, her onesie hanging off the railing. Her filthy clothes would have to be washed then hung up to dry before she could go to the supermarket or risk her sneaky visit to Olive's deli bar. She thought of the wad of notes in her jean pocket, congealed, stuck together. At least it had stopped raining. Or had it? The sky darkened, turning overcast. It started to rain again. She started to fret.

'I could be stuck here on my own for hours while he sinks to the depths to find breakfast.'

Her tummy rumbled. She was still pondering her ridiculous predicament when she heard the low growl of a man,

'Is that really you, with him?'

She recognized his voice at once, 'Yes, it's me.'

He was appalled at her behaviour. There was no doubt in his mind as to what she'd just done with him, no doubt at all. She'd enjoyed sexual intercourse with an aquatic, 'had it away,' as his mate always said, with one of them. His stomach heaved. He controlled the muscle spasms, his contractions, tensing his abs until the primal urge had abated. Instead, he took his anger out on her,

'What in hell's name do you think you're playing at, lying in a muddy pond in the pouring bloody rain, having sex with one of them. You look like a mermaid, know that? A bloody mermaid. What do you look like?'

'A mermaid,' she repeated, quietly, obediently.

She covered her breasts and sank into the water whispering to him as she went, 'Down!'

He didn't move, just lay motionless sound asleep in the shallows. She knew he was asleep, touching his heart one last time as she sank. The man glowered at her as if she were crazy, which in truth she was – nutty-mad as a rampant March hare on fertility drugs. What other explanation could there possibly be for her errant behaviour? He pricked his ears for her, like a deer being stalked,

'What was that?'

'Down. I've been feeling down, lately. What with losing my job, my little room, and that.'

The rain eased. The man pulled down his wet olive hood, revealing a wet olive deer hunter hat, a damp olive tee-shirt. Everything about the man was olive, camouflaged, except his face. His face was kind and round and warm, in spite of his anger at her. He cared about her, deep inside his stone-hard heart, loved her in a strange way. Love can make you kill.

She watched him pull the oily rag out of his olive fleece, systematically polishing dry the barrel, body, stock, and sight of his sniper rifle. A stray bullet of awe flew out of her mind.

My man, she boasted proudly, saves patient's lives, then hunts, and takes them away! He doesn't shoot clays. Oh, no! My man shoots animals. Wonder if he'll shoot my lover?

To her relief, the man broke the rifle. He then proceeded to break her heart.

'What did I say about coming here, playing with them? Told you never to play with them, didn't I?'

'You did.'

'Then why did you?'

'I can't help myself. I get these urges. I know I shouldn't really. I can't help how I feel. I love him.'

Him? So, now there was only one of them left. The mate he'd seen floating in the shallows. Her dead foal must have been his. He felt a gram of pity for them, for her. She had nothing left to live for, only him. Feeling a rare surge of sympathy for her, the man took off his olive fleece, and extended it to her. She rose up out of the carob-coloured water, his naiad.

'Here, put this on before you catch your death,' he said kindly, 'Are those your togs lying in the mud over there?'

She blushed, donning the warm fleece, struggling with the zip, stepping out of the water. The zip was stuck, she couldn't do up her zip, his zip. Her manatee of love slid from sight, out of mind, safely, in the murky depths. The fleece barely covered her torso.

She blushed, smiling, laughing at herself, 'I can't do the zip!'

'Here, let me help you.'

Her ginger-red hair was matted, stuck to her scalp. He could see pale freckled flesh where her hair had thinned. Her hair ran, like thick treacle down her neck, her chest, adhering to her skin, gluing to her firm round breasts. She looked beautiful, all dripping wet like that. He quickly zipped her up, taking safe care to look over her head.

'How does that feel?'

Her heart leapt in time with the rhythm of his voice.

'It feels lovely and warm and dry, thank you.'

He smiled for her, a kindly, caring, considerate, warmly meant smile. The sun broke thru the trees, warming their spirits, dancing vainly upon the surface of the chocolaty mere. She watched his line of bubbles fade then disappear, as surely as her love for him began to fade. She padded around the pond, knelt, and gathered up her dirty clothes. When she looked up, the man was there, standing over her, beaming, holding out his Jack Pyke olive hunter's trousers for her to wear. She received them from him, as if they were his alms.

'You're very kind,' she grinned, appreciating his hairy, bandy legs, the olive welly socks, staring at the broken gun hanging, at an angle, over his strong arm, 'What do you shoot?'

'Oh, the gun, you mean?'

'Yes, the gun. What do you kill?'

He sensed a protective, defensive bitterness in her voice mixed with sudden apprehension: her concern for their survival? Wondering where her animalistic love for them would end.

'It's not what you think,' he explained, 'I shoot targets, clays, at my local club. I've never shot an animal in my life. Look, you're covered in mud, soaking wet, hungry, I imagine. My mate died last year of breast cancer...'

'I'm so sorry.'

He could tell from the timbre of her voice, she meant it. The baggy hunting trousers swung from her hips like heavy drapes onstage. She hitched them up, clutching them to her waist.

'I keep a cottage on the edge of the forest, not far from here. It's only small, but there is a spare room, with a warm bed, hot bath, soup on the cooker, hoagie on the plate...'

'I'm not sure I should.'

'Promise, I won't go near you. You're free to leave whenever you want. I want to help?'

She'd nowhere to live. Nothing to eat. No bed to sleep in. She was covered in mud. What did she have to lose? She cast her last lingering glance over the lake where they mated.

She left her manatee of love, left him for a real man.

He lay under the surface, wracked with heartache, searing pain, yearning for his lost mate.

The man was as good as his word. He did keep a cottage on the edge of the forest - not far from there. It was only small, delightful, a doll's house for grown-ups, rose beds and wild cherry trees, an overgrown thatched roof, grubby wattle-and-daub walls, leaden windows. A woman's house, a home without a woman. A house without a woman isn't a home at all. She wondered if, maybe, she could become his woman, his mate, wondered if she could commit herself to a new life, at home with him, cooking his meals, washing his clothes, ironing his laundry, sharing his bed,

~ 245 ~

'This is beautiful,' she said as he threw open the weathered oak door, inviting her inside.

His face broke into a happy, I-want-to-look-after-you, kind of grin, 'Mind your head!'

She stooped to avoid bumping her head on the low lintel aware that by entering his abode she was crossing a kind of personal threshold, risking her life on a man she barely knew.

'Give me your wet things,' he said taking her muddy clothes from her, 'I'll put on a wash.'

He let her into his living space, letting her go first. She smiled well, feeling herself relax.

'This is beautiful and homely and warm and..' the sight before her took her breath away.

The door opened into a living room with a stone floor scattered with old runners and rugs, whitewashed walls, a low uneven ceiling, an open hearth, a stairway winding out of sight. In one corner of the room stood a Welsh dresser stacked with willow pattern China plates, tureens, jugs, cups, saucers. There was a faded oak leaved table with solid oak chairs. The walls were coated from floor to ceiling with framed pictures, photos of the most beautiful woman she'd ever seen. She turned to face the man and saw that he was weeping. She held his hand. Neither of them spoke. She'd never forget his mate's haunting blue eyes, her sad-spoilt look, the solitary misery written across the man's face, for as long as she lived.

Shivering, dripping wet, still clutching his baggy trousers to her waist with one hand, she tightened her grip, reassuringly, with her free hand. He cheered up, loving his warm glow inside, the wonderful feeling of having someone to care for after all these years.

'You're shivering. There's a hot bath, warm bed, fresh clothes waiting for you upstairs. Shall we go?'

His mate's clothes, she reflected, following the man up the winding staircase as far as the bathroom. She watched him deposit her wet clothes in a wicker snake basket underneath the hand basin, run a steaming hot bath, laced with lavender scent bath foam and relaxing aromatherapy oils. There was a loofah, a lady's bath hat, back scratcher, a bar of coal tar soap on a rope, her pink towels hanging off a heated rail. All for her! Sheer, unadulterated luxury, the likes of which she'd never known. He ran her bath for her, turned off the taps, turned to go.

'Have a lovely bath,' he smiled at her, affectionately, 'The spare room's over the landing. I'll turn the bed down for you. Have a good sleep. Call me when you're ready for supper.'

She let his trousers fall to the floor, unzipped then took off his fleece. He caught a glimpse of her, nude, on the bath mat. Her beauty was intolerable. She reminded him of his mate. With her mannerisms, her face, her lust for life. When she replied, he had to look away,

'I will. Thank you for being so kind to me.'

'Don't mention it.'

He went to his bedroom and lay flat on his back on the bed thinking of his dead wife. She climbed into the steaming hot bath, sank up to her neck, shut her olive eyes, and dreamed of them, mating in the shallows.

After she'd washed the mud out of her hair, rid herself of him, and scrubbed their dirt out of her pores, she stood up in the bath rinsing off her body under the shower. Bliss! There was a tideline, their filthy scum, stained around the bath when she climbed out. She found a green scourer, and pulled the plug, scrubbing the ceramics clean, as the water level fell. Once she'd scraped the bath spotless, opened the windows to release the steam, towel-dried her gingery-red hair, limbs, and torso, rolled on his mate's deodorant, smoothed her face with her scent, dusted her flesh with her talc, and purged clean her teeth - using her toothbrush - she went to bed.

Her bedroom was twee: affectedly quaint, pretty, and sentimental; the walls were covered in bright portraits of the man's dead mate: heartfelt mementos, cameos of a stolen love.

The Florence antique pinewood bed, pleasantly decorated with an olive floral quilt, duvet, and matching puffed-up pillows, looked comfy, rustic, enough for her to get a good day's sleep. Ignoring the bedside table lamp, a guide to forest walks, and a brass alarm clock, she threw open the dusty curtains letting morning daylight pour in, pulled back the covers, and leaped into bed. Tired out, she fell asleep the moment her head hit the pillow.

He nudged her bare shoulder, shaking her gently when the sun was at its highest, coaxing her awake at noon. She blinked the sleepiest bits out of her eyes, acclimatizing herself to the harsh sunlight that washed the room with warmth,

'Can you draw the curtains closed, please?' she asked him, squinting.

He drew the curtains, switched on the beside lamp, stooping out of view, reappearing with a decorated beanbag crowned with a wooden tray. Sitting on the tray were: a big bowl of piping hot tomato soup, an oatmeal hoagie split lengthwise, toasted, dripping with melted butter, an open jar of crunchy peanut butter, an overripe pear, a glass of sparkling mineral water, and a ramekin of black cherry yogurt. She felt as if she were taking her breakfast at a five-star hotel, she'd never been so pampered by a man before. His smiling face said it all: he was loving every second of caring for her, nursing her better, loving her like his mate.

'I made you some lunch.'

She sat up in bed so that he could rest the tray on her lap, 'That's very kind of you, thank you. I'm starving.'

'You must be,' he smiled, placing the tray-bag on her lap, 'When you've finished, leave the tray on the floor. I'll collect it when you've had a good sleep. You must be exhausted, after all that.'

He left the worst line unfinished. No point flogging a dead horse. After all, she wouldn't be seeing him again.

She took a spoonful of soup from nearest the rim of the bowl where it was coolest, didn't want to burn her mouth. She ate the soup savouring every mouthful, tearing off big chunks of hoagie to chew between slurps. He turned to leave the room. She swallowed, too soon, burning her throat, searing the roof of her mouth, in her run haste to blurt out the question.

'Hello?'

He stood in the doorway, admiring her. She looked beautiful, sat up in bed like that, eating her soup and bread, 'Yes?'

'This was your mate's room, wasn't it, before she died?'

The man stared at his socked feet, nodding sadly, 'Yes, she used to love the morning sun.'

In so far as he could tell there was only one of them left, and one was enough. A vanishing breed. Last of the species. A male on the verge of extinction. A male, and him, her other male. Just the two of them, sharing secrets, at twilight.

The sun sank, reddening the treetops. A milky luminescence spread on the lake's surface, a brilliant white, blurring into yellowish orange then gold: the thin fog that heralded them.

The abyss, he supposed, wasn't so bad - now that she was there to share it with him.

'I can't live without her,' he told himself, as the sun set, 'How would I cope when summer ends, and the autumn chill sets in? How would I survive winter, the frost, snow, the ice?'

'I'll stay warm with her. I love her, dearly. Why should I ever want to live without her?'

He waited by the far bank, camouflaged in olive green, indiscernible from the treeline.

'Where are you?'

A raft of bubbles appeared in front of him.

Her manatee of love lay just below the surface, eying the man using the periphery of his vision, not knowing who he was, what he was. Assessing him on instinct. Assuming he was female.

He came alive at sunset. He surfaced. Swimming up, down, around the liquid chocolate lake. The aquatic led a simple life. He felt emotion, yearnings, for his dead mate, her foal. Heartache over his new love. He felt lonesome, never lonely, plundering his way through his solitary existence until it was time for him to die.

He'd breathed, swam, fed, slept, excreted, until she came into his life: to be with him at sundown for as many sunsets and moonrises as he could wish for. He heard her wild swim call!

The moon rose high in the night sky, casting eerie shadows over the dingy lake's surface. He rose to the surface. The lake became a churning, bubbling, cauldron of swells, whirls, wash waves.

The man cried out to him, chanting her magic spell, 'Up! Up!'

And he was there for her floating on his back, showing off as usual, wanting her to swim! He grinned at her, lurking below the surface, his otter's snout, seal's whiskers, his catfish rubbery lips, twitching with delight. She made him content, happy, a happy contentment he hadn't felt since his mate gave birth to their foal.

He rolled in front of her, belly-up, exposing his muscular chest, his smooth pelt.

Her pet is all it was. Her tame pet. And she'd let it go.

It was just an animal, after all, granted a living miracle, a relic from some far-off distant past, an alien?

'Please tell me it isn't an alien.'

Wasn't.

Furious with them, he reached for his sniper's rifle.

The man had never killed an animal in his life.

She was woken by the sound of gunfire, a volley of shots, fired in quick succession.

The shooting stopped.

She felt him die inside her. She felt nauseous, sick, a sickness that she'd never felt before.

She felt them stir inside her.

And, all the while, the foals grew in her belly.

Two Girls

AFTER THE BITTER CHILL OF WINTER, THE SNOW AND ICE OF FEBRUARY, Spring couldn't come soon enough for Kaitlyn and Madison. Throughout the drab lockdown, the vibrant forest had sustained them, freeing them from its suffocating constraints: online studies, incarceration with their frightened parents, to explore a fantasy world of adventure, life without masks.

Their return to school re-established daily rituals for the girls. They hardly saw each other during schooltime. Every morning Kait would meet Maddie off the school bus at the stop in front of the charity shop. After school they would kiss before Madison boarded the bus, and Kait watched her tired pale face, her veined hands, waving goodbye from a rear seat.

Except for when they walked-and-talked in the forest.

The forest was bordered by Pouting Hill, a busy country lane which wound its way from the traffic lights by The Stag and Hounds, past the Golf Club, to the junction with Forest Road, opposite the village green. Kait, oldest and tallest of the girls, held Maddie's hand as they crossed the road, entering the forest discreetly, out of view, beyond a sharp bend in the road. Then they were free to roam, to wander, wherever, however they wished. The hilly path stretched for three miles as far as the woodland car park, the starting point for organised walks, cycle rides. There, the path veered left, before making its steep, winding descent past Lover's Common to a narrow opening in the hedgerow, the Tennis Club, and the murder house.

~ 253 ~

March was chilly, frost-free, wrap-up-well weather: rainy, gusting winds, falling trees, in mid-month. It was unsafe for the girls to walk through the woods so Maddie took the bus.

Spring arrived with a flourish of cherry and hawthorn blossom in the hedgerows. On the sunniest, warmest, driest day of the month, with sunbeams highlighting the virgin leaves in the trees, Kait led Maddie deep into the forest, in rolled-up shirtsleeves, open collars, swaying, polyester skirts, holding hands.

'Where are we going?' asked Madison keenly, her pale face flushing, starting to perspire.

The birdsong ceased. Leaves rustled, in the trees. She felt the grip on her wrist intensify, her lover's lilting, dulcet tones.

'Somewhere where they'll never find us.'

They trod her path of mystery alone.

After a while, Kait halted in her tracks, turned to face her girlfriend, and grinned, 'Take off your shoes and socks.'

Maddie's eyes lit up, sparkling sapphires, her face stretched, cheeks risen, high, just like her rib cage when she breathed in sharply, indenting her mouth with such happy dimples.

'Why?'

'You'll get muddy feet otherwise.'

Muddy feet! The thought of it! Us, two girls! Playing together! In the mud! Muddy legs!

Maddie was a child at heart.

The eastern spur of the leafy avenue: beech and oak, the forest's thoroughfare, changed. Narrowing to a soft-mud path bordered by budding hawthorns, cruel brambles, and hazel. There were uncommon surprises dotted here, there, gaps in the thicket, wild cherry trees straining to burst into bloom. Remnants of some ancient orchard? Shooting bluebells yet to flower, straining for the sun. There was a bend in the path ahead. Kait smiled at Maddie, cherishing her childish happiness, loving the influence she exerted over her mate. Her girl would walk the plank for her, shin the tallest tree, scale the highest peak, swim the iciest stream. There was nothing in the world she wouldn't do for Kait - when she was a child.

Today, Maddie was her child. She watched, excited, as her adorable lover, her sole reason to live, got down on bended knee, and took off her sandal, her anklet, revealing her slender thigh, her skirt hitched. Kait had model's legs, smooth round knees. Unlike her knobbly knees, her pallid creamy skin, her sinewy calves, and thighs. Chick's legs she called them. Kait's chick. The socks and sandals were her idea, being childish, fun in the forest! Doting on her every word, Maddie followed suit. The sight of eighteen-year-old girls dressed in socks and sandals at school had raised their teacher's brows, given the other girls a laugh that morning!

They would never understand these two girls.

Standing very still, Madison bent her left knee, raising her calf behind her, reached back, prised off her sandal, and peeled off her sock. One of Kait's model's legs was bare, she noticed. She was bending, on her other knee, working off her sandal, the sock, standing. Mud, she had mud on her knee. Maddie watched her brush it off. She wanted to lick it off her smooth, round knee. While she bent her right knee and raised her calf, picking at her buckle,

~ 255 ~

pulling off her sock. Kait's legs were bare. Her legs were bare! Fun! In the forest! Kaitlyn's jaw kept moving, saying something odd, shoes and socks, held, in both hands…

Wipe the wisp of hair off your face, Kait. So that I can see you. So that I can be your child.

She wiped the wisp of copper hair off her face, grinning – fully - at Madison, and said, 'Shall we get our legs all wet and muddy?'

Breathless with excitement, fretting - nice frets, dreaming - wet dreams, fun-filled-panic attacks, Maddie could barely speak.

'Yes, lets! Hurry, Kait! Let's, yes! Kait, hurry!'

Please! I want to know your secret!

Kaitlyn Hart. Madison Hendricks.

Two Girls.

Went, around, the bend.

In the shady, narrow, muddy, path.

Cleft watched the girls undress. The short girl with the bronze-tinted shoulder length hair, parted down the middle, grey eyes, big nose, thin lips, slightly jagged teeth, was the sexier of the two girls, more self-conscious. She stood to take off her shoes and socks, refusing to go down on bended knee, to bare her thighs, in case a voyeur saw them, naked. It was the tall girl who intrigued Cleft. She appeared to exert an unhealthy influence over her mate. The childish girl couldn't take her eyes off her. And yet she bore such a shy smile on those melancholy, cracked lips of hers, a sadness in her eyes of midnight blue, and, on her lower lip, a prominent, ugly, brown scar.

From Cleft's hidey-hole, the gap in the thicket, she could almost reach out and touch the girl with the thick drape of copper hair brushing, scratching her eyelids, the bridge of her nose.

She wondered what would happen if she did.

It had to happen.

Madison felt the goosebumps rise on her bare calves and thighs as she slid, first one leg, then the other, incrementally into the stagnant pondwater. The fermenting broth, a rotting stew of decaying leaf mulch, dead rats, and birds, lumbricids, and snails, was deeper than she expected, wetting the hem of her skirt. She wondered if there were eels in the pond, leeches, bloodsucker lampreys, imagining them all attaching themselves to her arms, legs, and body. Kaitlyn, come to rescue her, biting them off, chewing them off, with her jagged, incisive teeth. Sucking them off Maddie's wet breasts with her mouth. She felt herself go,

Didn't mean to! Oh, no! What will mummy say when she sees me like this? All covered in sticky-clingy pondweed, pond slime, algae, sloppy-stink mud. Take off my clothes, Kait, wash me, cleanse me… touch me!

Slip! Trip! Fall! Headfirst! Into the murky water. Mads plunged, headfirst, into the filthy mire, digging her toes in deep, smearing herself, her crisp cotton shirt, her polyester skirt, in thick grey gunge, bobbing her head upward, sputtering froth and bubbles, weed, crying.

'Help me, girl!'

Kait, being the taller of the two girls, kept her hem dry as she waded through the disturbed swell of mud and mulch, swirling around, engulfing her best friend. Grabbing her by both arms, she dragged her to the far bank, appreciating Maddie's crocodile tears, her plaintive cry.

'Will I catch the lurgy, Kait? Please don't let me catch the lurgy. I'll so miss you if I do?'

Maddie was shivering, despite the unseasonal warm spring sunshine, trembling, a wibbly-wobbly jelly girl, all tingly in her wingly, rippling on the outside, nervy-girl in her insides. Kait smiled at her, knowingly, shaking on the bank.

Clumsy girl's lost her socks and sandals during her one-girl water fight. Maddie's socks and sandals are nowhere to be seen. How can she ever go home looking like that?

Her satchel lay on the grassy bank. Kait dipped inside, took out her phone, and checked. She breathed a sigh of relief,

No signal! There's no signal! We're alone in the forest. Where no-one will ever find us!

Clumsy girl was hunched up in a sodden heap on the bank, arms wrapped round her soppy wet shoulders in a vain bid to keep warm. Kait threw the redundant satchel into the thicket with the phone, and any hope of contact, reached under Maddie's armpits, and hauled her to her feet,

'Won't let you catch the lurgy,' was all she said.

There were beech trees, hazel, pussy willows, a prickly holly tree, then - rhododendrons.

~ 258 ~

Rhododendrons! Here in the heart of the forest! Whoever heard of such a thing?

Kait giggled, the child who springs out of bed, better, feeling better, after her prolonged illness: measles, chickenpox, mumps. The child released within her, she took a longing, yearning, look at Madison: all bedraggled, begging, beautifully muddy for her, beckoning her mate to follow her. Then she disappeared into the soft, broad-leafy hedgerow.

Maddie shrugged and shivered, stamping her bare foot, cracking twigs in her frustration,

'Aren't you going to undress me?'

Silence, all around her. Then…

The sound, of, heavy, breathing.

Somewhere, behind, her.

She dare not look!

A cold drip of fear ran down her back.

Madison Hendricks scarpered, a frightened bunny rabbit, ran for her life, to Kait, to safety.

Or so it seemed.

Cleft decided to stalk them, knowing where they were headed. She left her den and strode as far as the bend. The dewpond stretched from a knot of silver birch and pussy willows on her left to dense undergrowth on her right.

If she wanted to pursue her quarry, Cleft would have to wade the pond. She cursed silently.

This is turning into a muddy nightmare. Is she worth it?

She closed her eyes, seeing the tall girl, down on her bended knee, soiling herself, skirt hitched high, baring her slender thighs, her crotch,

Mmmn, she's worth it! There's only one thing for it…

Cleft shielded her eyes from the sun and stared ahead. The girls were nowhere to be seen. She shrugged, found a tussock of dry couch grass to kneel on, took off her jogging shoes, her prim new sports socks, pulled down her tracksuit bottoms, and waded into the stagnant water.

The short girl's anklets were swelling with bilge in the middle of the pond, about to sink, like her scuffed sandals, Cleft noted salaciously:

The clumsy girl's sandals have sunk into the muddy abyss. Those are her socks!

Wishing, she had a ship's whistle to pipe the sinking of the socks, Cleft ceased wading, tucked her bottoms, socks, joggers, under her left armhole, and raised her hand in silent salute. She'd find them, afterwards, for at the going down of the sun she would remember them.

After all: finders' keepers, losers' weepers!

How would the short girl's toes taste on her palate when she sucked them all clean? she wondered, licking her lips fervently with the upturned tip of her tongue. For that matter, how would she taste? Cleft wobbled as her perfectly manicured left foot slid and slipped on a submerged slimy boulder, rinsing her thighs, tainting her pure-soft skin with nature's rich wild broth of decay. She closed her eyes and dreamed, all smiles: suck-a-toe-in-turn.

The sun beamed down on her from its noon high, casting twinkles on the rippled surface, burning her face with ultraviolet light, warming her body as she waded to the other side. Cleft shook her legs dry as best she could, pulled on her tracksuit bottoms, jogging shoes, stuffed her socks in her pockets, then found the hidey-hole in her rhododendron hedge.

She felt a nausea, a sick bile, rising in her parched throat, swallowed hard, her excitement.

'No going back now,' she told herself, 'Your fetish, carnal need, darkest secret, two girls, await you. In you go, girl! In you go!'

No-one's land. Maddie found herself standing in the cool, leafy, umber shade of no-one's land. The hidey-hole in the hedge. Nature's passageway. A portal. Her one-way invitation to paradise or purgatory, suspended, saturated, someplace between the wood and the why? There was a kissing gate, timbered, coaxing her to enter forbidden territory. She pushed the gate with her wet cuff, wary of catching virus off its splintered surface, passed through the gap, and stepped inside.

She was blinded by the light, roasted by the heat, loving the cellophaned-body effect as her shirt, bra, and panties clung to her, sticking to her bristling skin, sensuously, sensually. Something slithery, sluggish, slippery: a leech, or a lumbricid, wormed its way inside her left bra cup, tickling her teat. Bugs, lice, flies, gnats, nipped and bit her folds, the creases in her skin: along her jawline, behind her ears, inside her armholes, elbows, knees, belly, navel. Making her itch like billy-ho! Maddie didn't seem to mind. Maddie was her child.

Kait admired her, the child-girl in her, her calves and thighs caked with drying mud, her matted hair stuck onto her scalp, dirty-urchin face, the shabby ruins of her school uniform.

Her mind wrestled with the mud. Mad's mud. Clumsy girl's crisp white cotton shirt had dried in the unseasonal heat, and stained khaki. Her skirt was filthy, spattered, with khaki.

My precious army girl!

She couldn't take Mads home to her mum and dad, Steph, and James Hendricks, looking like that. Steph would have her daughter's guts for garters. Then there were the onlookers to consider: walkers, passers-by, men-in-the-street: the knowing glances, mocking chants, derisive laughter: the shameful humiliation Maddie would endure. Kait's embarrassment. Chance meetings with schoolmates. Taunts, jeering in the playground. Animals bullying.

Maddie had an enchanted look on her face. Beguiled! Bewildered! Kait took her hand and led her, inside the summer garden. It wasn't spring. It was summer, *inside*. Roses climbing over weeded flower beds, fruiting apple, cherry, pear trees, buttercups on a lawn, a mossy garden path which led to…

'Wh-what's that?' asked Maddie, shaking herself, vigorously, to check that she was real.

A shed? A shack? A shambles?

Something unworldly, unnatural, unfriendly, about the place made her tighten her grip on Kait's hand.

A summerhouse?

It was the strangest place they had *ever* seen. A flight of hardwood steps led up to a crude, sheltered veranda, enclosed by metal trellis covered in flaky white paint. At the top of the stairs, across the entrance, stretched a solid, cupric metal chain - without its missing sign:

DANGER! UNSAFE! NO ENTRY!

'Shall we go inside?' suggested the taller girl, in a funny-odd voice.

Maddie, quite forgetting what it feels like to be shrouded in mud, shrivelled up, crawling, all over with lice and lumbricids, soaked, sored, bruised, bitten, bilious yet unbowed, said, 'Wh-what is it, Kait? Please, tell me what it is!'

There were no windows in the wooden walls. The roof was a grassy thatch. The only way in was through a thick-plank-grey wooden door, which hung ajar, enticing, inviting them.

'K-kait? Wh-what is it?' Maddie repeated.

Her best friend wasn't listening. Her lover let go of her hand, peering through the sunshine at the glimmering sheen which lay beyond the weird hut, and stretched, as far as her eyes could see. Kait left her standing on the path, crossed the lawn, and stood at the very edge,

'Come see what I've found!' she cried.

Madison hurried to her playmate's side, seizing her hand - for a sense of security. A little bit scared. Just a bit. Nothing made sense here in the arbour-within-the-woods. The heat for a start, why was it so warm? She cast her mind back to Geography. Felt her heart leap,

Micro-climate! Maybe we're in a micro-climate, a bubble of summer warmth, surrounded by trees. Hidden from view! Anyone's view? At least,

~ 263 ~

that horrible heavy breathing noise has stopped. Have Kait and I finally found our paradise? Hope so! Can't afford a holiday. Couldn't go on holiday. Even if I wanted to. Can't go away with my Kait: mummy say it's unhealthy, daddy won't let me. If they could see us now! I like it here. With Kait. Like it! A lot! Perhaps we can stay here, forever, where no-one can ever find us. Hope so! I love Kait. She's my world!

'Look!' cried Kait.

Maddie opened her eyes. And looked.

At first she though it was a swimming pool, the water was *so* clear and clean. She could see the bottom, the floor, chequered black-and-white floor tiles, old-fashioned. Victorian? There were submerged red and amber brick walls enclosing the pool at its perimeter and partitioning the space into rooms. At least, they used to be rooms, once upon a time. There was a convenient flight of steps, at the far end of the pool, a fool's descent, a flooded...

'Cellar!' the two girls both cried at the same time, 'A flooded cellar!'

Kait swivelled round to face the wooden outbuilding, taking Maddie with her.

'This,' she said, waving her arm from left to right, 'All this, must have been someone's property. Once. The house. The garden. The Summerhouse! It is a summerhouse, Mads. Children might have played here.'

Her voice was tinged with sadness, so much so that Maddie shared her sense of loss, her grief, Kaitlyn's overwhelming desire to reconcile their present with someone else's past.

'Who do you think lived here then, Kait, a family?'

Her mate spoke slowly, 'A rich family I expect. Only the rich can afford a summerhouse.'

Madison suddenly felt weak. Wearied by it all. It had been an exciting adventure but the sun would go down sooner or later taking away its warmth, dusk would set in. They had yet to wade their way back through the pond, find their way home through the dark forest, and.

'I'm tired out,' she complained, 'Think we should take a bath, have a rest, make our way back, before it gets dark?'

'Are you saying it's our bath time?!' her lover smirked, not a smile, just a naughty smirk.

'Yes! Bath time!' Maddie craved her, pleaded for her touch, 'Will you undress me, Kait?'

'Only if you undress me, too!'

'Yes! Yes! Hurry! Hurry!'

Cleft, concealed in her hidey-hole, watched, enthralled, as the tall girl hastily unbuttoned her friend's filthy blouse, peeling it off her back, a crusty scab. Her skirt came off next, stiff with dirt. She freed her lover's breasts, unlatching three hooks, teasing off her cups, revealing her pale breasts, the dusky nipples, flicking off the clinging leech. The girl stood still as a garden gnome, quivering inside, tingling with excitement, as Kait pulled down her dirty pants, threw them on the ground, kissing her blushing cheeks, whispering, softly, in her ear,

'Take off my clothes, Maddie.'

Cleft could barely bring herself to watch the tall girl's denouement, such was her pent-up lust, her self-imposed restraint.

Maddie, meanwhile, was all fingers n thumbs, fiddle, flaff, fizzing in a frisson of wanton, selfish need. Her hands shook, digits dithered, as she unpicked the five remaining buttons on her girl's blouse, fluffing the cotton shift out of her skirt, pushing the material back over Kaitlyn's angular shoulders, hearing her murmuring instructions in the background,

'Fold it neatly for me. Leave it on the path.'

Clean! She wants me to keep her clean!

She did as she was told, then she unclasped and yanked off Kait's skirt, folding it, neatly.

Cleft gasped as the lip-servant stripped off the tall girl's bra and briefs - denuding her.

Kaitlyn Hart was easily the most beautiful girl that she had ever had the pleasure to stalk.

For once in her, shallow, life, Madison Hendricks was lost for words, such was the nature of Kait's twin imperfections: the scar over her mouth, remnants of her hair lip, the raised blue varicose vein: her vascular graffiti: which crept over her floppy right breast, swelling her nipple. The imperfections enhanced her natural beauty, her healthy ruddy complexion, the smooth silkiness of her skin, her astonishingly shapely physique. Maddie wanted to kiss her scar, to lightly run her soft fingertips along her bulging vein. But Kait was having none of it. She ran up to the flooded cellar, abandoning her stunned mate.

'Come on! Let's go for a swim!'

Maddie stooped and picked up her soiled clothing, in litter-picker fashion, 'I can't swim!'

'Then stand on the steps and wash yourself. You look like a tramp!' called Kait.

'A lovely tramp, though,' she added, joyfully, 'My precious little tramp.'

I love you so much, Maddie mused, You're always so kind to me.

It was time for the two girls to splash around naked in the water. Kait perched with all her toes clasping the rough edge of the makeshift swimming pool estimating correctly that the water was little more than two feet deeper than her height. She dived in headfirst. Her friend watched, admiring her as she scythed through the crystal-clear water as far as the steps, rolled underwater, then swam back to her.

Kait trod water for her, spoke in sputters, 'It's really warm! Come on in!'

Madison shook her head in disbelief, 'No way! It can't be warm. It's still only Spring!'

'Don't believe me then. Come in and feel it for yourself.'

With that Kait about turned and struck out for the steps. Her lovechild was waiting there, dipping her toes in the water. Kait was right. The water was warm. Mads sat on the stairs, enjoying her natural bath.

Perhaps there's a warm water inlet to the lake. Hang on! This is a cellar, not a duckpond!

She rubbed the horrid khaki stains out of her clothes, rinsing them off in the clean water, got up, and padded to the summerhouse, leaving her idol to enjoy her swim. There were no familiar forest sounds, she noticed, no animal rustling leaves or birdsong. Her paradise was perfectly at peace, at one with her sense of wellbeing, her emotional fulfilment, her overwhelming happiness. Maddie had never felt so free. She quickly strung her clothing along the metal trellis to dry in the sun, ready for later, when the two girls returned home - without her shoes and socks.

'Try explaining that to mummy and daddy,' she tutted.

Someone, close by, laughed at her. Laughter, coming from the hidey-hole. Cruel laughter. Taunting her. Jeering at her. Scolding her for being such a stupid girl. Maddie ran away.

Don't look back, girl! Don't look back!

Kait was partially submerged, sitting on the cellar steps, rubbing her neck, when Maddie appeared, panting heavily, unfit, out of breath. She said, before the other girl could speak.

'I've been bitten. Don't worry. It's only a scratch. Probably just a mozzie.'

Her little tramp ignored her, bending at the waist, hands on hips, gathering her breath,

'I think we're being watched.'

Kait instinctively covered her breasts with her hands and slunk down into the water, like a scared hippo in retreat only smaller. She smiled to herself. So, they had a secret admirer? Someone had witnessed their exotic schoolgirl burlesque, her denouement by Maddie. She sighed,

Wonder who he is? Probably some crafty old bugger escaped from the local care home!

It wouldn't have been the first time that she'd attracted the attention of older, mature men.

'Where?' she said.

Maddie wrung her hands, and shifted from foot-to-fit, nervous, glancing over her shoulder at the gap in the rhododendrons. The hidey-hole was empty. There was no-one there. A solitary light aircraft flew overhead. A mild breeze blew, rippling the surface of the pool, chilling her damp head of hair. She heard a sharp crack – a dead branch broken underfoot? The birds sang their hearts out. The treetops swayed in the breeze. The forest came back to life. Maddie began to wonder if her imagination had played tricks on her all along. She did have a hyperactive imagination, childish dreams, subliminal excursions into her own private la-la land. When she felt emotionally vulnerable. When she was Kait's child. Truth be told, she felt a bit stupid,

'I thought I heard laughter in the forest,' she said, flushing, 'I thought I heard someone laughing at me.'

'Laughter? At you, Mads?'

'Mm.'

Her mate was intrigued, 'What kind of laughter?'

'Horrid laughter.'

'Why would anyone laugh at you?' asked Kait, her face splitting in a mildly amused grin.

Madison threw up her hands and stared at the sky, which was clouding over, like her face.

'Don't believe me, do you?'

'I'd say you're imagining things. You do imagine a lot don't you?'

Maddie clasped her hands behind her back and swayed, blushing profusely, the little girl who is caught red-handed stealing candy from a sweet shop,

'I suppose so.'

'You're filthy! Come into the pool and let me bathe you.'

The mood changed to sultry, steamy, soporific. The urchin entered the pool, desperate for Kait's touch, longing for her kiss. She sat between her lover's smooth legs and slid into the warm water, right up to her neck,

'Tilt your head back, so that I can wash your hair.'

Maddie relaxed as Kait washed all the muck and pondweed, a dead water boatman, and a live pond skater out of her manky brown hair, loving the sensation of her fingers rubbing her scalp. She closed her eyes and dreamed as Kait explored her earlobes, her cheeks, her thin smiling lips with her fingertips, hearing her quietly murmur.

'Sit on my lap.'

Maddie shifted herself up the stairs, sat on her lover's lap, then opened her mouth to admit her tongue. They kissed deeply, throatily, drinking each other's saliva, tickling tongues: tasting their palates, making their tonsils twitch.

After several, breathless moments, Kait whispered, 'I love you, girl.'

She ran her hands lightly over Maddie's full off-white breasts, cleansing them, pausing to tease her dusky rose nipples, stiffening her tiny red teats making her gasp with pleasure. Ploughing, delving, deeper, massaging her flat tummy, probing her deep navel, squeezing her taut abs, caressing her soft hairy mound, tenderly, gently, fingering, parting, entering, her lover's intimate cleft.

This is why I live, mused Madison, her body sensitizing, tingling, I live for her, for Kait.

'Oh, that feels good,' the young girl moaned, 'That feels so good.'

The clouds burst, a summer shower, ripples formed around their bodies as Kait made love to her childhood sweetheart. They didn't care wet, naked, in love.

Kaitlyn made her wish: if only we could stay here, in love, forever.

The rain teemed down in stair rods making it hard for Maddie to breathe. She began to panic. Kait read the alarm in her lover's eyes. Maddie was prone to panic in extreme rain, when under extreme pressure. It was the child in her, her little girl mentality, struggling to cope with the real world. Kait removed her hand.

'Let's get you inside, girl,' she said, lovingly, 'I can love you inside.'

Maddie gasped, seeing stars, her head spinning with love, their intimacy, 'Must we?'

'You can love me, too?'

The two girls separated. They stood. They climbed the stairs out of the flooded cellar and raced through the pouring rain, through the garden. To the summerhouse! The trees were a hazy blur of dark and light green, the grass was soaking wet, slippery under their feet, the salmon pink roses hung their heads in shame, withering under the onslaught of the driving rain. The girls ran for the summerhouse, oblivious to their saturated surroundings, oblivious to their clothing which lay strewn across the freshly mown lawn, or hanging on the trellis, soaking wet. They mounted the four steps to the veranda, pulled open the door, and stepped inside. It was dark inside. There were no windows. Kait left the door wide open, so that they could see each other.

Inside the summerhouse, lying on the bare wooden floorboards, was a single mattress. A shock - or a pleasant surprise?

It was Maddie who broke the silence,

'I wonder who lives here?'

Kait assessed the mattress: pink-and-white stripes, spotlessly clean, wide enough for two.

'Search me! A tramp? No, this is too good for a tramp.'

She looked around her. Other than the mattress, the room was empty. There was a dry, musty smell, the smell of dust when the covers are removed from furniture in a disused room. It struck Kait that the summerhouse hadn't been occupied for ages.

So why the mattress?

She felt Maddie's soft hand give her forearm a gentle squeeze, felt her hold her hand, her child,

'P'rhaps we should go home, Kait.'

The rain pummelled down on the veranda. Kait sang slowly as if she were in a trance.

'It's raining, it's pouring, the old man is snoring…'

Maddie chuckled. Kait was playing games with her! She loved it when Kait played games,

'He went to bed, and bumped his head, and couldn't get up in the morning!'

Kait smiled her twisted smile and led her lover to the mattress. She let go of her hand.

'We can't go home in this rain, can we? Let's go to bed until the rain has gone away.'

 She lay down on her back with her arms outstretched, her pendulous breasts heaving with excitement.

'Lie on top of me, girl,' she murmured.

Maddie went to her, lay on top of her, brushed the copper kiss curl off Kait's face. They kissed, open-mouthed, in the French-style. Kait took the girl to her breast, suckling her, as if she were a new-born babe. Maddie ran her tongue along the length of Kait's varicose vein, loving the sensation of the swelling on the tip of her tongue, as her mouth reached her nipple. Kait cupped her fat breast for her lover, so that she could feed her, feed her babe. Maddie slathered, slobbered, and licked Kait's rose pink nipple, teasing her realm of tiny teatlets, sucking voraciously on her corky teat.

Kait whispered sensually while she fed her, 'Lie on top of me, the other way round.'

She unlatched her babe from her breast and gently forced her off. Maddie clambered into her new position: lying on top of Kait with her head between her lover's thighs. Kait put her arms around Maddie's waist, holding her in place. They kissed each other, deeply, in their most intimate places.

Cleft stood in the doorway, watching the two girls make love, watching the tall girl, Kait, pressed against her lover. There would be plenty of time for her to touch and play with her afterwards. She had all the time in the world for beautiful Kait. Not for the sexy girl, though. She didn't fancy the clumsy, childish, sexy, little, girl at all, only wanted Kait.

She slammed the door and locked it.

Maddie raised her head from between Kait's thighs, 'Why has it gone so dark?'

It wasn't just dark inside the summerhouse. The wooden shack was pitch black, without a shaft of light. It was impossible for the girls to see each other, only feel, they could feel.

Kait relaxed her grip on her lover's waist, 'The door must've blown shut in the wind.'

'But there isn't any wind?'

'Then it must've shut itself.'

'I'm scared.'

Kait hugged her girl as best she could, then eased her off her, feeling her weight removed, 'Don't be scared, Mads. We'll soon get out. Then we'll put on our clothes and go home.'

'Our wet clothes,' Maddie corrected, getting to her feet.

'Yes, our wet clothes,' Kait reflected gloomily, then brightened, 'Things could be worse.'

'How, Kait? How could things be worse? Shut up in this horrible place, nothing to see, nothing to eat or drink, no clothes to wear. I want us to get out of this dump and go home.'

Kait clambered to her feet and searched for a tell-tale chink in the wall, feeling blindly with her hands,

'Feel along the wall until you find the door, then push. Ouch!'

Maddie's voice, in the dark, 'What's the matter?'

'I've got a splinter in my finger.'

'Oh, no Kait!'

'Oh, no Kait! Oh, no Kait! Oh, no Kait!'

'Stop it, Maddie!'

'It isn't me! It isn't me!'

'Oh, no Kait! Oh, no Kait! Oh, no Kait!'

'Stop it! Stop it!' she screamed.

The mocking voice fell quiet. There was someone outside the summerhouse, mocking Kait. The sound of hysterical laughter, cruel laughter, outside. A woman's laugh, or the laugh of an effeminate man. They heard her laugh cruelly. Both of them heard her laugh, this time.

'Oh, no Kait! Oh, no Kait! Oh, no Kait!'

'Stop It! Stop It!' they screamed. The voice fell quiet then nothing. They were alone.

Kait cried, 'No! Come back! Come back! Let us out! Let us out!'

The two girls beat their fists on the splinter-wood wall, making a terrible din, screaming their heads off. Cutting and bruising their fists. Kicking at the wall, furiously. Cutting and bruising their bare feet. Screaming themselves hoarse. Kait felt Maddie's body sag against hers, felt her giving up all hope, despairing.

'What are we going to do? What are we going to do? We can't stay here! Can't stay here!'

'Someone will find us,' Kait assured her.

'Who? Who will find us? You told me no-one would ever find us here. You told me that!'

The darkness, the hard drumming of rain upon the veranda, the onset of panic in her babe, tipped Kait over the crazy edge, the ridge of hysteria; it was Kait who lost her cool, lashing out at her mate, shaking her by the bare shoulders, slapping her cute little pixie face.

'Shut up, Mads! Shut up!'

Maddie started to cry. They both did. The two girls slumped to the ground, wondering if they would ever be found.

*****

It was left to Cleft to tie up all the loose ends. She picked Maddie's clothing off the metal trellis, then gathered Kaitlyn's clothing off the muddy ground, tying it up in a wet bundle, destined for the clothing bank that she passed on the way home. The hungry and the poor would appreciate the white cotton shirts, their swaying polyester skirts, in the heat of the desert, maybe not their bras and panties. She disposed of them, burying them under the heavy logs in the swollen, muddy, woodland pool.

Then, she made her way to the forest path - and home.

Belle

SHE FELT PERFECT. AT ONE WITH HERSELF: body, soul, and mind. The camera zoomed in on her. A full body shot of her, standing in front of a floor-to-ceiling moving montage of death:

A wailing mother holding the bloodied body of her dead child. The shell of a burning school, target of a direct strike. Angry men screaming hatred, firing AK-47s into a smoke-filled sky. The occasional moans of the wounded, the dying, the grieving.

Conflict: when would it ever end?

The night was hot, humid, stultifying outside. She had come to work wearing little more than an airy leaf print dress, bared arms, and legs. Huge sunglasses covered half her face. Silver bangles mustered on her right wrist.

Jessica Cleft didn't just read the news. These days, Jessica was the news. Her move into advertising health spas, bubbling hot tubs, full body massage, medicinal baths, showers, skimpy bikinis, and sexy lingerie, had brought her legions of adoring fans: midults, women, bisexual, transgender, gay, men of all ages, the lecherous grey pound.

Her no-holds-barred Saturday night radio show on Flex: Strong Women Speak! had inspired disillusioned women to be liberal, to have fun, to achieve personal fulfilment, to take pride in being a strong woman, just like her. Her Sunday adult show, starting half an hour after the end of Flex TV News: Play with Jess!, she did strictly for laughs, for her personal self-gratification.

Jessica Cleft was a living controversy, a legend, an enigma, who no-one really knew. A secretive woman with a public face, private face, and an emotionally disturbed dark side.

The camera zoomed in on her body. She looked great! In her hands she clutched a sheaf, notes she didn't need. The cameraman focused on her perfect face. Jessica began to read.

'In today's other news, Police investigating the disappearance of schoolgirls Kaitlyn Hart and Madison Hendricks, 18 and certified by child psychiatrists as emotionally vulnerable, have extended the search area to include Holly Lakes, Deep Lake, Aisling Brook, and the dewponds of Chipping Forest. The girls, described as inseparable by schoolfriends, have not been seen since the morning of Friday 14th May. Police have issued a fresh description together with a recent photograph of the two girls.

They are appealing for anyone with knowledge of their whereabouts to come forward in strict confidence with information, however trivial it may seem. This evening, the girls' distraught parents made an emotional appeal for their safe return…'

The playroom door swung open and she was there for him, effortless yet elegant Belle, his adorable wife. Slim, supple, lightly tanned, with a smattering of freckles on her chest, shocks of auburn café crème hair slung off her face, cascading onto her pert breasts. Her face creased in a broad, dimpled, smile. She raised her eyebrows - her surprised look - scratched her shoulder (the mosquitoes always bit her skin in the garden), and said,

'Think we should get changed, honey, don't you? Hot tubs bubbling. Pink gins are on the side. Ready for our wild night in!'

Marc Pritchard switched off the wall-sized plasma screen with the remote and appraised his soulmate. She always looked immaculate for him no matter how busy or tired she was, with Sienna, running the home, cooking the meals - when he wasn't away on business. Tonight, she was flattering him, wearing her tropical, feminine, botanical, lustrous top, freckled arms bare, silhouette sage green, slim leg jeans, glam shimmering rose belt, bare feet. She had started to undress already for the tub. God, he loved this woman.

'You're the best, sweetheart. Best mother, best wife, best lover I could ever wish for. You and Sienna make my life.'

She scratched her shoulder, and spoke, Deep South, Florida, 'Why, thank you, sugar. You're not so bad yourself! Now get your ass off my couch. Need to get changed for that hot tub. Don't want to miss the show, do we?'

Marc buttoned up his stoneground shorts at the hip not the waist. His waistline had gotten too fat for shorts. Too many late nights, junk food at the office, on the job. His Vietnamese red silk shirt still fitted, just, the one with the dragon emblazon, the distinctive logo which translated as Same, Same, But Different, tight around his right man boob. His left chest was shallow, his nipple missing, sutured, stitched, sewn as best the surgeon could, severed in a knife attack. He stood up, scratching the six-inch scar where his left breast used to be - before the bastards lopped it off. The scarring made his skin itch, hurt his mind, made him bitter, angry, always,

'How's my little girl?'

Belle beamed with pride. Sienna, her bundle of joy, cute, sweet as nectar, sharp as the knife that cut a twenty-centimetre wound in her when her baby girl was born by Caesarean section. His brave woman showed it off: her pride, shaved herself bare: her love, no pubic hair to cover her daughter's scar line. No way! Belle wore her scar with pride, for them.

'She's bouncing on the trampoline.' Before he could protest she added, 'I'll put my baby girl to bed before the show starts, won't I? She'll be all sleepy head, ready for bed…'

'…by the time you kiss your darling heart goodnight.'

Marc tried to hug the love of his life, to kiss her on the lips. She shook him off, her radiant smile unsmeared.

'Later, honey, later! Now, go and get changed.'

Belle went to her boudoir to prepare herself. Marc went to his walk-in wardrobe to find some trunks. They chatted through the plastered wall, planning ahead as they undressed.

'Belle?'

'Yes?'

'Did you plug in the radio?'

'Marc Pritchard! What do you take me for, stupid?'

'No, I take you to the hot tub, we down some gins, we do the show, then, I take you!'

'Maybe,' she said, smiling smugly to herself, 'Maybe I'll take you!'

He put on his tightest thong. She dressed in her tiniest bikini.

Happy, in love, so excited, they made their way down to the garden, to their bubbling tub.

*****

'Watch me do a forward roll, Daddy!'

'I'm watching! I'm watching!'

Marc relaxed in the hot tub and watched his sweet Sienna bounce higher and higher on her trampoline. She flipped over headfirst, head-over-heels, landing with a firm thump at the centre of the mat. He breathed a sigh of relief: no bones broken, no twisted neck. He dreaded to think what he would do, how he would cope, if his little Goldilocks fell on her face, broke her neck, or swallowed her tongue. Sienna's daring exploits on the bouncy netted turret were one of the few risks he permitted himself in his private life.

The greatest risk, he kept secret.

The proud father closed his eyes, rested his strong arms on the rim of the tub, then opened his hairy thighs, thrilling to the forceful sensation of bubbles frothing in his crotch. He took a sip of pink gin, refreshing his palate, licking his lips at the notion of Belle preparing herself for him. Her sexy musk, that carnal link between her smell, her body's odour, and his seduction, his nasal-oral-optical-tactile-stimulation, his arousal, by her.

He checked his sub aqua diver's watch, moving the phone in closer to him. The jacuzzi extension was his idea - purely for personal pleasure. He opened his eyes, staring at the night sky, the thick blanket of black clouds obscuring all but a thin smattering of stars, a faded crescent moon.

Where is she? We're due to perform.

Sienna, tomboy in a pink dragon t-shirt and floppy red shorts, sat cross-legged on the mat watching him.

'What is it, Daddy?'

It had been a tough week of constant interruptions, late calls, false leads, restless nights. He blinked open his weary eyes, 'Just dreaming.'

'Happy dreams?'

Marc wasn't paying attention. His mind was elsewhere. In the forest. By a muddy pond.

'Sorry?'

The girl sucked her withered thumb and looked at him, 'Are you having happy dreams?'

'Yes, happy dreams.'

He thought of the two girls, still missing, the hell their parents must be going through, thankful it wasn't his treasured daughter the team of frogmen were searching for, smiling.

'Show me another forward roll.'

The girl stood, wobbled a bit on the trampoline, then started to bounce, higher and higher.

No traces or clues. That's what he didn't understand. Despite endless appeals, house-to-house interviews, pulling in the usual scumbag of suspects: perverts, stalkers, prowlers, paedophiles, trolls, voyeurs, for questioning; the investigation had yet to yield a lead. Add to that the fact that Madison

Hendricks was baby-cute, emotionally regressive, bordering on a child, mentally, and it was difficult to imagine how the girls could have survived in the forest undetected. The weather, when they went missing, was atrocious - endless rain, an occasional heavy shower, thunderstorms. Yet there had been no sightings. No-one had come forward since the girls were seen, by a passing motorist, entering the forest.

The team had begun the gruesome task of dredging the dozens of dewponds scattered around the forest, diving into lakes, searching for bodies. Pritchard was in no doubt that this was where the search would end: in the discovery of two drowned girls. Pressure was building from on high, the girl's distressed parents, the media, to find the girls, to achieve some kind of closure. Marc struggled to cope. The notion of having the blood of two dead girls on his hands was too much to bear, tearing at his insides.

He needed a break, and he needed relief. He shook himself awake, increasingly impatient, concerned at the risk he was taking with her, in the tub tonight,

Come on Belle.

He heard his daughter giggle. Sienna climbed off the trampoline and ran to be with him. He felt her soft little fingers tickle his shoulder.

'Daddy?'

'Yes, precious.'

'Will you and Mummy be handsome in the tub tonight?'

Handsome! Her favourite word! Who did she learn that word from? Mummy? Had to be!

'I hope so,' he replied, grinning from ear to ear, 'I really hope so.'

The little girl clapped her hands with glee, 'Good! I like it when you and Mummy are handsome. Handsome as the day I was born!'

Marc took a large swig of gin, swallowing hard: the thought of his adorable, beautiful wife, running his fingers along her scar.

'Daddy?'

'Yes, Sienna?'

'Do you love Mummy?'

'I...'

'Come along, young lady,' Belle interrupted, 'Think it's bedtime, don't you? Let's get you to bed.'

Marc couldn't bear to watch her, not in front of Sienna. His blush, his embarrassment, the pole-like swelling propping up his thong, her feline display, her beautiful face, her body, her musk, was too much for him to bear in front of their child.

She smelled of vanilla.

Long touted as an aphrodisiac, the scent of vanilla causes arousal and stimulation in men. Vanilla may be soft, almost sweet, but it has a strong, intense, aroma, an animalistic effect.

Sienna, just five, starting school next term, was bright, smart, too smart for her own good sometimes. She would notice them, make one of her smart childish comments, tell all her friends at their birthday parties, in the park, on the slide, the swings. Tell their mummies all about them, the strange games they played, handsome, in the steamy, bubbly, tub.

'Must we, Mummy?'

'We must. Say goodnight to Daddy.'

Marc felt Sienna's small lips kiss his shoulder, the faintest touch, heard her tiny whisper, 'Night, night, Daddy.'

'Night, Sienna. See you.'

He had no idea when he would see his precious girl again. Her voice faded as she was led away to clean her pearly teeth, comb her golden hair, say 'Night, Mummy, love you, lots,' read her story - about the little girl who lost her name...

The telephone rang.

Marc swivelled at the hips and reached for the phone, tearing the receiver from its cradle, pressing speaker to high with his index finger. He downed his third pink gin, relaxed, and sank into the tub, his heart pumping hard in his butchered chest. The twinge made him wince. When he finally took the call, his speech was slurred.

Wearily, drowsily, he spoke, 'Yeah? Hello?'

'Mr Pritchard? Mr Marc Pritchard?' a young female voice said warily, at the other end of the line.

'Who's that?'

The voice calmed, 'Hello Mr Pritchard, this is Celine from Flex Radio.'

'Marc,' he insisted, 'Call me Marc.'

'Ha! Hi! You're live on air with Play with Jess in ten minutes. Is Mrs Pritchard with you?'

He looked around. Where was she? They were due to perform tonight. Human sealions!!

'No, but she will be.'

'Can I just check a few details with you then, for Ms Cleft?'

Ms Cleft. Of course, she'd be a Ms! Cleft, what a name!

Marc felt as if his thong might tear open, revealing his swollen appendage, any time now. First, Belle, playing easy to love, horny as hell. Now, the girl-on-the-phone, her posh, dulcet tone. She sounded nervy, young, 18? 19? 20? Her first assignment on radio? Play with Jess. The pleasure inside him, the intense emotional stress, played with his heart. His heart felt like bursting out of his chest. Hurt? Would it hurt him when it did? *Hurt.* Meal Scene. Crew. *Nostromo.* The *Alien.* Bursting out of his chest. How much more of these women could he take? He grabbed another pink gin, his fourth. Bitter, it tasted bitter. He panicked, more sweating, more palpitations, more heartburn.

So, babe, he asked himself, what have you spiked my gin with this time? Panex ginseng? Maca? Tongkat Ali?

He grinned. Spanish Fly was his trusted ingredient for Belle's libido enhancement. Not that she needed any encouragement tonight.

His mind drifted into erotic-half sleep mode. Marc slept for what seemed like five minutes.

'Marc. Marc? Marc!' shouted Celine, 'Are you still there? You're live on air in five!'

The midult shook himself awake, 'Yeah? What?'

Celine bombarded him with questions, 'Your wife's name's Belle, right?'

'Yeah, that's right.'

Angostura bitters! Why didn't I think of that? Pink Gin! Angostura turns gin pink. Sorry Belle, I trust you, babe, I trust you…

'You have a daughter, Sienna, right? She's five, off to school to next term? Marc?'

'Yeah, sorry Celine, my little girl.'

'You live in Aigburth?'

Where's that for chrisake?

'By the forest. In Essex.'

'Essex. How lovely.'

'Last question. Do you have your absolutely right word ready for Jess tonight?'

'Yes,' he gasped, 'We have it ready.'

'Thank you, Mr Pritchard. Enjoy the show!'

'Don't mention it.'

Celine looked up at the studio clock, then glanced at Cleft, 'You're live in two minutes.'

The clouds parted overhead. The night sky bristled with stars, twinkling in their blackened canvas. Marc thought of all the insignificant lives before him, those lives yet to come. He swigged his gin. His heart pumped with irregular beats in his strained chest. He needed a break, a holiday, needed relief. He felt Belle's soft warm hands on his shoulders, felt her slide her palms over his chest, her fingertips stroking his livid scar, felt happier than he'd ever felt in his life.

Fame beckoned! Tonight, they would perform for an audience, live on air, human sealions in their bubbling hot tub. He savoured his woman's marine animal scent, her husky, sexy voice, murmuring in his ear.

'Take off your thong, honey.'

Heart pounding like a steam hammer, wincing with the muscle stretch in his torn breast, the pleasure pain of his woman, he wriggled out of his thong, leaving it lying limp on the rim of the frothing tub. Belle climbed the non-slip steps into the spa pool, facing her man, and took off her teeny-weeny bikini top.

She stood between his thighs, letting him untie her miniscule g-string, so that it hung, like a ribbon, out of her crotch. Marc ripped it off. She sat in his lap, straddling him, kissing him. His face turned puce. Her breath aroused him. Sharp teeth nipped his earlobes. Soft puffy lips mouthed in his ear.

'Shall we perform?'

His heart skipped a big beat. Listen to the beat of his straining heart. She plied him with gin, pink gin, bitter gin. He burped wind. It was wind, all the time! Belle sat in his lap. They performed naked as the day they were born, human sealions in a bubbling hot tub.

'You're about to go live on air,' Celine informed them in the background, 'Ready?'

'Yes!' Belle hissed.

'Okay then, on the count of ten…

10…9…8…7…6…5…4…3…2…1…'

'And our next loving couple are Belle and Marc from Essex,' Jessica announced, 'Are you there, guys?'

Belle felt between her thighs, caressing her husband's scrotal sac, swollen with semen, ripe with sperm to create her second baby, fondling his rigid, turgid, throbbing gland, then pleasured herself on him. Marc groaned as she used her vice-like muscles, clenching him, squeezing him to bursting point. He heard her murmurs,

'Yes, we're here. This is Belle.'

'Hello Belle, where are you speaking from?'

Marc opened his mouth to speak, his attempt to communicate thwarted by a deep kiss, by his wife. Belle broke off, panting, immersed in the throes of her exertion, pelvic gyrations.

'We're, we're, we're, sitting in the hot tub downing pink gins, aren't we, Marc?'

Her husband's heart weakened: the combined effect of the gin, the heat, the sex, the bitter tasting compound stirred into his drink by the love of his life. His heart was giving out.

Marc just managed to say, 'Yeah, gins-in-the-tub.'

Belle bore down on him, bouncing in his lap, gripping his shaft with her birth muscle, thrusting her rosy-pink nipples in his face, his mouth. Her face suffused with blush.

Cleft contemplated the couple, merry if not drunk, frolicking in the bubbly, hot, tub. There was no doubt in her mind, judging by the ecstasy, the fervour, laced molten honey in the sensual woman's voice, her man's exhausted submission. The two of them were having sex in the tub. Having sex in a hot tub, live on air! Making passionate love on her show. Playing with Jess! She tried to stay calm, tried to keep her cool. It wasn't easy, given that:

Cleft's mind strayed to the two girls: Kaitlyn and Maddie. She had watched them making love in the summerhouse, hidden in the forest. She recalled the flooded cellar in the secret garden. Young, virile, beautiful Kait swimming naked in the crystal-clear water. Sexy Madison, sitting naked on the natural swimming pool steps, fretting, worrying, about her. How she had slammed the stable door, locked the girls inside the summerhouse, taken all of their clothing and buried it under a heavy log in a muddy woodland pond. Jessica began to feel aroused,

'Well, this is a first! I've never interviewed anyone in a hot tub! Are you ready to Play with Jess?'

Belle quickly stuffed her g-string and bikini top into her man's mouth, holding them there, making him gag, making it impossible for him to breathe.

She felt him claw her buttocks, felt him spurt his semen out inside her, his final, prolonged, deep, pelvic thrust, the limp, shrivelled retraction. Spent, shattered, stuffed, suffocated, subdued, he died inside her, of a massive heart attack.

The soluble aphrodisiac having served her well, she replied, 'Yes, Jess, I'm ready.'

I'm ready?

'Do you have your absolutely right word for me tonight?'

'Yes, Jess,' Belle gasped, coming back down to earth, 'My five-year-old daughter Sienna came out with the word when she saw us playing naked in the tub together under the moonlight.'

Playing naked in the tub together?

There was no-one watching in the studio. Jessica lifted the hem of her airy leaf print dress, massaged the soft inside of her smooth, paleskin bare thigh, and slipped her fingers inside her panties.

'You play with each other, naked, in the hot tub, Belle?'

'Yes, Jess.'

'You moon in the moonlight?

'Yep.'

Jessica closed her eyes and dreamed, imagining the couple making love in the bubbly hot tub, two girls making love in the summerhouse before she left them to die.

She murmured, 'What does Sienna say when she sees her mum and dad naked, playing in the tub at night?'

Belle dismounted her dead husband, went, and sat on the rim of the tub, waggling her toes in the warm water, a tangled ivy tattoo shining on her slender back, mischief in her mad grey eyes, the blood of her dead husband on her hands.

She lifted the receiver, set the speaker to silent, and uttered Sienna's magic word, 'Handsome, Jess. She calls us handsome.'

'Belle, that word is so absolutely right?'

Jessica's fingers were sticky. She pulled them out of her panties, took out her hands, and pressed the airy leaf print dress against her thighs. The interview was over.

'Belle, look, it's been lovely speaking to you. Would you like to say any dedications?'

'Yes please, I'd like to dedicate tonight to my lovely daughter Sienna, Marc my handsome husband, to all of my family and friends who are listening, and, especially, to you Jessica.'

Cleft thought of Kaitlyn Hart and Madison Hendricks, their feeble, whimpering screams,

How close had Pritchard come to finding the two girls? The lonely forest path. The muddy woodland pond. Her secret garden. The flooded cellar. Her summerhouse. Before Belle called her husband telling him to come home, quickly, to take Sienna to hospital? Sienna, his treasured little girl who

~ 293 ~

sprained her ankle when she tumbled off the trampoline? How close had Pritchard come - to finding her?

Cleft thanked Belle for her lovely word, for handsome, for Sienna. Then she cut the call,

'That was Belle and Marc from Essex having fun, playing, mooning, in their bubbly hot tub with a pink gin or three,' she announced, 'Handsome. Like that word, don't you? This is *Night Fever* by The Bee Gees...'

Jessica Cleft left the studio at midnight. Outside, on her way to Oxford Circus tube station, she found a shady shop entrance, and rang the private Essex number. Belle answered her call immediately.

'Thank you, my sweet lover,' the killer said, 'For your dedication to me.'

Pritchard's naked body was where she left it, floating, tossing about in the frothy hot tub. She really ought to call an ambulance, the Police. Well maybe not the Police, not just yet.

After all, accidents happen during violent sex, don't they?

Belle recalled the tangled ivy tattoo on Jessica's slender back when they met at the health spa. How they had agreed to meet again. How Belle had the same leafy motif tattooed on her back, to demonstrate her dedication, her love, and affection for Jessica. Cleft's deadly secret,

'Your secret's safe with me, honey,' she soothed, dipping her feet into the frothy jacuzzi, kicking her husband's corpse,

'Your secret's safe with me.'

Occasionally

EVER SINCE I WAS A LITTLE GIRL I've been frightened of the dark, things that go bump in the night, faces at the window, black mirrors. That sort of thing. I write about them: dark, erotic, fantasies. Those of you who know me, and read me, will understand why.

You see, I'm an insomniac. I wake up in the middle of the night with a story idea, write it down, go downstairs to the kitchen, and make myself a midnight feast of milky mint tea and hot toast. I live on my own in Marriage House, a red-brick farmhouse with a black slate roof, encircled by a dense hedge of dark cypress, well-established ivy climbing its walls. She knows the place well. I unlock the door and breathe in the cool night air, so rich, with the aromatic scent of pine.

I let her in.

The intruder stands behind me. Her mouth, nostrils and chin are covered by a thick black mask. Her shaggy teak hair hangs over her face, scratching her crazed walnut eyes, accentuating her baggy-lined eyelids, her umber weals of tiredness. She looks exhausted. I feel the tip of a knife blade press into the side of my neck, hear her excited voice for the first time.

'Do what I say and you won't get hurt.'

I decide not to nod my head, standing quite still, while she puts on my blindfold. The blindfold is made of coarse black linen. She fluffs my hair out of the way, then ties the knot securely at the nape of my neck. I feel its torn edges tickling my skin. The blindfold covers the bridge of my nose and eyes ending above my forehead, at my hairline, my grey-streaked widow's peak.

'Hold your hands behind your back.'

She arrests me. I obey her, clasping my hands to the small of my back while she ties my wrists. I feel her cord cut into my flesh. I'm dressed for bed in a loose black chemise and panties. My world is black tonight. My entire world is black. I feel her soft hands, slim fingers, grasp my shoulders and turn me around. I am her dummy. Her robot. Her wish is my command. The tiled floor feels cold under my bare feet.

She propels me towards the kitchen door. I relish the warm tufts of carpet between my toes as we cross the hallway. She pushes me upstairs. I am bat blind. I can't see her but I can feel her, sense her apprehension, smell her nervous sweat.

At the top of the stairs, we turn left. My midriff brushes against the smooth banister. I feel myself being guided. I am forced to take three steps forward. She shoves me face-down on the bed. I twist my head to the right to breathe, careful not to let her blindfold slip, then I plead for my life.

'I keep the key to my safe in the top right bedside drawer,' I explain. 'The safe is located under the pillows in the left-hand bedside cupboard. Insert the key and turn the dial to the right. Inside the safe you'll find my passport, my most expensive, precious jewellery, my purse, a key, and a red notebook. The key opens my jewellery box which I keep under the bed. In there, you'll find my diamond necklace, diamond earrings, diamond pendant, gold bangles, bracelets, pearls. The notebook contains all my passwords, details of my bank accounts. Take all of it, but please, don't hurt me.'

The effort of revealing my innermost secrets leaves me drained of energy. I want to sleep, to dream, fantasize. Make her go away. I exhale, shutting my weary eyes. I listen to her reassuring me.

'I'll hurt you if you misbehave. I don't want your money. I want us to play games. You will play games with me, won't you?'

She presses the tip of the knife blade firmly into the side of my neck. I agree to play her games.

She unties my wrists as my reward, and asks, 'Do you wear stockings?'

'Occasionally, you'll find a pair of black stockings with a red suspender belt in the top drawer.'

She looks around. We're alone in the moonlight. She speaks to me as if I'm a ragdoll, a corpse,

'Don't want to see you like this.'

She rolls me onto my back, then dresses me, drawing my stockings up my taut calves, over my knees, up my thighs, carefully attaching them to my ruby red suspender belt. I feel exhilarated. Can't wait for our next game to begin.

She leans forward and kisses me, tasting my flavour with the tip of her tongue. I feel her hands idly wander up the soft insides of my thighs. For a moment, she stands perfectly still. Then she lifts off my chemise.

Other than my panties, stockings and suspender belt, I am naked. She unties my blindfold and lets me watch. She is wearing a red short-sleeved sweater, faded skinny jeans, a silver belt.

I marvel as she applies my make-up.

My stomach is daubed with a tattoo of a magnificent scarlet rose in full bloom, its petals dripping dew. At my rose's heart she lays a solid diamond charm sparkling violet, indigo, amber, emerald shards of light. Her beautiful phenomenon takes my breath away.

I sink into my bed transfixed. Slowly, my petals unfurl. My intimate charm protrudes. She extracts her surprise from my navel and lays the iridescent gem in the palm of my hand. I ask her if I can keep it. She tells me, I can wear it as her keepsake, and gently replaces it in my navel.

'Sit up straight for me.'

I sit up for her. She puts on my blindfold. I let her take off my panties, stockings, and suspender belt. I am nude for her now, ready, eager, to play her next game.

'Lie on the towel.'

I feel the coarse texture of my beach towel lying on the bed beside me. I lie on it. Safe. I feel safe. On my towel. Happy, content, warm, secure, and satisfied.

She tells me to keep still, 'Play dead, relax for me, let your body go limp.'

I close my eyes under the blindfold. My arms flop to my sides. My legs go slack. I fall asleep, dreaming that I am lying on her beach. I perspire. She rakes the sweat strands of hair off my face, affectionately brushing my cheeks. I feel her place a warm bottle of suntan oil near my body, sense her squeezing a blob of oil onto her palm.

'Lie on your front.'

I roll onto my front and lie with my chin resting comfortably on the backs of my hands. She ties back my hair with an elastic band. Excited, I grip the edge of the bed. Although her tender touch will caress the whole of my body, she lightly covers my buttocks with a soft towel. She will soon strip it off of me when my skin falls under her soothing magic spell.

Delicately, she glides her hands over my shoulders and neck, up and down my arms, kneading warm oil into my flesh. She rubs my back using long, deep strokes, pressing herself against me, so that I can feel her breasts, her hot breath on my cheek, fleeting kisses on my ear lobes, jaw, neck, spine.

Slowly, softly, her tongue licks my lower back. I quiver as she removes the towel and spreads my legs apart. Gently, she massages my inner thighs. I tense as her fingertips gently brush my outer lips.

'How does that feel?'

'Mmmn.'

I roll onto my back. Once I've settled, she lubricates my chest, pouring oil all over my breasts.

'Be gentle with them,' I plead, 'They're sensitive.'

She massages my shoulders, working up and down my arms, using the balm to lightly skim my breasts with the palms of her hands, pausing to tease my stiff teats, circling my aroused nipples. Sending blissful sensations tingling through my body. She removes the blindfold, so that I can watch her undress.

Breathing heavily, taking in deep gasps, she slips out of her sweater, jeans, bra and panties. My jaw falls at the sight of her, naked, uninhibited. Her beauty intoxicates me. She licks her lips salaciously. Her eyes are eyes half-shut.

We embrace. She holds me tight, enjoying my hand buried in her soft belly, pressing her mouth against mine, her dewy, rose lips. Our membranes adhere, bound in an infinitesimal moment of intimacy. We pause to catch our breaths.

She is crying. Tears of joy moisten her fiery cheeks. Her smile illuminates her face. Her soft lips brush my ear. I lie back and arrange myself on the crumpled towel.

She licks my tummy, plucking out my charm, tasting the salt in my navel. With my leg hiked over her shoulder, she kisses my inner thigh, massaging my soft outer lips. By now, I am all dreamy, dripping wet, and smothered in oil. She kneels between my legs.

I gaze into her shiny eyes, the luckiest woman in the world. She covers my eyes with the blindfold. I feel her tongue. My face flushes. My breasts swell. My heart races. I grit my teeth, flex my hips, arch my body upwards.

'What're you waiting for?' I slur, 'Want you.'

She pours warm oil all over me and massages my cleft. My skin feels soft, smooth, scintillated, blushing, I'm on fire.

'Oh God!'

I thrill to petit mort. She grips my hand and combs my hair. A single tear trickles down my cheek from under the blindfold. Gently, she removes the damp cloth and kisses my face dry. We lie in our passionate embrace, our bodies entwined, her head snuggled to my sweaty breasts.

'I love you,' I say dreamily, 'You're my world.'

She tells me, she loves me, too. My heart races with excitement. Her eyes sparkle like stars on a clear summer night. She smirks mischievously, twirling a strand of her straggly teak hair, and murmurs in my ear.

'What would you like me to do next?'

'Kiss me.'

She kisses me, a longing, loving kiss. She is all I have left in the world. A tingling sensation passes through my body. Her cheeks blush roses.

She asks me, 'Do you know what it means when we kiss like that?'

I only know I love her more than life itself. I sit up for her. She ties on my blindfold and forces me to stand in front of the bed. She maims me gracefully, silently drawing the garotte tight around my neck. I thrash my head from side to side. My brittle nails tear out my assailant's hair.

My elbows pummel her ribs. I strain and stretch, kick and bite. She clings on, until my near-death. Calmed, I relax onto her chest. I fall asleep, dreaming of the time when she made love to me. My neck still entwined, my sad head flops forward, my dead eyes staring into her empty space.

She waits by my bedside for me to come to. I open my eyes. The blindfold has gone. She hasn't put on any make-up. Her beautiful teak hair is a bedraggled mess. Her eyes are bleary, blotched blood-red with tiredness.

Dawn breaks at last. Sunlight streams thru our window. She climbs onto the bed to be with me. We kiss and embrace,

'Have you missed me, Jacqui?' she says.

'Have I!'

She gently strokes my cheeks, and kisses my breasts, 'What kept you?'

I roll my eyes in disbelief. We lie hand-in-hand on the bed, enjoying the hot sun on our bodies. I am content with her. She is naturally very beautiful. I want to spend the rest of my life with her.

My thoughts turn to lockdown. I'm frail, sick, vulnerable, forced to stay indoors. I sunbathe with her, make sweet angelic love to her upon our crumpled bed, then whisper naughtily to her, 'I hope you packed my bikini.'

My girl glances at me, smiling, 'As if I'd forget. Honestly! What do you take me for?'

She takes me in her arms and holds me tight, stroking my hair, smothering my lips with kisses.

'My true love, girl,' I murmur, drawing her naked body snug and close to mine, 'My true love.'

Ever since I was a little girl I have been frightened of the dark, things that go bump in the night, faces at the window, black mirrors. That sort of thing. I write about them: dark, erotic fantasies. Those of you who know me, and read me, will understand why.

You see, I enact them with her.

We live out my dreams.

Fantasies are our life.

Nightmares are my death.

Printed in Great Britain
by Amazon